Exposed

A Detective Jade Monroe Crime Thriller
Book 5

C. M. Sutter

AUTHOR'S NOTE

This book is a work of fiction by C. M. Sutter. Names, characters, places, and incidents are products of the author's imagination or are used solely for entertainment. Any resemblance to actual events or persons, living or dead, is entirely coincidental.

ABOUT THE AUTHOR

C.M. Sutter is a crime fiction writer who resides in the Midwest, although she is originally from California.

She is a member of numerous writers' organizations, including Fiction for All, Fiction Factor, and Writers etc.

In addition to writing, she enjoys spending time with her family and dog. She is an art enthusiast and loves to create handmade objects. Gardening, hiking, bicycling, and traveling are a few of her favorite pastimes. Be the first to be notified of new releases and promotions at: http://cmsutter.com.

C.M. Sutter

http://cmsutter.com/

Exposed:

A Detective Jade Monroe Crime Thriller, Book 5

Darryl Sims, a long forgotten murderer, has been locked up in a maximum security prison for the last twenty years. Only when the family farm is repossessed for back taxes and sold to a megastore does the full extent of his heinous crimes—and the crimes of his son, Max—finally surface. When the property is excavated, skeletal remains of women that have gone missing over the years are exposed.

Max is now on the run with Jade Monroe closing in. Worthy adversary that he is, Max eludes capture and continues his killing spree.

With Darryl Sims calling the shots from behind prison walls, Max has been given his most important task to complete. This final murderous act rocks Jade to her core and makes her question the very career she loves most.

Stay abreast of each new book release by signing up for my VIP e-mail list at:

http://cmsutter.com/newsletter/

Find more books in the Jade Monroe Series here:

http://cmsutter.com/available-books/

Chapter 1

He looked up from the task at hand and peered down the driveway. One could never be too careful, and an extra ounce of caution couldn't hurt. Max couldn't remember the last time somebody came down that driveway to pay him a neighborly visit—it was too long ago. The only cars that came and went belonged to the sheriff's department, and the deputies harassed him weekly. The spring rain that pelted the landscape created pools in the driveway's potholes. That in itself would have dissuaded a visitor from stopping by. He scratched at that annoying tic above his left eye and got back to work.

At thirty-nine, Max lived on the large compound, in that creepy farmhouse, alone. The thought of marriage never crossed his mind. Women were bothersome and good for only one thing—cooking. He liked his privacy far too much, anyway.

He tapped the dirt with the head of the shovel and gave the site a long, thorough look. Nothing could be out of place—that wouldn't do.

"Damn it," he growled when he noticed the pink tip of her nose poking through the dirt. He swung the shovel over his head and smacked the soil with as much force as he could muster. Mud sprayed in every direction. He heard the hard crack of metal against bone, then he cocked his head and smiled. He filled the shovel with one more scoop of wet dirt and dropped it over that spot. "Good enough." Max pierced the soggy ground with the shovel's blade and wiped the mud off his face with the back of his forearm. "That will teach you to look down at me." He chuckled at the irony, grabbed the shovel by the shaft, and crossed the driveway to the house.

Inside the large screened porch, Max stripped down to nothing and opened the door to the kitchen. The pile of wet clothes and muddy boots remained behind.

After his shower, he dressed and took a seat at his usual spot in the kitchen. The rickety wooden table had seen better days. Dry, crusted food had now become a part of the surface and would take hours of elbow grease to remove, if he cared. He stared at the fly that seemed to enjoy the fresh crumbs. Max slowly reached for the swatter that lay on the floor. He hoped he wouldn't scare the fly away. With his right hand, he lifted the swatter above his head and came down on the fly with a violent smack. He slid the mashed body across the table and dropped it to the floor. Yellow Boy, the stray cat that shined around occasionally, sniffed it then walked away.

Max glanced to his left, then to his right. His father would have been at the head of the table, to his left, his mother to the right, and Grandma would have been directly across from Max, facing him. He sat alone—two out of the three were dead, and Darryl Sims was in prison for their murders. While he sipped black coffee that had been in the pot since yesterday, Max browsed the newspaper's classifieds to see if his ad had posted. It was time to hire a new cook and housekeeper.

Chapter 2

Clark stormed out of his office with Monday morning's newspaper in hand. "What's going on with Max Sims?"

"Apparently nothing, boss." My response was sarcastic and tiresome. Our deputies had been to the Sims homestead five times in the last two months. Max had been served three eviction notices, and he still hadn't budged.

"The newspaper says the groundbreaking ceremony has been put on hold until he vacates the premises."

Jack huffed. "Then that big-box Swedish housewares store will never get built. Do you have any idea what the buzz was like in town when it was announced who bought that chunk of land? The county is going crazy with anticipation, not to mention the jobs it will bring in."

Billings spoke up. "Lucky for me, though. Now I have a good excuse to ignore Lynn's pleas. She's constantly harping on me about buying new furniture."

"Enough is enough. Jade, you and Jack go out there and give him a final warning. Max Sims has two days to vacate, or he'll be under arrest for trespassing."

"Man that sucks. Trespassing on your own family homestead," Clayton said.

"It isn't his home anymore, and he's had plenty of time to pay the property tax. He's five years in arrears, for Pete's sake." Clark jerked his head. "Go on, get it done. He's holding up progress."

I rose and put on my shoulder holster, slipped the chained badge over my head, and grabbed my purse and phone. I nodded at Jack. "Ready?"

"Ready as I'll ever be," he said as he put his sports jacket on over his shoulder holster.

Jack grabbed a set of keys off the rack behind the dispatch desk, and we exited the building.

"I'm driving." I held out my open hand. Jack dropped the keys into my palm, and I unlocked the cruiser doors when we got closer. "What do you know about Max Sims?" I asked as I turned left onto Washington Street.

"Other than he's the son of a convicted murderer?"

"Yeah, other than that." I stopped at the red light and waited.

"Not a lot. Seems whenever the conversation of the Sims place comes up, Max is described as a recluse with antisocial tendencies and just plain weird. People say he'll never leave that farm. So far, it appears they're right."

I gunned the cruiser through the green light and continued east. "True, but this will be his final warning to vacate. We'll have to take him in if he doesn't leave."

Jack chuckled. "At least he'll have a place to stay, but I don't know if there's a bunk big enough for him."

I swatted his arm. "The jail is a temporary solution. Does he have any money or relatives?"

"I don't know a damn thing about the guy, other than he gives me and everyone in town the creeps."

The Sims family homestead was located on Highway G, southeast of North Bend and just outside the city limits. With plenty of room for the enormous store and parking lot, that one-hundred-acre parcel was the best choice when the Swedish store chain bought it at a foreclosure auction four months back. With the paperwork signed, back taxes paid, and transfer of ownership complete, groundbreaking was scheduled to begin when the snow melted. The house and outbuildings were supposed to be razed first to keep squatters and vandals at bay, but Max was delaying the progress. He should have left months ago.

"I've never actually been here," I said as I turned into the driveway. "The deputies always took care of the fun stuff."

"Yeah, but apparently they didn't make much of an impact by taping eviction notices on the door."

"Well, let's see what he thinks of us."

The driveway went back nearly a quarter mile. Ahead stood the two-story clapboard farmhouse. To its right and across the driveway were the milk house and another building about the same size. Made of fieldstone, that one was probably the summer kitchen from back in the day. Farther down the driveway, and beyond all of the other buildings, stood the barn. Its worn, aged facade lacked paint, and tall weeds surrounded it. The crumbling structure bowed inward at the roofline and gave the appearance it might collapse any second. Next to the barn stood the long-abandoned cement silo, and broken fence boards lay scattered on the ground like pick-up sticks.

"Wow. This place is a mess, and the driveway is nothing but potholes. You'd think he'd be happy to leave," Jack said.

"Yeah, unless he has no place to go." I pointed toward a black van and an old tractor parked against the barn. "He must be home."

"Let's find out."

I did a wide turn at the house and aimed the cruiser back toward the road. I killed the engine, and we got out. Jack and I did a visual scan of our surroundings. We didn't need a blitz attack from anyone popping out from behind a shed. Everything seemed quiet. The rain had decreased, and the gray storm clouds looked a little less threatening. I glanced at the ground—no recent tire tracks other than the ones I'd just made. I cocked my head toward the house.

"Shall we?"

We took the four cement steps up, then I gave the porch door a hard knock. If he was home, he had to see us coming.

Jack pointed through the screen at the eviction notices torn up and strewn across the floor. In a pile before the kitchen door lay wet clothes and muddy boots. "Looks like he's here."

I knocked again and called out his name. Silence. "He's probably watching us through some crack in the wall."

"Avoidance isn't going to make his problems go away. So, now what?"

"Now we snoop. If he *is* watching us, he won't like us

milling around. He'll poke his head out sooner or later. Come on. Let's check the van."

I tried to stay on the grass as much as possible. I hadn't planned this trip, so walking through the mud in tan leather flats wasn't something I had anticipated.

The screen door creaked open, then slammed closed. We turned to see Max Sims, a huge man that was six foot four and pushing three hundred pounds, staring at us. His graying hair was slicked back behind his ears and touched the nape of his neck, and a full gray beard covered the lower half of his face. His forehead furrowed with anger and forced his bushy eyebrows to touch each other above his nose. He crossed his arms defiantly over his wide chest.

"Making yourself at home, are ya? What do you want?"

I wasn't in the mood for his attitude, and my hair was beginning to frizz. I lifted my badge from inside my jacket.

"I'm Sergeant Monroe from the sheriff's department." I thumbed Jack's chest. "This is Jack Steele, my partner."

"I asked you what you wanted."

"We're here as a final warning, Max. You need to vacate this property. You don't own it anymore, and legally, you're trespassing."

He laughed loudly and charged toward us.

Jack reached in under his jacket. "Stay where you are!"

"Or what?" He continued coming. The threatening expression on his face told me he wasn't kidding.

I pulled out my service weapon and pointed it at him, center mass. "Do you really want to do this?"

He stopped twenty feet from where we stood. "Get off my property."

"You have until noon on Wednesday to vacate, or you'll be removed forcibly. We aren't coming back alone, Max. Do yourself a favor and leave. If you're still here when we return, you'll be arrested."

He snickered a curse at us, returned to the house, and slammed the door at his back.

"That went well," Jack said as we climbed into the cruiser and drove back to town.

Chapter 3

Max cleared his throat before answering the phone. The only person calling would be someone responding to his ad, and he didn't want to scare them away.

"Hello," he said as he tried to soften his gruff voice.

"Hello, my name is Deborah French, and I'm calling about the ad in the paper. Is that position still available?"

Deborah French. Nice name.

"That depends. You sound awful young."

"I'm twenty and very responsible. The last few years of my grandmother's life, I helped out quite a bit. I'm a good housekeeper, and I know how to cook."

"In that case, yes, the job is still available." Max got comfortable on the overstuffed couch then reached for the ball gag. He twirled it in his hand and rubbed where the teeth marks were imbedded in the rubber. "I'd like to show you the place and explain the duties before I make a final decision, though. Are you able to stop by?"

She hesitated briefly on the other end. "Can you tell me just a bit more?"

"Sure. The pay is twelve dollars an hour, and you're only required to be here from noon until six. It's a mix of light housekeeping, lunch, and dinner, then you can go home. I'm not a big fan of breakfast." Max rose and walked to the built-in china cabinet. He gave the handles a jerk and opened the double doors. As he continued the conversation, he browsed the selection of cutting tools his father had left him. "Do you live in North Bend?"

"Um, no, but close by. My family moved to the area last summer."

Good, she doesn't know our history.

"So are you going to stop over? I'll tell you what I like for meals, and you can take a look at the place. You said you're experienced. I'll give you my decision after you make lunch." He laughed at his own comment.

"Oh—okay, I'll come over now if you want."

"Wonderful. Here's the address."

With the phone back on the cradle, Max trudged up the staircase to his bedroom. Inside, he changed out of his denim overalls and put on a decent pair of pants. He smoothed back his hair so he'd look a bit more welcoming. He checked the time—11:30.

I'll kill her later. I want a decent lunch first.

He waited on the wingback chair near the driveway side window. He'd see her coming once she turned off the road. He looked at the combination clock and barometer hanging on the wall of the living room. Now it was nearly noon. Max got up and paced. He was anxious to get started. In a few days, he'd be forced from the farm, and he'd have to find a new killing and burial site.

The sound of crunching gravel interrupted his thoughts. Max went to the window and peered out. A car, dodging the rain-filled potholes, was approaching the house.

Good, she's here. Now the fun begins.

Max crossed the living room and pushed the kitchen curtains aside. Everything was in place and waiting. Through the screened porch windows, he saw her park the car. He watched as she got out and closed the car door behind her.

Just right—young and pretty.

She walked up the steps to the porch and knocked twice.

Max opened the creaky screen door and grinned. She appeared startled by his size but smiled and said hello.

"You must be Deborah French. I'm Max Sims. Come on in. We can talk in the kitchen." Max reached out and shook her hand, then moved aside and allowed her to pass.

Deborah French had long brown hair that glistened with the slightest bit of moisture from the outside air. He wanted to smell it then rip it from her head. Those large brown eyes would watch everything he intended to do to her. And that prominent beauty mark on the right side of her full lips? He'd cut that off her face. Max sized her up quickly. She couldn't weigh more than one hundred and ten pounds.

Easy enough to carry wherever I want to take her.

Max pulled out the chair where his grandmother used to sit and offered it to Deborah. "Here, have a seat. Go ahead and ask anything you want."

"Oh, okay. You said you'd tell me the kind of food you

like. Am I supposed to shop for it or just prepare it? And the light housekeeping involves what?"

He smiled widely, and she blushed. "I buy my own food, so all you have to do is prepare it. The light housekeeping involves washing dishes, vacuuming, and doing laundry—nothing else. Want to start now? It *is* lunchtime. I have bread, cheese, and baked beans. How about grilled cheese sandwiches?"

"Okay, that's easy enough. Should I just dig in?"

"Absolutely. What do you like to drink?"

"Do you have soda?"

"Sure do. I'll get the drinks."

Max watched as she prepared the sandwiches at the stove, her back toward him. Slipping the ground-up Rohypnol into her soda can was a cakewalk, and it dissolved immediately. He gave the can a swirl. Max put the sodas, plates, and silverware on the table, then placed a napkin to the left of each plate. The melted cheese sandwiches went from the griddle to a platter. Deborah set the platter on the table along with the bowl of baked beans.

"I guess that's it. Does lunch look okay?"

"It looks perfect, and I'll pour the sodas. I prefer glasses to cans on the table."

He noticed how her speech began to slur after fifteen minutes. A double dose worked quickly on someone her size. At the half-hour mark, her head fell into her plate of beans.

"Yep, looks like you've had enough."

Max pushed his chair back and stood, then yanked her

head out of the plate by her hair. Her head flopped backward. He slid the plate to the side, wiped her face with the napkin, and lifted her off the chair. He planned to introduce her to his favorite tree in the woods.

Chapter 4

"How did it go at the Sims house?" Clark asked after Jack and I returned from lunch.

Jack huffed sarcastically and took a seat. He rearranged the pen cup and straightened the slew of files on his desk.

"Care to tell me what the huff means?"

"Let me explain, Jack. In a nutshell, I had to draw my weapon on him."

"What the hell for?"

"I felt we were in imminent danger, boss. When a giant that weighs almost twice what Jack does comes at us with that look in his eyes—"

Jack interrupted. "Yeah, what she said. We gave him a warning to stop, but he kept coming."

"And he knows we're returning in two days, right?"

I nodded. "It's going to be tough getting him to vacate, Lieutenant. I wonder what will happen to all his belongings. He doesn't have enough time to clear that place out."

"Not our problem," Clark said. "He's had plenty of warnings to leave. Everything will likely be sold at public auction, then the house and buildings will be torn down."

"I'll tell you one thing, he isn't going to leave willingly. I wish he'd just disappear." I looked around the bull pen. "Speaking of disappear, where did Clayton and Billings go?"

"They went to Waupun Correctional Institution to interview Tony Lynch one last time. If he doesn't give up the location of Jillian Wiley, he's getting transferred to Boscobel. He can play with the big boys there."

"Wow—that place is no joke. I thought USP Atlanta was on the table so he could be near his family."

"Not unless Jillian's body is actually found and identified. Tony isn't getting any deals in advance. You know, Darryl Sims is in Boscobel, and it was your own father that put him there."

"My dad did? He was a rookie detective twenty years ago, wasn't he?"

Clark chuckled. "He sure was. We were both pretty green back then."

"Yeah, and I bet you two have a lot of stories you could share," Jack said. "Maybe Max is weird because of his old man. Darryl *did* murder the grandma and mom in the very house Max still lives in."

"Yeah," I said, "but wouldn't that make you want to leave—like a long time ago?"

Clark raked his hands through his hair. "We don't know what's in his mind, even now. Max was still a teenager when those murders took place. Even young adults are impressionable, for sure. Could be why he's a little off himself."

"What happens if he's still at the house when we go back?" I asked.

"We're going in with four deputies and heavy-duty handcuffs. He's going to sit in a cell for a while until he cools off. After that, if he causes any more trouble, he might become a permanent resident."

My cell phone rang on my desk. I picked it up and saw that Amber was calling. "Excuse me, guys. I have to get this." I walked down the hallway to the empty conference room and went inside. I closed the door behind me.

"Hey, sis, what's the word?" I heard cheering in the background. "Is that Kate?"

"Yes, and we both passed every preliminary exam. We start classes next week. Yay! There's a laundry list of supplies we need to buy before then."

I laughed. "There sure is. I'll help you guys out with that, and I'm so proud of both of you. Which academy are you going to?"

"The closest school is in Pewaukee. We'll buddy up and ride together every day."

"I can't wait to hear more. Both of you meet me at the Washington House at six—my treat. You can tell me everything over dinner."

"Sounds great. Talk to you later."

I couldn't wipe the smile off my face when I clicked off the call and went back to the bull pen.

"What's up? You look like the cat that ate the canary," Clark said.

"Amber and Kate just got accepted into the police

academy. I'm so happy for them."

Jack fist-bumped me. "That's cause for celebration."

"Then stop in at the Washington House after work and buy them a drink. I'm picking up the dinner tab."

"Congratulations. We'll both be there," Clark said as he returned to his office.

I heard his chair groan when he plopped down.

Jack glanced at the clock.

"Got somewhere to be?" I asked.

"Yeah, I'm going upstairs to interview the punks from the Sanfrony Auto Mall break-in. Maybe sitting in a cell for the last few weeks has improved their memories. Six people were on those videotapes of the break-in, yet we only have three upstairs."

"Want company? I'm not busy right now."

Jack jerked his head toward the beverage station. "Sure thing. I'll call John, and you grab the coffees."

Jack held the door open and let me pass through with a coffee in each hand. We took the stairs to the second floor, where we exchanged wisecracks with John while a deputy linked up each of our car thieves in an interrogation room.

"Looks like you're good to go," John said.

Jack and I entered the first interrogation room and took our seats across from punk number one.

I sipped my coffee then smiled. "What's up, Manny? Feeling like a bird today?"

He smirked at me. "What's that supposed to mean?"

"Just wondered if you felt like singing. I guarantee you, there are two more of your punk friends in the next rooms ready to tell us a story. First one that talks wins the grand prize."

"Which is?"

"That's decided after we hear the names. Three of your boys haven't been accounted for yet."

He stared down at the table without speaking.

"Time's up. Let's go," Jack said.

We rose and walked to the door.

Jack looked back. "You snooze, you lose. We're moving on to room number two."

We went through the same process in the next room except we stretched the truth a bit. Actually we lied, but cops were allowed to do that.

Jack started the conversation with Mike Cross. "Here's your last chance to come clean, Mikey."

"The name is Mike."

"That's what he said, Mikey." I smirked and elbowed Jack.

Jack went on. "Manny has already given us one name. Actually, he threw you under the bus and said you're the ringleader."

Mikey smirked and curled his lip. "Like I believe anything you pigs say. Whose name did he give you?"

"That shouldn't be your first concern. I'd worry about what he told us about you." I leaned in and whispered in Jack's ear, just to unnerve our underage car thief and vandal.

"Yeah, I agree," Jack said as he opened the folder in front of him. "You could get an additional year or two at the state pen if what Manny said is true. Nice chatting with you, Mikey."

We pushed our chairs back.

"Fine, I'll give you the other names, but whatever Manny said is a lie."

"The names?" I turned to the next blank page of my notepad and waited with a pen in my hand.

Mikey slumped lower in his chair with a mix of fear and defeat written across his face. "John Pensley, Andy Gomez, and Billy Handler—they all live in town."

I smiled and cocked my head at him. "Now, doesn't that give you a warm, cuddly feeling to come clean? Jack, call the city boys and have those punks picked up. We'll get back to you soon, Mikey. I'll even bring you a candy bar."

Jack closed the door at our backs as we exited the room.

"Toss them back in their pens, John." I jerked my head toward the interrogation rooms. "We have all the information we need for now."

Downstairs, after Jack made the call to the North Bend PD, we returned to our usual routine when we weren't on an active case—sorting files, signing off documents, and answering phone calls. I was anxious for Clayton and Billings to return from Waupun. With any luck, Tony Lynch would show some empathy for Jillian Wiley's family and tell them where her body was located.

At four o'clock, I heard the beep of numbers being entered into the keypad on the bull pen security door. The boys were back.

I set my pen down and closed the file folder I was reviewing. Clark walked out of his office and pulled up my guest chair.

"Well, let's hear it," he said as he pulled his right leg to rest over his left knee.

Clayton ground his fists into his eyes. "No luck, boss. That bastard won't tell us anything."

Clark groaned. "I guess he can go rot in Boscobel, then, and serve his time there. Indiana and Illinois can have him after his life sentence in Wisconsin for killing Tamara Simpson."

"Okay, guys, I'm heading home to change clothes." I looked down at my feet. "And shoes. Guess the muddy driveway at the Sims homestead didn't bode well for these tan flats. By the way, you two didn't hear the news." I grinned at Billings and Clayton.

"Yeah, what's that?" Billings asked.

"Kate and Amber are beginning their police training next week. They both passed the interviews, background checks, and physicals. We're having dinner at the Washington House at six. Stop in and have a drink."

Clayton poured himself a cup of coffee. "Good for them. I bet they're super excited."

"Oh, they definitely are. Anyway, I'll catch you guys later." I walked out of the bull pen, said good night to Peggy and Jan, and exited the building. The clouds were breaking up, and the sky was beginning to clear. I inhaled a deep breath of spring air. This time of year always made me happy. Summer was right around the corner.

Chapter 5

He watched her as she finally regained consciousness. The sun had slipped behind the two-story farmhouse, and shadows filled the wooded area where she was being held. The rain had stopped, and a light breeze rustled through the budding trees. She lifted her head and looked around, groggy. The realization hit her quickly when she saw him. He sat on a chair in the woods, ten feet away, and smiled at her, a cigarette dangling from his lips. The smoke swirled above his head. Deborah couldn't move. She couldn't scream. Ropes held her tightly against the tree's rough bark, and the ball gag kept her silent.

Max stood and walked over to her. He slapped the side of her face. "Here, let me help you wake up."

Her eyes bulged with fear, and tears streamed down her cheeks.

He squeezed her face in his large hand. "Pay attention. Now, see this tree over here?" He walked three feet to his left. Her eyes followed. "These marks on the tree show how many women have died right where you're standing. You're tied against the sacrificial tree. Don't you feel honored?" He laughed wickedly and approached her, his face only inches from hers. "This homestead is a killing field, Deborah, and a burial ground. It's been in the family forever, and now it's all going away. My old man has been in prison for years because of the cops in the area. I had to pick up where he left off. You understand, right? I have everything ready for you. Check it out." He heard her rapid breaths and muffled moans as he forced her head toward the pit he had dug in the ground. The hole was the perfect size for a body. "See, nice digs, huh?" He roared out a belly laugh. "That was pretty funny if I do say so myself. Is there anything you want to say?"

The stench of his breath filled her nostrils. She nodded and pulled back against the tree.

He released the ball gag. "Nobody will hear you, so it's useless to scream. What do you want to say?"

"Why? Why are you doing this to me? You don't even know me." She choked through her words.

"Because I like it." Max plunged the skinning knife into her chest and watched as the life drained from her body. Her eyes remained open and fixed on him. He stared at her until her head dropped to her chest. "Guess that's my last one for a while." He loosened the ropes, and her knees folded. Her body fell to the ground, and Max rolled her into the hole then grabbed the shovel that was propped against the chair. He flicked his cigarette butt into the grave and threw the first shovelful of dirt on top of her.

The deed was done, and the earth accepted her body,

just as it had with the dozens before her. Max took his seat on the chair and watched as the evening turned to darkness and the stars lit the sky. He had to get the incriminating possessions out of the house. Anything that once belonged to his father and had been passed down to him needed to go. He'd load the van tomorrow. The knife collection and bondage devices had been kept in the barn's loft twenty years ago when the police raided the farm and took his father away. The collection was never discovered. Max had remained in the home all these years and continued where Darryl left off. Killing was in his blood, and he had learned everything about it from his father at an early age.

Chapter 6

The sun blasted through my window and woke me at six o'clock. My head pounded with every beat of my heart. I squeezed my temples and hoped the pain would stop, but it didn't. I fumbled with the alarm clock until I found the shutoff button—I didn't want to hear that shrill blast. A bottle of aspirin was calling my name, but I wasn't quite ready to be upright.

Bits and pieces of last night came back to me as I lay with my head buried under my pillow—I needed darkness. What started as a low-key dinner held in honor of Amber and Kate's acceptance into the police academy turned into a free-for-all that could have rivaled any sorority or fraternity's alcohol-induced party. I chuckled through my pain and tried to remember how I got home. I gradually crawled out of bed.

With my arms outstretched, I walked forward and used the walls of the hallway for support, just in case I tipped over. Two bodies lay in the family room—Kate on the recliner, Amber on the sofa. They both slept, Kate with her mouth open and Amber with her arm dangling off the couch. I was sure by now she had lost all the blood flow to that limb. I prayed that someone had set up the coffee last night, but my prayers went unanswered. Kate stirred when she heard my banging in the kitchen.

"What's going on?" She cranked the recliner's lever and sat up, then groaned. "What am I doing at your house?"

I laughed at the wild mop of hair on her head while I searched for aspirin. "I bet we look the same right now, and I have no idea why you're here. I don't remember coming home."

"Me, either. Is the coffee ready?"

"Can you give me a second? I still don't have my bearings, and aspirin comes first."

I heard Amber moan. "My eyelids are stuck. They won't open."

"Then keep them closed," I said. "Where the hell are the aspirin?"

"Probably in your medicine cabinet."

Kate got up and shuffled to the kitchen. "Go find your aspirin. I'll make the coffee."

"Does anyone know how we got here last night?" I asked as I went back down the hallway.

"Jack drove us home, I think. I'm pretty sure our cars are still downtown."

I returned with the bottle in my hand and passed out the aspirin. "How the hell am I supposed to get to work?"

Kate plopped back down on the recliner. "Call a cab. You and Amber can split the cost since both of your cars are downtown. I walked to the Washington House—that much I remember. But I have no idea why I ended up here."

After downing four aspirin, I took my coffee and headed for the shower. Maybe a dose of scalding water would revive my brain.

Kate yelled down the hallway as I dressed for work. Thankfully, my headache was starting to subside.

"Jack is here."

"What?"

Someone banged on my bedroom door, and I opened it a crack. Kate stood on the other side.

"I said Jack is here."

"Jack, as in my partner, Jack Steele?" I heard him laugh from the kitchen.

"What other Jack do you know?"

I walked out with the comb in my hand. I did a double take at him, then the clock. "You're normally asleep at this hour. What the hell is wrong with you?"

"Somebody has to drive you to get your car." He chuckled at our appearances. "Do any of you remember last night?"

The three of us shook our heads.

He smirked. "Then maybe it's for the best. I'll help myself to the coffee. Amber, you better get dressed if you want a ride to your car." He looked at Kate and laughed. "Guess you slept in your clothes."

We were downtown fifteen minutes later.

"Thanks for the ride," Amber said as I lifted the passenger seat and let her and Kate out. Amber walked to her car, and Kate headed the two blocks to her apartment. I sat back down in the passenger seat for a moment and cradled my head.

"Still hurting?" Jack smiled. "You girls really lit up the Washington House last night."

"I don't want to know about it. We didn't piss anyone off, though, did we?"

"Nope, not at all."

"Good. Thanks for the ride, partner. I got it from here."

"Do you want me to stop and get you more aspirin?"

"Nah—thanks, anyway. I have plenty in my desk drawer." I climbed out of Jack's Charger and clicked the key fob to my Cobra. The door locks sprang up, and I climbed inside. I gave Jack a nod as I backed out of the parking spot and headed to work.

Inside, I sat at my desk with my head in my hands. I glanced up—Clayton, Billings, and Clark looked as bad as I did. The bull pen was quiet save the occasional moan that came from one of us every few minutes.

"How did you stay sober, Jack?" Clayton asked.

"I wasn't *that* sober, but at midnight I switched to soda. You goofballs guzzled booze until last call."

"Jade, will you share your bottle of aspirin with me?" Clark asked.

"Sure, boss, but you have to come and get it."

By noon, I was back to true form. Other than nagging headaches, everyone else said they felt human again too.

"Are you capable of eating?" Jack asked.

"I think I can handle soup and crackers. Want to go to

Omicron? They have the best chicken dumpling soup in town."

"Sure. After lunch I want to swing by the Sims house. Maybe Max will already be gone."

"Do you really want to piss him off even more than he is? We told him he has until tomorrow to be out."

"I know, but we can still drive by slowly and see if he's making an attempt to leave."

The drive to Omicron took only five minutes, but as always, the line to be seated was long. That restaurant had been in North Bend for twenty-something years and was a favorite of the geriatric crowd. We went there because the food was good. Luckily, we were seated ten minutes after we'd arrived.

"Coffee?" the waitress asked while holding a carafe of leaded and unleaded. We both took the leaded.

"I'll have a bowl of the chicken dumpling soup too."

"You got it, hon."

Jack ordered the breakfast special, which was served all day long—two flapjacks, two sausages, and two eggs prepared any way he liked. He took them over easy.

"I'm really looking forward to that store being built. It's already behind schedule because of Max."

Jack agreed. "I think they want to be open by next Christmas."

"Ugh. We just got through with the cold. I don't even want to think of it again quite yet."

"Winter in Wisconsin is inevitable, Jade, unless you have other plans?"

"I'm still giving that some thought."

Jack sipped his steaming coffee and gave me the right eyebrow raise. "You aren't serious, are you? You just bought your condo."

"Owning a house isn't a life sentence, Jack. People flip places all the time and move somewhere else."

"But you're a lifer here. What about work?"

I jerked my head at the waitress who was approaching with a platter.

"Here you go, folks. Enjoy your meal." She smiled, topped off our coffees, and left to wait on another table.

"Let's eat. All this talk is just speculation, anyway." I dug into my soup and plucked out the first dumpling.

We left the restaurant at twelve forty-five and continued south to Paradise. Jack turned left and went two miles to Highway G. The Sims homestead was a mile farther on the right. With the trees along his driveway still in the budding stage, we were able to see in as we drove by at a crawl.

"Humph—there he is, loading the van," Jack said. "That's a good sign."

"He can't possibly be taking everything unless he's hired a moving truck."

"Guess it's a moot point. Whether he has everything or not, he still needs to be gone in twenty-four hours."

We headed back to the station. With all likelihood, the groundbreaking ceremony could take place on Friday. After that, they'd bring in the heavy equipment and get started.

Chapter 7

He looked over his shoulder and smirked when the black cruiser passed slowly by his driveway. He knew the entire town was itching for him to move out and move on. Nobody cared about Max Sims. He had lived in the shadow of his infamous father and overheard whispers for the last twenty years. He had turned into a recluse with a chip on his shoulder.

Max had lived at that farm his entire life. Without a plan going forward or another place to call home, he was more than angry and lost about what to do next. He needed to talk to his father.

With the last cutting tool in his tote, Max carried the bin to the van and placed it in the back. He'd return later and grab anything else his father thought was important or possibly incriminating, then leave the homestead for good.

Yesterday, Max had called the Wisconsin Secure Program Facility in Boscobel to set up a visitation with prisoner number 450-A72—his father. The hour-long visit was scheduled for four o'clock. Darryl Sims would tell his son what to do.

Max pushed up the sleeve on his plaid shirt and checked the time—1:15. He'd leave in forty-five minutes. There was enough room in the back of the van for a few more items. He flung the wooden cellar doors open, and they hit the ground with a hard thud. He swiped at the cold cement wall until he found the light switch then flipped it on. The basement was nine steps lower. The damp, pungent air hit him halfway down. At the bottom of the stairs hung another light fixture, he pulled the string and the area in front of that locked door illuminated. The key buried deep in his pocket would open the padlock to the room Max hadn't entered in years.

He turned the key in the knob and gave the door a hard shove. Years of basement dampness had the wood swollen and the framework warped. He shoved it again. This time he put his shoulder into it. The door creaked while it scraped against the basement floor. Cobwebs stretched as the door gave way. Spiders and centipedes scurried and looked for a new place to call home. Inside the dark room, Max swatted at the air and wiped the webs from his face. He remembered the light was centered in the room. He felt the pull string and gave it a tug—surprisingly, the bulb came to life after all that time.

Max looked from side to side and remembered the day when his mother and grandmother were executed in that room. They were the last women his father killed, and Max had kept that twenty-year secret, never uttering a word about the rest. Nobody knew what lay buried within the woods and fields on that property. The police had no idea there were more women—many more.

Darryl Sims had been spotted one day as a deliveryman set a box on the porch. The Sims patriarch had exited the basement through those outer doors, his clothes and hands stained with blood. The horrific sight frightened the deliveryman enough to go straight to the North Bend Sheriff's Department. After the carnage was discovered and before Darryl was taken away, he whispered to Max how he'd saved the best for last.

Darryl was a psychopath—a vicious, evil man. To remain in his father's good graces, Max joined in on the horrendous acts Darryl inflicted on women. In time, Max began to enjoy it, but he wanted no part in the deaths of his own flesh and blood. He refused to help his father that day. Law enforcement had always viewed Max as a victim—they had no idea there were more women beneath the ground.

The stained basement floor gave testimony of the murders that had taken place twenty years earlier. Max crossed the room and stared at the dark spots. Arm chains hung there, still bolted to the stone walls. He pulled out the hammer from the pant hook in his carpenter jeans. With all his force, he hit the wall with the claw until the mortar crumbled and the chains fell to the floor. With a swipe of his foot, they slid across the room. Max picked up the chains, pulled the light string, and walked out. The last open spot in the van was filled with a box of ladies' purses that had been kept as souvenirs over the years. It was time to go—a three-hour drive lay ahead of him.

Chapter 8

"Boss, should we go ahead and let the mayor know that Max Sims will be gone by noon tomorrow?"

"You mean by any means necessary?" Clark groaned at the thought.

"We did see him loading totes into the back of his van. He might surprise us all and go peacefully."

"Well, we can only hope. I'll call the mayor now so he has time to inform everyone. He'll likely have a photographer, the investors, and of course, the representative of the store present."

"Do you have a minute, Lieutenant?"

Clark leaned back in his chair and rolled his neck. "What's on your mind, Monroe?"

"Just wondering why everyone in town looks at Max Sims as a pariah. He didn't kill his mom and grandma—his dad did."

"It was a big deal back then, Jade. Darryl Sims was a mean and vicious son of a bitch. Murder didn't happen in North Bend, let alone two women from his own family.

Your dad said Max never shed a tear about the murders or when Darryl was sentenced to life in prison."

"But Max was already an adult by then."

"Yep," Clark said. He shook his head as if he were trying to erase the memories. "Max was nineteen at the time of the killings, but he was stone cold, just like his old man. People assumed he'd turn out like Darryl—a bad seed."

"Has he ever been arrested for anything?"

"Nope, not a thing. Seems like he's always minded his own business. I recently heard that Max was nearly broke. His grandma left him some money, but I guess that's almost dried up. I suppose he had to choose to either keep up the property tax or have money to live on. It looks like he decided on the latter."

Jack peeked around the corner. "Am I interrupting?"

"Nah—we're good. I have to call the mayor now, anyway." Clark picked up his desk phone, clearly ready to call.

"You might want to hold off for a minute."

Clark set the receiver back on the cradle. "What's up?"

"I just got a call that a local twenty-year-old female has gone missing. The mother said her daughter was going to interview for a housekeeping job yesterday, then go out with friends afterward. When she noticed the bed hadn't been slept in, she assumed her daughter bunked at someone's house last night."

I leaned against the doorway with my arms crossed in front of me. "And?"

"And the daughter hasn't answered her cell phone or

returned text messages all day. Her mother called everyone she could think of. Nobody has seen the daughter—not even yesterday."

I shrugged. "She's old enough to go missing if she wants to."

"True, but the mom is adamant that her daughter isn't that way. Supposedly, she's happy, optimistic, and hardworking, that sort of thing."

"Who is this girl, and where does she live?"

Jack checked his notes. "Says here she lives just this side of Slinger, and her name is Deborah French."

"Pretty name. Should we go interview the family, Lieutenant?" I was already at my desk with my purse slung over my shoulder.

Clark waved us on. "Yeah, and keep me posted."

I turned back before we walked out. "Will do, boss."

Jack called Deborah's mother and told her we were on our way. We climbed into the nearest cruiser in the lot, with Jack behind the wheel.

"Give me your notes so I can program the address into my GPS."

Jack reached into his back pocket and pulled out his notepad. He handed it to me, and we were off. "Shouldn't take more than twenty minutes to get there," he said as he turned right onto Washington Street.

I stretched my seat belt over my chest and buckled it. "I'm not glad that anyone has gone missing, so don't take this the wrong way, but I do like to stay busy."

"Yep, I'm on the same page. Hopefully we can get this

straightened out quickly and find the daughter. It would be nice to have something end happily." Jack cocked his head at me.

"What?"

"Just wondering what you and Clark were talking about, that's all."

"You mean earlier?"

"Yeah."

"I asked him why everyone in town dislikes Max Sims. He said it's because the townspeople assumed he was like his old man—mean and psychotic. I guess my dad told Clark how Max never shed a tear about the murders or even when Darryl went to prison."

"Yeah, he's definitely an odd duck."

I pointed at the green road sign ahead. "This might be our turnoff." Right then, my female-voiced GPS assistant told us to turn left at the next intersection. I looked down at the road map on my phone. "It shows we only have a mile to go."

Jack nodded.

I spoke up again. "Okay, turn left and then right. If this is correct, we should see Liberty Lane coming up."

Jack did as I instructed and slowed at the next right—Liberty Lane.

"Good, now we have to find house number 630. Looks like the even numbers are on my side. Here it is, the tan two-story."

Jack pulled into the driveway and parked. We exited the car, and I pulled my chain badge out from inside my blouse. Jack wore his on his belt clip. The house was a typical subdivision home, clean with a well-manicured lawn. Everything looked completely normal, and the neighborhood was nice. We walked up the sidewalk, and Jack rang the bell.

A woman peeked around the sheer curtain on the sidelight. I smiled and showed her my badge. She opened the door widely.

"Sorry, please come in." She stepped aside and welcomed Jack and me into her foyer. "I'm Lynn French, and I'm not usually this cautious during the daytime hours." She extended her hand and shook both of ours. I introduced Jack and myself.

"Shall we?" She motioned toward the living room, and we walked in and took a seat.

"Mrs. French—"

"Please, call me Lynn."

I gave her a thoughtful smile. "Okay, Lynn, what time did Deborah leave home yesterday?"

"I believe it was around eleven thirty. She said the gentleman that placed the newspaper ad mentioned something about her making lunch for him."

"That's an odd request."

She nodded. "I thought so too, but he said he was going to decide whether to hire her or not based on her abilities."

Jack didn't think it was so unusual. "Many people make employment decisions based on the skill of a potential employee. Would you want me to cook for you, Jade?"

I chuckled. "Guess you do have a point. Lynn, do you still have that newspaper ad?"

"Give me just a second. I think it's in the recycling bin." She excused herself and went around the corner to what I assumed was the kitchen. We heard newspapers being shuffled.

Lynn was back in less than three minutes. She gripped yesterday's classifieds between her fingers. "Here we go. The ad is circled in red marker."

She handed the section of newspaper to Jack, and we read it together.

"You said the ad was placed by a man?"

"Yes."

"Did she happen to mention his name?"

"Um—Mike, maybe, or Mark. I'm sorry, I was in the middle of something when she said his name. Now I can kick myself."

"No problem. We'll track the phone number. Is there a Mr. French?"

"Yes, but he's out of town right now. I've been keeping him posted."

"Ma'am," Jack said, "would you write down a handful of Deborah's friends and their phone numbers so we can start on their interviews?"

"Yes, that's easy. She only has about five close friends. We moved to the area from Alabama last summer. She doesn't have a wide circle of friends yet." Lynn picked up her cell phone and scrolled through the numbers. Jack handed her his notepad, and she transferred each phone number to it.

"There you go, detectives." She gave Jack his notepad

back. “I’ve spoken to each of her friends, and they all said the same thing—they didn’t see Deborah yesterday. I’m beside myself with worry.”

We stood and handed Lynn our cards. “We’ll get on this right away, Mrs. French. By the way, did Deborah say where the man lived?”

She sighed. “Again, I wasn’t paying close enough attention. I know she said it was about twenty minutes east. She was figuring what the mileage would be if she actually got the position.”

Jack wrote that down then shook her hand. “We’ll be in touch, and feel free to call either of us if you think of something else or hear from Deborah.”

“I certainly will. Thank you.”

She closed the door behind us, and Jack and I climbed into the cruiser. I stared at the newspaper clipping as Jack backed out of the driveway.

“Something bothering you?”

“I’m not feeling good about Deborah. I’ll get Billy on this phone number right away and see what pops.”

Chapter 9

Max arrived at the small town of Boscobel. He'd have to enter the village, then turn back east to get to the penitentiary. Surrounded by farm country, he felt right at home in the area—he'd been going there for years. The prison was a maximum security facility for men, often holding the worst of the worst.

Max reached the parking lot of WSPF and followed the long sidewalk to the visitors' entrance. He'd have a thirty-minute wait while Darryl was being processed for the visit. Every third month, inmates were allowed one special circumstance visit through a Plexiglas divider. Normal visiting hours were between eight and three o'clock daily in the visitors' center. Max considered this visit a very special circumstance. He showed his ID when he signed in, then a guard led him to a holding area where he was searched for contraband. All of his loose items needed to be placed in a locker where he'd retrieve them after the visit. The locker key was the only thing allowed with Max into the visiting booth.

"Number four, you're next," the guard called out as his eyes scanned the few people sitting in the waiting area. "Please stand." Max did as he was told. "Come this way, sir." Max followed.

He was taken through one more room before he reached the visitation area. A final check for disallowed items was performed, then the guard nodded. The heavy steel door slid open, and Max was ushered through.

"Take a seat there." The guard pointed at a stool. "Prisoner 450-A72 will be out shortly, and your half hour will begin once he's seated." The guard turned and left the way he had entered.

Max waited. He rearranged himself on that small stool several times. His back began to ache. He rolled his neck and drummed his fingers on the stainless steel counter and waited some more. He finally heard movement coming from the hallway beyond his view. Voices echoed off the stark walls, and footsteps sounded on the tiled floors. A door opened, and Max saw Darryl pass through.

Darryl Sims was thin, unlike Max, but also tall. His dark blond hair had grown long, and his face was as wrinkled as old shoe leather. His disheveled appearance made him look much older than his sixty years. Prison hadn't been kind, and he was still as mean and nasty as ever, except to Max.

"Your half hour starts now," the guard said.

Darryl took a seat across the counter from Max, separated by the divider. They spoke through the six-inch screened circle located in the center of the window.

"Good to see you, son. What's going on?"

Max ground his fingertips into his temples. "Damn cops. You know the property is sold and the developer is pushing to get me out of there. Every few weeks, the sheriff's department sends a deputy to the house, and they smack an eviction notice on the door."

"Right—did something change? They've been doing that for months."

"Oh yeah, you could say that. Now they're threatening to lock me up if I'm not out by tomorrow."

Darryl rubbed his forehead. A worried expression furrowed his brows. He leaned forward and spoke in a whisper. "What about the field and woods?"

"No clue." Max noticed where the closest camera was, then he cupped his hands around his mouth. "I have to get out of there and hide somewhere. When those bulldozers come in, all hell's going to break loose."

Darryl smirked. "They'll think I did all of it. I'm a lifer, anyway. What difference does it make?"

"I don't want them asking me questions. You know what pressure does to me. That damn sergeant drew her gun on me yesterday."

"What?"

"I told you I'm not good under pressure. There were two of them. One was a man, and the other was a woman. The woman said she was a sergeant at the sheriff's department. Stupid bitch pulled her weapon out and aimed it right at my chest. She said her name was Sergeant Monroe, and she thought she was hot shit with that gun in her hand."

"Monroe? How old did she look?"

"Younger than me. Early thirties, I'd guess—why?"

"I wonder what the odds are of her being Tom Monroe's daughter."

"Who is that?"

"You might not remember names from twenty years ago, but I sure as hell do. They're burned in my mind forever. Tom Monroe, a young detective at the sheriff's department at the time, was the man that arrested me and testified against me in court. It's because of that bastard, and Judge Gardino, the judge that sentenced me, that I'm doing a life term here."

"What do you want me to do, Pa?"

"Have you emptied out the house?"

Max huffed. "And done what with the stuff? They gave me two days to vacate. So far I've loaded the van with anything that could incriminate me." Max's eyes darted to the cameras located at each corner. He whispered to his father, "I have all the weapons and memorabilia out, if you know what I mean."

Darryl nodded. "There isn't a computer in the house, right?"

"Nope, I just have my smartphone."

"Okay, once you leave, you'll have to hunker down somewhere that you'll get Internet service. You need to find out about that woman and Tom Monroe. Get their history, find out where they live, and see if they're related. Look up that judge and his family too. It will keep you occupied. Go through the house again and grab anything and everything that you can jam into the van. Look through papers, old documents, and bank statements—burn everything except what you need." Darryl paused as if in thought. He pressed his wrinkled forehead with his fingertips. "Listen carefully, son. Years ago, your uncle Lee had a cabin in a secluded woods south of Green River Falls. Do you remember the place?"

"Yeah, I think so. I'm sure I could find it again."

"Good. That might work, and as far as I know, it's been vacant for years. Go there and lie low for a month or two. You can fish for your dinner. Go to town when you need to use the Internet, otherwise keep your phone turned off. There probably isn't electricity at that cabin, anyway. Find out as much as you can about that bitch sergeant and Tom Monroe. See what he's up to these days. Get information on that judge and his whereabouts too. Come back next week during regular visiting hours and update me. Remember, keep that phone off unless you're using it. Cops can track any kind of phone by the closest cell tower."

"What am I supposed to do for money?"

"Call the banker and tell him to release the trust fund your mama set up years ago. It was being held back until you turned forty. You always had your grandma's money to live off of, anyway. You might get penalized for drawing it out early, but what choice do you have?"

Max nodded.

The metal door slid open, and the guard entered. "Your time is up, Sims. Back to your cell."

Darryl gave his son a wink and walked out of the room.

Max left with a new mission. He didn't have the private

sanctuary where he'd conduct business anymore. For now, his new focus would be on that woman from the sheriff's department—Sergeant Monroe—her family, and Judge Gardino.

Max memorized Darryl's instructions and returned to the homestead to spend his last night there. He'd start a bonfire and burn everything that could be incriminating. In the morning, with a loaded van, he'd leave the residence for good.

Chapter 10

"Sorry, Jade, but it's a burner phone. It's going to take a court order or a stroke of luck to find out who owns it."

"The stroke-of-luck part being we ping its location?" I sat downstairs in the tech department, talking to Billy about the phone number on the ad.

"Yeah, but it's not going to give us a definitive location, just a triangulated area. Call the newspaper and find out who placed the ad."

"I will, but I was hoping to go an easier route. They'll want a warrant, and that's going to take time. I'll see what Clark says." I stood and pushed the roller chair against the wall before I walked out. "Thanks, Billy."

He nodded and got back to work. Upstairs, I knocked on Clark's office door.

He glanced up from his computer screen and waved me in. "What's up, Jade?"

"Boss, can you request a warrant for me?"

"Why?"

"To speed things up in this search for Deborah French.

Jack is out with Billings and Clayton interviewing Deborah's friends, and I was going to work here and figure out who owns the phone number attached to the ad."

Clark leaned back in the oversized leather desk chair. "And?"

"And Billy hit a dead end. It's a burner phone. A court order to identify the owner of that phone number would take the same amount of time as a warrant for the newspaper ad. It's a horse apiece."

"Let's see what the guys have to say when they get back." The lieutenant looked at the clock. "It's almost closing time at the courthouse, anyway. I'll make a decision on the warrant tomorrow."

The security door between the bull pen and the dispatch counter opened at five thirty. Jack, Adam, and Chad walked through. Clark rose from his desk and joined us.

"What's the word?" he asked as he pulled up a chair.

Jack sat while Clayton and Billings filled their coffee cups.

"Not a lot, boss," Billings said as he headed to his desk. "Clayton and I interviewed three of the girls, and Jack took the only guy and the last girl on the 'friends' list. Apparently the girls work together at a coffee shop in town. Yesterday was Deborah's day off, and she'd mentioned how she was going to look for additional part-time work. They were supposed to get together last night and hang out for a while, but Deborah never showed up. Each friend said they tried her cell phone, and none of them got through."

Jack opened his notepad and looked over his own

chicken scratch, his eyebrows furrowed.

"Have anything else to add, Jack?" Clark asked.

"Just double-checking. My notes are primarily the same as what Billings said. Nobody talked to her yesterday at all. The text messages went unanswered too. One girl"—Jack flipped the page and looked for her name—"Macy Link, showed me the texts she sent out starting around six o'clock last night. Deborah didn't respond to any of them."

"Doesn't sound good, boss. Did any of you talk to the manager at the coffee shop?"

Jack turned toward me and spoke up. "I went there, but the manager was at a different location. The assistant manager showed me Deborah's schedule for the week. It looked like she was supposed to close for the next three nights. Brent, the assistant manager, said Deborah was responsible and never missed work."

"Okay, we have a missing girl that was last known to be going to an interview for a housekeeping job. That was what time, Jade?"

"Around noon yesterday, sir."

"And nobody has seen or spoken to her since?"

"That's how it appears, boss." I rose, filled my coffee cup with water, and guzzled it.

Jack smiled. He knew I still had cotton mouth from my hangover.

"Okay, the courthouse offices are closed, and no judge in the county will answer a personal 'after hours' call from me. I'll request a warrant for the newspaper ad and the cell phone number first thing in the morning. Jade, grab Billy before he leaves. I need to know what prepaid phone carrier that number is attached to."

"Got it, boss." I left the bull pen and ran downstairs to catch Billy before he clocked out for the night. I caught him as he was locking the tech department door. "Billy, Clark needs to know the cell phone carrier for that burner phone. He's going to try getting the information about the owner. If he hits a brick wall, he'll go the usual route."

"Warrant?"

"Yep. Which do you think will go faster, the phone or newspaper?"

"The newspaper, just because it's local. The cell phone service belongs to a nationwide carrier. A lot of red tape is involved with that. Anyway, good luck, and the carrier is Talk-Time."

I groaned. "It would have to be one of the largest ones."

Back in the bull pen, I gave Clark the information.

"Okay, everyone go home and get some rest. I'm thinking we're going to get pretty busy tomorrow. Don't forget, we have to deal with Max Sims too." He wrote down the cell phone carrier name while he spoke. Jamison and Horbeck walked in as we were packing up. Clark waved us on. "I'll update them. Good night, guys."

The four of us walked out together. "Who wants to go out for a beer?" Billings asked.

"I ought to smack you, and thanks, but no thanks. I'm going to drink warm milk when I get home, but I have a fun idea. Let's place a bet on Max."

Jack nodded. He was all in.

"Okay, we each throw five bucks in the kitty. Write down which way you think it will go. He's still there or he's gone when we show up tomorrow. Whoever wins gets the money or has to split it with likeminded winners."

"What if we all win?" Clayton rolled his eyes at me and laughed.

"Then we keep our money and yours too—smart aleck. We'll figure it out in the morning. Night, guys."

Chapter 11

After a surprisingly decent night's sleep, I woke refreshed and ready to tackle the day. I wanted to get the Max Sims ordeal out of the way and concentrate on finding Deborah French. Two cups of coffee and a piece of raisin toast would hold me over until lunchtime.

Amber woke and started the coffee while I showered. With the towel wrapped around my head, turban style, I anticipated my first cup of Colombian roast as I walked to the kitchen. A plate of scrambled eggs was sitting at my spot on the breakfast bar, and a cup of coffee sat alongside it. Amber turned off the stovetop burner and dished up a plate of eggs for herself.

"I swear I'm going to gain twenty pounds with you living here." I plopped down on the barstool and dug in.

"No you won't. If you eat my food and lay off the doughnuts, you'll be fine."

"Humph—you might be on to something."

I finished breakfast and dressed. Polly and Porky tweeted happily when I opened the blinds and let them enjoy the sunshine. With their food dish full and the water changed, I said goodbye to them, Spaz, and Amber, and left through the garage. Each of us at the office had promised to be at work by seven thirty. We had that bet to take care of, then we'd see how soon Clark could get the warrants. We wanted to act on them as soon as possible.

Clark was on the phone when I arrived in the bull pen. Billings and Clayton sat at their desks, knee-deep in their morning busywork, and I had the files to look over for our latest guests that had recently checked in upstairs. Jack entered with a box of doughnuts. I groaned and sat on my hands while everyone else dug in.

Clark shoved half a glazed doughnut in his mouth and began talking. "Anyway, that was Judge Gardino on the phone earlier. He said he would try to expedite the warrants. He could possibly have them as early as nine o'clock."

"Good to know." I signed off on the paperwork that would hold our eighteen-year-old criminals upstairs until their pretrial hearings. I closed their folders. "So do we actually have to wait until noon to go out to the Sims property, boss?"

"We gave him two days to vacate, and I believe you and Jack told him noon today, didn't you?"

"Yeah, I guess we did."

"Then we have to wait. You know he'll fight leaving if you go early. Sit tight and call Deborah French's mom. Give her an update."

I dialed Lynn French's house number. A male voice picked up.

"Bob French speaking."

"Hello, Mr. French. This is Sergeant Jade Monroe from the Washburn County Sheriff's Department. I'm calling to give you and Lynn an update. You haven't heard from Deborah, have you?"

"Unfortunately not. I couldn't stand being out of the loop. I had to get home."

"Understood, sir. I wanted to let you and Mrs. French know that we're expecting warrants this morning to get the name of the person who placed that housekeeping ad. We do have a warrant for the phone number too, but I think the person's name will suffice. This isn't a large community."

I heard his sigh through the phone lines. "So you may have something to go on before noon?"

"It's a good possibility, sir. We'll keep you posted." I hung up right as Clark's phone rang. We sat on pins and needles and waited as we watched through the wall of glass that separated the bull pen from the lieutenant's office.

He gave us the thumbs-up and finished his phone call. Clark stood, slapped his hands together, and came out of his office. "Jade, you and Jack head over to the courthouse and pick up the warrant for the newspaper office. Clayton, get on the horn and call Talk-Time headquarters and tell them we have a warrant for the identity of the owner of that phone number. Billings, head over to the courthouse too and pick up that warrant. Get it back here fast. We'll likely have to get the local boys to serve it. Where is Talk-Time's headquarters?"

"They're in Indianapolis, boss," Billings said as he left the bull pen with Jack and me.

"Want a ride or would you rather walk?" I asked as we headed to the cruiser.

Billings groaned. "I'll walk—too many doughnuts, you know."

Jack climbed in behind the wheel, and I sat in the passenger seat. The courthouse was right around the corner, but we'd be continuing on to the newspaper office on Sixth Avenue with the warrant in hand.

Luckily, the warrants were ready and took only a few minutes to pick up. Billings had his too and walked out at the same time we did.

"Good luck, Adam," I said as we climbed back into the cruiser. We were downtown in less than five minutes.

City News had remained a staple on the corner of Sixth Avenue and Maple since the turn of the century. The old brick building had numerous additions on the back, but the facade remained the same as I remembered from childhood, when my dad insisted I have a paper route. I argued that a paper route was a job reserved for boys, but my pleas fell on deaf ears. For two years, I rode my bicycle to every house behind Main Street and tossed a rolled-up newspaper onto their front porch. Doing that helped me become the best female softball pitcher throughout my high school years.

Jack parked in a diagonal spot a few feet from the entrance to *City News*. We exited the cruiser and walked inside. A bell above the door dinged when we entered. Everything inside the front door looked the same as I remembered, down to the hard, wooden guest chairs lined up against the wall.

A receptionist greeted us as we approached the counter.

"Ma'am, we're from the sheriff's department and have a warrant for an advertiser's records. Can you help us with that?"

"Oh dear, of course not. I'll get the office manager, Mr. Emerson." The woman pushed back her chair and disappeared through a side door.

Jack and I took seats on those uncomfortable wooden chairs near the entrance and waited. Just as Jack picked up the newspaper lying on a side table, a fortyish looking man came out through the same door the woman had entered. We stood and walked toward him.

"Mr. Emerson?" I said.

"Yes, officers, how can I help you?"

Jack handed him the trifolded warrant. "Sir, we need the name and contact information for the person that placed the ad listed within this warrant."

Mr. Emerson unfolded the document and stared at it. "What's this all about? Nobody called here for information."

"Would you have released that to us over the phone?" I asked.

He scratched his balding head. "Probably not."

"Then we saved ourselves a useless phone call. Could you please get that information for us? Time is of the essence."

"Certainly, I'll be right back."

Jack paced in front of the counter.

"What's wrong? Don't like those chairs?" I smiled and paced too.

The door opened again, and Mr. Emerson appeared with an invoice pinched between his fingers.

"Here you go. Please let us know if you need anything else."

I glanced down at the invoice and had to hold my tongue until Jack and I got outside. "Thank you, sir."

Jack gave Mr. Emerson his card, then we shook his hand and left. The bell dinged at our backs.

"Son of a bitch," I said as I slammed the cruiser door behind me. "The ad belonged to Max Sims."

Chapter 12

Jack backed the cruiser onto the street, hit the lights, then squealed the tires and took off. Taking Seventh Avenue was the quickest way to avoid all the stoplights and get out of the downtown area.

"I have to tell Clark what we discovered." I pulled my cell phone from my pants pocket. It slipped out of my grasp and tumbled into the footwell. "Damn it." I unbuckled my seat belt, reached down, and fumbled in the darkened area until I felt its smooth shape. "Got it."

Jack glanced over. "Take a breath, Jade."

"Sorry, I'm just so pissed off." With my phone tight in my grip, I scrolled through the names until I got to Clark's desk phone number. I hit the call icon.

"Jade, what's up?"

"Boss, it's Max Sims."

"What is?"

"The newspaper ad belonged to him. We're on our way to his house. That son of a bitch did something to Deborah French. We're running the siren and lights."

"Damn it, we're on our way. Don't approach the house until we're there. Promise me, Jade."

"I promise, boss, just hurry."

Once Jack hit the freeway, he let loose and blew past every car on the road. It would take under ten minutes to reach the homestead.

"I hope there are vests in the trunk," Jack said. "That guy is no joke."

"My sidearm is no joke, either. We're getting close, Jack. Kill the siren. He doesn't need advance notice we're coming."

Jack silenced the siren before we reached Highway G. The radio squawked, and I picked up. Clayton was calling from another cruiser. "What's your location, Jade?"

"We're about two minutes from the house, and you?"

"We're about three minutes out. The boss said to hold tight. We have two squads dispatched too. You should be seeing them any second."

"Yep, I see lights approaching. Okay, we're going to park behind a stand of trees a few hundred feet from the driveway and suit up. We'll be waiting for you guys."

"Roger that." Clayton clicked off.

Jack pulled to the side of the road and killed the engine. "Ready for this, Jade?"

"I'm more than ready. The poor girl could be held prisoner somewhere on that property. Is this payback because he's getting booted out? He's as clean as a whistle, for Pete's sake. I don't think he's ever had a parking ticket."

"Who knows—maybe the eviction sent him over the

edge. What kind of vehicle does Deborah have?"

"Her mom said she has a black Corolla."

Jack nodded then jerked his head to the left. "The troops are here."

Two squads slowed to a stop behind our cruiser. Tim Donnelly and Aaron Silver got out of one, and Mike Ebert and Karen Lawrence climbed out of the second car. They approached our vehicle.

"Sergeant, Detective, how do you want to do this?" Donnelly asked.

I looked at them and noticed the thick padding under their shirts. "All of you are vested up, correct?"

Every deputy nodded.

"Good, then we wait for the lieutenant. They should arrive any minute. Right now all we know is a young lady has been missing for two days, and Max Sims was the last person to see her. Mr. Sims is a large, angry man. Keep your heads on a swivel and protect your partner." I jerked my chin to the road behind the cars. "Here we go."

Two cruisers pulled up and stopped on the shoulder. Clayton and Billings exited one, and Lieutenant Clark, the other.

"What have we got?" Clark asked. "Any movement from the farm?"

"Haven't checked yet, boss. We were waiting for everyone so we could coordinate a plan of action."

Clark pointed at the deputies. "Lawrence, get your binoculars out. Look for movement—you too, Silver."

"Yes, sir." Lawrence grabbed the binoculars by the strap

and pulled them out of the backseat. She propped her elbows on the squad car's trunk to steady herself. Silver mimicked her stance at the squad car in front of hers.

"I don't see any movement, sir, not even a stray cat," Lawrence said.

"Silver?"

"No, sir, not even by the barn, but I do see a ribbon of smoke. Looks like it's coming from behind the milk house."

Clark grouped us together. "All right, we're walking in. Use the trees for cover and stay low. He could be watching us from anywhere. Don't forget about those outbuildings. Clear the summer kitchen and milk house first. We wouldn't want him jumping out from behind one of those buildings. You know the family history, so stay vigilant. We're taking him alive, people. It's the only way to find out where Deborah French is. Any questions?"

We all shook our heads.

"Turn your radios and shoulder mics on, and be prepared for anything. Let's go."

Jack and I led the way. The deputies followed us, and Clayton and Billings flanked the lieutenant. We communicated with hand signals as we approached and cleared the outbuildings. I ran for the barn while the deputies kept an eye on the windows on that side of the house. If Max was watching me, the deputies would see movement. Clayton covered me from the milk house, and Billings crouched behind a large boulder and watched the front door. Clark covered the porch, and Jack circled the perimeter of the barn to clear the outside.

Voices crackled over my shoulder mic, each one giving me an 'all clear' from their position.

"Jack, how does it look behind the barn?"

"Nobody in sight. I'm coming up front. Wait for me."

I pressed myself against the side of the barn and out of sight of the house windows. Jack met up with me.

"Ready to go in?"

"Yep. We'll pull the doors open and hit the ground. If Max is in there, he'll have the advantage. We'll be sitting ducks with the sun at our backs. Get in and down fast. Crawl to the closest point of cover."

"Got it, partner. Let's do it."

Jack grabbed the left handle, and I grabbed the right. On three, we both pulled the double doors open and hit the dirt. On hands and knees, we scurried to the nearest area of cover. Our eyes had to adjust to the darkness, and we had no idea if there were lights in the barn.

I rolled over onto my back on that dusty floor and squinted at the walls. I was beginning to see outlines and shapes. I called out to Jack. "Everything okay where you are?"

"I'm good. Max Sims, if you're in here, come out where we can see you with your hands in the air. We're armed, and we'll use these guns if necessary."

The barn was silent until a scurry above my head made me spin with my gun drawn. Two pigeons flew out of the barn into the daylight. I took a deep breath and let it out slowly.

I pulled the flashlight out of my vest pocket and turned

it on. The beam of light bounced off the wall boards. I saw the light switch on Jack's side of the door.

"Jack, follow the flashlight beam. The wall switch is by you."

"I see it."

I heard Jack crawl across the floor, then I saw a hand reach to where the wall was illuminated. He flipped the switch, and the barn lit up. I rose cautiously—there were way too many hiding places and plenty of dark corners.

Jack's eyes focused on the center of the barn. Mine followed, and I saw the same thing.

"Holy shit." I spoke into my shoulder mic, "Boss, we need a few more people to help clear the barn, and Deborah French's car is sitting dead center in the middle of the room."

I heard the lieutenant curse and click off. Within a minute, Clayton and Billings were at our sides.

It took forty-five minutes to clear the barn. While we were doing that, the deputies and Clark cleared the house. Max Sims, his van, and most likely Deborah French were in the wind.

Clark met up with us in the barn and walked around Deborah's car. He ground his hands into his scalp as he peered through the windows. "Her keys are in the ignition. We need Kyle and Dan out here to process this car. Let's check out that smoldering fire."

Jack called the forensics department and gave Kyle the address. We needed them at the farm right away.

We gathered around the mound of ash. On the ground

lay remnants of paper that hadn't burned completely away, along with a few glowing embers.

Clark stared. "I'm guessing he burned everything that could prove interesting to us. There's got to be a lot of ghosts in those closets." Clark looked toward the house and shook his head.

I imagined his memories of twenty years prior.

"Jade, get on the horn and have Billy pull Max Sims's license plate number. We need to put a BOLO out for that van. This has now elevated to a hostage situation."

"What's left in the house, Lieutenant?" I asked.

"Looks like everything"—Clark turned his head toward the ashes—"except whatever that stuff was."

With my arms crossed in front of my chest, I thought about our next move while I kicked a few coals around. "The question is, how long does it take for a fire to go out? Max couldn't have gotten far."

Silver spoke up. "That depends, Sergeant. If it was only paper, probably not long, but if he threw a bunch of logs on top of everything to hold the papers down, this fire could have been started last night."

I looked at him quizzically, with raised brows.

"I used to be a Boy Scout, ma'am."

"Uh-huh." I smiled at Silver.

"Kyle and Dan need to fingerprint the house before we start going through things. This certainly wasn't on the agenda. I figured by this afternoon we'd be done with Max Sims and this property would be turned over to the developer." Clark groaned.

"Now what?" I asked.

"Now I've got to call the mayor—this farm is a crime scene. Jade, I want you and Jack to go back to the station with me. The rest of you stay out here. Dan and Kyle shouldn't be long. Help them with whatever they need." Clark jerked his head. "Come on. Let's go."

Back at the station, Clark, Jack, and I sat in the lieutenant's office. I had just made a fresh pot of coffee—we all needed it.

"What's the plan, boss?" Jack asked.

"We don't know where he went or what Deborah's condition is, but I want both of you to go to the French home and have a sit-down with the folks. They need to be told what's going on. I have to explain this mess to the mayor. I'd hate to see that Swedish company pull out. I know this situation will push their groundbreaking back even more."

"The barn is clear other than the car. Dan and Kyle will take that back to the crime lab, anyway. The only thing in the house we care about is forensic evidence of Deborah being there. We kind of figured the belongings would be removed when they tore down the house, right?"

Clark looked at me and wrinkled his forehead. "Yeah, so what are you getting at?"

"Why can't they start breaking ground? There's nothing that says they have to start with the house. We just assumed they would to keep vandals out, but if there's a police presence, vandals aren't going to be an issue. The field will likely be the parking lot, so why not let them start there?

They can hold the ceremony and take pictures far away from the house. It isn't like the groundbreaking ceremony is open to the public, anyway."

Jack agreed and poured coffee into each of our cups.

"Once forensics is done with the house, and our job there is complete, the developer can move forward in that area too."

"That might work as long as we temporarily cordon off the house. The rest of the property is theirs to start however they want." Clark took a deep breath and sighed. "Okay, wish me luck. I'm sure this news isn't going to make the mayor happy."

"Boss, a woman's life is at stake. I'm sure he'll understand."

Chapter 13

After several attempts at finding the property, Max finally caught a glimpse of gravel hidden beneath weeds at the road's edge. These days, everything was grown over and easily missed. He parked next to what looked to be the forgotten driveway and decided to walk in and check out the situation first.

He climbed out of the van and looked both ways down the road. The vacation season was still several weeks away. School hadn't ended yet, so most of the summer cottages along the road stood empty. The area was deserted—perfect in his opinion.

What was once the driveway that led back to the small summer cabin now looked more like a deer path. He nearly stepped on a garter snake that slithered by as he walked the narrow trail.

Max remembered his uncle's cabin was a hundred yards off the road and north of the lake. When he was a kid, the families would gather several times at that cabin during the summer months. They'd swim and fish. Women would fry the fresh catch every night for dinner. Those were the normal days, the happy times before Darryl developed a bloodthirst and pulled Max into his murderous lifestyle.

Max let go of those thoughts momentarily and continued on. He had no idea if the cabin still belonged to his father's brother or if it had been sold years ago. From the looks of the driveway, he assumed it was abandoned. The weeds were deeper now, nothing but a tangled mess of high grasses, and the path began to disappear beneath his feet. He stopped and stared into the thick woods. Seeing anything more than fifty feet ahead was difficult. Max squinted and shielded his eyes with his hand. The sun filtered through the canopy and cast shadows on trees, yet the occasional ray would slip through the foliage and pierce the forest floor.

Up ahead, he saw what he thought was a roofline. Max turned in that direction and walked another fifty feet. He found the cabin—dilapidated and abandoned. It would offer him a good place to hunker down until Darryl came up with a plan. The nearest town of Green River Falls was three miles up the road. Max could get Internet service at most coffee shops since this was a high tourist area. Except for his large size, he could easily blend in with the summer crowd.

Max reached the three wooden steps that led up to the porch. Missing and rotting boards made the porch floor a hazard. He'd have to watch where he walked. With a wide step, he crossed over an area with several suspicious boards and stood in front of the door. He gave it a shove—it resisted. Another hard push with his shoulder forced the door open. It creaked and scratched its way across the wide plank floors.

Damn it, why don't I have a flashlight? I may have to go into town right away.

Max stepped in cautiously. The three-room cabin smelled musty. Critters scurried toward the open door. He stepped out to the porch again and unlatched the shutters that covered the windows. That offered him just enough light to see the layout of the main room. An old cast-iron stove stood at the far left side. Cabinets and a sink were next to it. He remembered that to be the kitchen area. A massive fieldstone fireplace covered the wall opposite the stove. A shredded couch, now home to dozens of field mice, stood against the north wall, and a wooden table and a few scattered chairs filled the rest of that room. Max treaded lightly, being mindful of the floorboards as he walked farther in. A small bathroom with a sink, toilet, and a corner shower was to his left, beyond the main room, and one bedroom with four twin beds was directly to the right. He peeked around the door to that room—the beds were questionable. Evidence of animals occupying the cabin was everywhere. It was time to go into town and get the necessary supplies.

Green River Falls was a small tourist community with a year-round population of just over three thousand people. In the summer months, that population swelled to ten thousand. The area drew in visitors for the fishing, water sports, and gambling. A large casino that brought in thousands of people daily stood just east of town.

Max hadn't been to this part of Wisconsin since he was a kid. He grinned as he drove the main street of town and rubbernecked at several familiar stores that had withstood the test of time. At the local hardware store, he picked up a cooler, broom, several sponges, a lantern, and a mop bucket. The grocery store, located a short block away, provided food, beer, and ice.

After he returned to his new home in the woods, Max spent the afternoon cleaning the cabin. If he was going to stay for an extended period of time, it had to be decent enough to sleep in.

Chapter 14

Jack and I were expected. I saw a man who I assumed was Mr. French watching out the front window when we pulled into the driveway. This was the part of my job I liked least. We had no proof that Deborah was dead, but knowing the Sims family history made that possibility much more likely. Maybe the apple didn't fall far from the tree after all.

I tipped my head toward the house when Jack parked. "Mr. French is waiting for us."

Jack glanced at the man staring out the window. "Yeah, and he looks like he's expecting the worst."

We exited the cruiser and took the sidewalk to the front door. The door opened before we had a chance to knock. The man on the other side extended his hand and welcomed us in. Lynn French stood behind him.

"Officers, we haven't officially met yet. I'm Bob French."

"Mr. French," I said as I gave him a firm handshake, "I'm Sergeant Jade Monroe, and this is my partner, Detective Jack Steele." Jack extended his hand too.

"Please, come into the living room," Lynn said as she led the way. "Coffee?"

I looked at Jack and nodded. "That would be nice—black for both of us." I didn't want to start a discussion until Lynn returned, so I made small talk with Bob for the time being. "So, Bob, what do you do for work?"

"I'm in machinery sales and travel quite a bit."

I smiled.

Lynn returned to the living room with a tray, four cups, and a coffee carafe. "We take ours black too. Please, help yourself."

We did, and then Jack took the lead. "We have an update to share with you."

Mr. and Mrs. French grasped each other's hand. Lynn looked as if she was holding her breath.

"Unfortunately the home Deborah went to for her interview is owned by a reclusive, somewhat strange man. We don't have any information about his personality or what his intentions were, but we do know that twenty years ago, his father murdered his mother and grandmother."

Lynn burst into tears. Bob cradled her in his arms.

"Ma'am, as of right now, we have forensic evidence that Deborah was indeed in the house. Her fingerprints showed up on an empty glass, and the soda can next to it contained traces of Rohypnol."

"That son of a bitch." Bob spat the words and held his head in his hands.

"Why are Deborah's prints in the system?" Jack asked.

Lynn wiped her eyes and coughed into her fist. "She

wanted to be a massage therapist and went to school for a year. To get a county license, she had to be fingerprinted. That was in Alabama. The rules are different up here, so she never pursued it."

"Understood." I wrote that down. "We searched the property, and there's no sign of this man or Deborah, but her car was found in the barn. There's a statewide BOLO out for this man's vehicle, but at the moment, that's all we have. Do you own a second home or vacation property? Is there any place that he would insist she take him to hide out?"

"No, nothing like that—this house is all we have. We've only lived in the area for a year, and that's because of Bob's job promotion. We had to move to Wisconsin. We should have stayed in Alabama, where Deborah was safe. It was our home and where all her closest friends lived."

Lynn began sobbing again, and I turned toward Jack. There was nothing more for us to tell them.

"Ma'am, we're going to do everything in our power to find this man and bring Deborah home to you safely. We're so sorry this has happened to your family." We stood and thanked her for the coffee. Jack and I shook their hands, said we'd be in touch, and left.

"Damn, that never gets easier," I said as we took the sidewalk back to the cruiser.

We pulled into a drive-through restaurant on our way back to the station. We each ordered the same thing: a double cheeseburger, fries, and a chocolate shake. I jammed the straw into the hole in the lid of my decadent drink and sucked in a mouthful, then chomped on a handful of fries.

"So, what are we supposed to do—sit around and wait?" I asked as I unwrapped Jack's burger for him.

"Thanks," he said as he gripped the wrapper in his hand and took a bite. "What if we went to Boscobel?"

"Why?" I bit into my burger and waited as Jack swallowed the handful of fries he'd just popped into his mouth.

"To talk to the old man."

I smirked. "Do you really think that rat-bastard is going to tell us anything? Why would he squeal any information to us about Max and his possible whereabouts when he's a lifer? There isn't a deal on the table for Darryl."

"Don't know. Maybe he'll reveal something without even realizing it."

"Maybe. Let's see what the boss thinks."

We jammed our fast-food wrappers in the bag, and I balled it up. At twenty feet, I launched the bag at the garbage receptacle outside the building's entrance and scored. I held out my hand, and Jack punched knuckles with me.

"You still have it going on, Monroe."

I grinned. "Ya think?"

Inside, we exchanged our usual pleasantries with Jan and Peggy, then crossed into the bull pen. Clark was in his office and on the phone.

We took our seats and checked phone calls and emails and filed paperwork while we waited. Clark finally pushed back the chair and exited his office. He ground his fists into his watering eyes and grumbled something about his springtime allergies.

"What's up, boss?"

"Just got grilled by the mayor, but I guess I can feel his pain. He's under the gun with the developer and the Swedish company to get the ball rolling on this multimillion-dollar project."

"What did he think about starting in the field away from the house?"

"He said he'd get back to me. If the developer is okay with it, they'll start breaking ground first thing in the morning."

I poured a round of coffee for all of us. "That's good news. At least it will get everyone off your back. I think we need to find some recent pictures of Max and get his face on the news. That should help track him down."

"Not a bad idea, Monroe, but recent pictures? Who would have taken them?"

"You're probably right, boss, but I bet Marie can age enhance some older ones. Jack, you want to head out to the farm to see if we can find some old photo albums?"

"Sure, we've got nothing else to go on."

"Hey, boss?"

Clark turned my way. "Yeah?"

"What do you think about interviewing Darryl Sims?"

"Maybe at some point, but not yet. He has no incentive to tell us anything. Right now we need to focus on finding Deborah French." Clark entered his office and took a seat. "Clayton and Billings are still at the farm. Have them give you a hand."

Jack nodded, and we left.

We pulled into the Sims driveway fifteen minutes later and saw the flatbed loading Deborah's car. Kyle and Dan approached us before they left.

"Whatcha got?" I asked.

"Same as before. Deborah's prints inside the house. It's obvious she wasn't the one that put her car in the barn."

Jack smirked. "More like someone who's six foot four?"

"Exactly," Kyle said. "The driver's seat was pushed back as far as it goes."

"Okay, we're going in the house to look for pictures of Max. We need to get his photo on the news."

"Good luck. The deputies are searching the house from top to bottom. You might want to ask them first if they saw any pictures. It might make things go a lot faster."

"Roger that," Jack said. "We'll catch up with you guys later."

Dan and Kyle climbed into the forensics van and left behind the flatbed truck.

We walked inside and found a handful of deputies still searching the house with Clayton and Billings.

"Hey, guys, have any of you found pictures of Max anywhere?"

"We haven't," Clayton said as he turned toward the others. "Anyone else?"

The deputies responded that they hadn't either.

"So, what's been searched so far?"

Adam spoke up. "We've done a quick sweep of the entire house just looking for anything obvious lying around. Nobody has conducted a thorough search yet."

"Got it. Let's focus on the living room and dining room. Everyone look for photos with people in the pictures, nothing else."

"Yes, Sergeant."

For the next hour, eight of us pulled out drawers, opened cabinets, looked under couch cushions, and rifled through every book on the shelves.

"Who saves *National Geographic* magazines that date back years?" Billings asked.

I chuckled. "Surprisingly a lot of people do. My question is, who in this house would have read that magazine?"

"Um… these magazines go back to the early nineties, so maybe the mom and grandma."

"No kidding? Let me take a look." I walked over to where Adam stood and stared at a wall of *National Geographic* magazines. "That's really weird." I sat on the floor and grabbed a random magazine. The cover showed the indigenous aborigines of Australia and was dated September 1994. The cover was interesting enough, but I didn't want to get sidetracked from the task at hand. I fanned the pages, and something fell to the floor. I looked down and saw the back side of a Polaroid photograph. "What's this?" I picked up the photograph and flipped it over. "What the hell? Take a look at this, guys."

Jack, Clayton, and Billings surrounded me. We stared at a picture of a young woman, likely in her twenties, lying nude in a wooded area. She appeared to be asleep.

"Why would this picture be in a magazine? Is this Darryl's wife?" Jack asked.

"The age doesn't fit. Everyone, over here—start going through these magazines," I said. "Why didn't we think of this before?"

"What's that?" Billings asked.

"Look up Darryl's case online. Clark said that trial was a media sensation back in the nineties. There have to be some pictures of Darryl, the murdered wife, and the grandma. Maybe there's even a picture of Max somewhere."

"I'm on it, Jade." Billings pulled out his cell phone, sat on a kitchen chair, and started his Internet search.

"Sergeant, you'll want to see this."

"What have you got, Lawrence?"

"Another Polaroid of a sleeping nude woman."

"Shit. Billings, have you found anything yet?"

"Working on it, boss."

Lawrence handed me the photograph. I compared it to the first Polaroid—they didn't match. I wrung my hands, and the gerbil wheel in my head began spinning a million miles an hour. "Go through every single magazine and don't miss anything. I have a feeling this is going to get a lot worse."

"Got it!" Billings pushed back the kitchen chair and stood. "Boss, bring those photos here under the light."

Jack, Clayton, and I stood at the table with Billings. We compared the photos to each other and to the picture of Mrs. Sims he found on the Internet in a newspaper article about the murders. The pictures didn't match each other, and neither of them matched the newspaper photo of Mrs. Sims.

"Was that guy some kind of pedophile too?" Clayton asked.

"These women don't look like they're under eighteen, but there's definitely something going on. They look staged." I placed the photos side by side. "The poses are identical, and the women look to be lying in the same location."

"Boss," Silver called out, "we found more pictures."

Jack thumbed his temples. "How do you want to do this, Jade?"

"Let's go through the magazines first and see how many photos we end up with. We'll compare them as far as poses and location. I have no idea where to go from there. Were these women drunk or drugged and how do we identify them? We don't even know where these pictures were taken or by whom." The only thing I was sure of is we were going to find out.

Chapter 15

By the time we left the farm, we had twenty-three pictures of different women. We went through every magazine twice to make sure we found them all. Clayton and Billings loaded the magazines into the trunk of their cruiser and took them back to the station. We had no idea whether they held a particular significance and why the photos were placed inside them. We'd have to go through every one to make sure there weren't messages or clues hidden within the pages.

Billings found a picture of Max online in a different article about the murders. The image was grainy, considering it was from the nineties, plus it was in black and white. Billy said they might be able to sharpen it up with their software program. He'd let us know soon. We were in for a long night, so Clayton ordered three extra-large pizzas. I called Amber and told her I wouldn't be home for dinner. She didn't mind. She said she'd invite Kate over to share a rib eye steak with her. So those of us at the station would break at six o'clock, eat, and then dig back in.

We congregated in the conference room with the Polaroids spread across the table. Clark pulled out the white board and stood it at the end of the room.

"Okay, people, put your thinking caps on. What are these pictures about, are they important or significant to anything, why were they in the magazines, who are they, and where were they taken?"

I started the brainstorming session. "Considering these are all Polaroid pictures, wouldn't it be correct to say they were taken anywhere between 1990 and 2005? I don't think anyone used Polaroid cameras at all after 2005. These days they're almost considered collectibles. And now, everyone takes pictures with their cell phones, digital cameras, or professional film cameras. Obviously, we can't pinpoint the era by clothing since all the women are nude."

"Maybe somebody was just into nude photography. They aren't posed erotically, but they are all posed in a similar fashion," Clayton said.

Jack groaned. We all turned toward him.

"Use your words, Steele," Clark said.

"What if each photo was placed in the magazine that corresponded with the month and year the picture was taken? We just pulled all of the pictures out."

I buried my face in my hands. "You're probably right, Jack, but what does *that* mean?"

"Who knows? We still have no idea who these women are, so I guess it's a moot point."

"Wait a minute," Adam said. "All of the pictures look like they were taken in the same location in the woods. The seasons change, and so do the trees. We can at least group the pictures according to the season. And notice," he said, as he jabbed the photos with his index finger, "there aren't any taken during the winter months."

"True. So, if those women were coherent and just posing as if they were sleeping, they certainly wouldn't agree to lie in the snow naked. But some of these photos are when the trees are bare. That has to be early spring or late fall. It's still awfully cold at that time. That means—"

Clark interrupted. "They were either drugged or dead."

Billy knocked on the half-open door. Clark waved him in.

"Show us something good, son," Clark said.

"I did the best I could, Lieutenant. Here's what we've got." Billy placed on the table the sharpened photograph they'd printed out from the newspaper article. He showed us what working a little magic could do. Even though Max was nineteen at the time, his facial features looked the same. His black hair twenty years ago was long and in a ponytail. Now being older, his hair was shorter and graying.

"Is there any way you can change the length of his hair and give it a salt-and-pepper color?" I asked, hoping he could do it with the department's software program.

"Yeah, sure. I'll be back in a few."

The phone in the conference room rang. Jan said the lieutenant had a call from the mayor.

"Go ahead and transfer it through, Jan," Clark said. He put his hand over the receiver for a second. "Here we go." Clark paced as the mayor spoke on the other end. "Uh-huh, yes, Mayor Gleason." He paused as the mayor spoke. "Of course, absolutely, and I don't think the house will be an issue anymore starting next week. Yes, that's good news. I'll keep you updated on our progress. Goodbye, sir." Clark hung up and rolled his neck. "They're breaking ground tomorrow morning, but the developer wants the house by next week. We have to make sure anything and everything that could lead us to Deborah French is out of there."

"What about these creepy photos, boss?" I asked.

"We need to find out about them too. Tomorrow, we're going to check the woods at the Sims property and see if there's an area that looks like this place on the photos."

Jack shrugged. "Those photos go back at least ten years. There aren't any trees that will still look the same."

"What about this white oak?" Clark tapped the tree on one of the Polaroids. "It's in every photo, and oaks are slow-growing trees."

"That could work," I said. "For now, let's separate the photos into seasonal stacks and see what we get."

Billy returned with the newly enhanced picture of Max. Other than his face appearing younger, everything else was right on target.

Clark handed the photo to me. "What do you think, Jade? You and Jack saw him last."

"I think it will work. Don't you, Jack?"

Jack studied the photo closely and nodded. "If we state his current age, height, and approximate weight, he'd be hard to miss if someone saw him out in public. I think we should get it on the news along with Deborah French's information and photo."

Clark slapped his hands together. "All right, get every news station in southeast Wisconsin on the horn. These pictures and descriptions need to be on the ten o'clock news."

We scrambled to make calls to the top news stations in our viewing area. We faxed the photos and details of Max Sims and Deborah French to every one of them.

With everything we could do for the night done, we closed shop and headed home at nine thirty. That would give me enough time to change into a pair of comfy sweats, sit down with a cup of tea, and watch the news. I was beat.

Amber and Kate sat next to me on the couch a few minutes before the news was set to begin. They each had a glass of wine in front of them.

I grinned at Kate. "What, no tea?"

"I'm enjoying wine more than I thought I would. Guess I've been hanging out with you guys too much."

I reached across the couch and patted her hand. "It's never too much. We love your company. Here we go. The news is starting."

The anchor greeted the viewing audience and went immediately to breaking news. Amber clenched her hands and leaned in, then looked over her right shoulder at Kate. "This is the kind of stuff we'll be doing before long."

"It's not always pretty, Amber, and far from glamorous."

"You're right. I didn't mean to be insensitive."

We watched the two-minute segment as the photos and descriptions were aired. The toll-free number that went directly to Horbeck and Jamison's desks was listed at the bottom of the screen. I had the other channels taped so I could play them back and compare the coverage from each station.

"Hopefully the calls will start coming in on the tip lines. I'm going to bed, guys. See you in the morning."

I lay in bed hoping for sleep but anxious to get tomorrow started. With any luck, we'd find that tree on the Sims property, but I still didn't know what that would tell us. I punched my pillow into a fluffy shape and shut down the gerbil wheel for the night.

Chapter 16

I woke at six thirty, went through my usual routine, and was on the road by seven thirty. My travel mug with freshly brewed, steaming coffee sat in the cup holder. I bit into the piece of peanut butter–coated raisin toast pinched between my fingers as I drove to the station.

I turned into the parking lot and was surprised to see everyone's cars already there. That gave me a bad feeling—something wasn't right. I parked and crossed the pavement at a quickened pace. Inside, at the dispatch counter, Jan stood and gave me a heads-up before I entered the bull pen.

"Jade, the lieutenant has been trying to reach you."

"What?" I dug into my purse and felt the void where my cell phone usually sat. "Damn it." I realized I had left my phone on the breakfast bar. "What the hell is going on?"

"I'm not sure, but it's a war zone in there."

"Great." I punched the code into the pad next to the door and walked in. All eyes turned toward me. I threw up my arms. "Sorry, I forgot my phone. What's the urgency?"

Clark came out of his office. "Jade, we've got a mess on our hands."

"Sightings of Max Sims and Deborah French?"

"No, nothing with reasonable merit has come in on that yet."

I slumped. "Then what the hell is going on?" I looked around the bull pen. Jack, Billings, and Clayton were on their phones. Horbeck and Jamison were searching through Internet articles and printing out documents.

Clark jerked his head toward his office. "Come inside."

I followed, and he closed the door at my back.

"Have a seat."

"Boss, you're worrying me."

"It's bad, really bad. The developer's crew got started at daybreak. There's a slew of machinery at the farm. Bulldozers, backhoes, front-end loaders, and dump trucks. You get the idea."

I nodded.

"Anyway, fifteen minutes ago everything came to a screeching halt. I already have forensics en route. They've unearthed human bones—lots of them."

I pushed my chair back and stood. "Son of a bitch—what are we waiting for, let's go!"

"We're calling in favors. By the sound of things, we're going to need help. And then there's the mayor. I'll have to deal with him."

"What do you want me to do, boss?"

"See what the guys need help with for the time being. I have no idea the quantity of remains we're talking about, but I'm sure this is way more than what we can handle alone."

"Do you think the Polaroids have anything to do with this?"

Clark raked his hands through his hair. "There's a damn good chance of it. Start searching the statewide database for women that went missing between 1980 and 1996 when Darryl Sims went to prison."

"Got it, boss. Does anyone know when Darryl actually purchased the property?"

"Don't know, but find that out too."

I closed Clark's office door behind me and turned back to look through the glass wall. He had just picked up the phone. I knew he was making the call to the mayor. This new discovery could very well put a permanent halt on the construction of the Swedish megastore. The investigation could possibly go on for years.

I approached Jack once he hung up from the phone call. "What were you checking on?"

"Depending on the quantity of remains, we might need the help of forensic archaeologists. I was checking with the crime labs in Madison and Milwaukee to see how many there are in the state."

"What did you find out?"

"There are four."

"How do we handle this kind of situation? If we let the bulldozers continue digging to see how many more bones they find, it's going to be an enormous mess. I think we need those forensic archaeologists."

"I agree, but maybe we should go to the site and see what Dan and Kyle can tell us before anything else."

"Okay, let's clear it with the boss first. Calling in the experts will have to go through him, anyway." I glanced through the glass wall again. Clark was still on the phone. "We better wait a few minutes. Let's get Billy to pull up the deed to the property and see when Darryl Sims bought it."

Jack and I took the stairs to the lower level. Billy and Todd glanced our way when we opened the door to the tech department.

"I heard there's a mess brewing," Billy said.

"Word travels fast. Can you pull up the property ownership records for the Sims place?"

"Sure thing." With a few keystrokes and clicks of the mouse, Billy had the deed front and center on his computer screen. "Says here that Darryl Michael Sims purchased the hundred-acre parcel on Highway G on April 9, 1987."

I tapped the desk with a pen as I sat next to Billy. "Well, that tells us what we wanted to know. Unless forensic archaeologists say these bones are from an Indian village two hundred years back, I'd venture to say Darryl killed a lot more women than just his wife and mother-in-law. Thanks, Billy."

"Yep, no problem."

Upstairs, and back in the bull pen, Clark was off the phone and sitting in the guest chair next to Clayton's desk. The missing persons website was running on Chad's computer.

"Are you looking for missing women from twenty years ago?"

Chad nodded, but he was laser focused on the images on the screen. He paused for a minute, rubbed his eyes, and leaned back in his chair. "The lieutenant wanted me to go back to 1980, but in 1980 alone, sixty-three women went missing in Wisconsin. This is going to take forever."

"Don't go back that far. Billy just looked up the deed. Darryl purchased the farm in April of 1987. Start there."

Chad changed the parameters on the website. "That should save a little time. I'll only have to search for missing women those nine years until he went to prison."

I looked at the lieutenant and addressed him. "Boss, Jack and I are going out to the farm to see what Dan and Kyle have so far."

"Okay, keep me updated."

Jack and I left the building and climbed into the first cruiser in the lot and took off. Our drive to the Sims farm was relatively quiet. I was sure Jack had plenty on his mind, just as I did.

I finally broke the silence. "Do you have any idea of the magnitude this discovery might create? What if every one of those girls in the photos are buried in that field? The worst part is, we have no idea who they are."

"Somehow, we'll have to find the fastest way to identify them. I'd say we should narrow the parameters even more. Why search statewide? If these bones turn out to be from twenty or so years back, I'd say Darryl didn't have a lot of time to browse the entire state looking for victims. He was probably an opportunist that snatched anyone he could locally. Even if he killed two, maybe three, a year over a few nearby counties, it probably wouldn't raise a local panic. Chances are, most of them could be from the Milwaukee area. He'd have a much larger pool of victims that could have gone unnoticed."

I shrugged. "Like runaways or loners?"

"Or even ladies of the night."

"I'll call Clayton back and tell him to stay within southeast Wisconsin for now." Jack pulled into the Sims driveway. At that point, only the forensics van, a few squad cars, and the groundbreaking crew's vehicles were at the site. I knew as soon as word got out, the place would become a zoo. We parked and exited the car. "Let's see what Kyle and Dan have to say."

We walked the hundred yards back to where the heavy equipment sat—shut down for now. People milled around, not sure of what to do next. Deputies had begun cordoning off the area, even though they didn't know how far to go with the tape, or even what to stake the tape to. Jack jerked his head toward the guys standing near the bulldozer.

"What do you have so far?"

Dan ran his fingers through his hair and groaned. "A mess, that's what. We have several jawbones with the teeth still intact, five pelvic bones, and two skulls. Don't know what goes to what, since everything is jumbled up from the bulldozer. We've never had a mass burial site, guys. I'm not sure how to handle this."

"Okay, if there are five pelvic bones for sure, we know there were at least five bodies buried here. Can you tell if they're all female?"

Kyle walked over and joined the conversation. "I'd say so. They're shorter and wider than what a male's pelvic bones would be."

"Who drove this bulldozer?" Jack asked.

A voice from behind us answered, "That would be me."

We turned and approached the man pacing the area.

"Sir," I said, "we're detectives from the sheriff's department. I'm Jade Monroe, and this is my partner, Jack Steele." He took off his work gloves and shook our hands. "And you are?"

"I'm Bob Chase, ma'am."

I nodded. "Nice to meet you, Bob. Can you tell us how deep you went down with the shovel?"

He sighed, as if in thought. "Yeah, it's usually three feet initially to loosen up large rocks. After the land is clear, we dig deeper, depending on if we're doing basements. Even if we're just doing footings, we have to stay under the frost line."

"So no matter what, it would always be three feet below the surface?" Jack asked.

"Yes, sir."

We turned toward the sound of vehicles pulling in and parking. I shielded my eyes and peered to see who was getting out.

"Shit. Here comes the mayor. I imagine the guy getting out of the truck is the man in charge of running this operation."

Bob spoke up. "Yeah, that's the owner of the development firm, Mr. Chesak. He's going to be pissed."

"By the look on his face," I said, "he already is."

The mayor and Mr. Chesak approached our group and asked who was in charge. Since I was the senior officer, I spoke up.

"I am, sir—Sergeant Jade Monroe here from the sheriff's department."

The mayor huffed. "Yeah, I just talked to the lieutenant earlier. What's going to be done about this?"

"I imagine the development stage will be shut down until we excavate the site and see how many remains are here, but I'm not the one that calls the shots—just my opinion. There is one thing I do know, though."

"Yeah, what's that?" Mr. Chesak asked. He propped his hands on his hips and gave me the once-over.

"This is either a crime scene or some type of ancient burial ground. Until we know which it is, this area is off limits to everyone except law enforcement, forensic archaeologists, and crime scene investigators. I'll have to ask you two politely to step back behind the yellow tape."

The grumbling and cursing from Mr. Chesak even made *my* face go red. "What am I supposed to say to the people from the Swedish megastore?"

I smiled just to irritate him. "Sir, that's entirely up to you."

He stormed away, climbed into his truck, and sprayed gravel as he peeled out of the driveway.

"Should we head back, Jack? We have to figure out what the next move is. I think Clark needs to call in the experts. Until we know how long these remains have been buried, we don't actually have a crime scene."

"Dan, is there any way you guys can date these remains?" Jack asked.

"To a degree, but if you want to know year and month—then no. If you want my best estimate on the fly, I'd say more than ten years but less than a hundred. Really old bones are dry, flaky, and brittle. There isn't any tissue or tendons left from the few bones we've found, but we need to look for more evidence before we can narrow down the time frame better. Being buried in a shallow depth like these bones were doesn't lean toward an ancient burial site. Plus, we haven't seen any artifacts like broken pottery, that sort of thing. We don't have carbon dating tools in North Bend, but forensic archaeologists certainly do. They can pinpoint things to a better degree."

"So an ancient burial site is pretty unlikely?"

Dan nodded.

"Is twenty years within reason?" I asked.

Kyle stared at the skull lying in the dirt five feet from them. He looked to Dan for confirmation. "I think we'd agree that twenty years is within reason."

"Okay, thanks, guys." I waved the deputies over. "Keep everyone out of this area except law enforcement. I don't care how important they think they are." I cocked my head toward the mayor, who was walking back to his car. "You get my drift?"

"Yes, Sergeant, we get your drift."

Jack and I left for the sheriff's department. Clark had to come up with something fast.

Chapter 17

He couldn't help himself—Max needed another woman. The bloodthirst he felt was much too strong, and blaming everything on Darryl made his task seem rational. Away from town and other people, and far off the road in that secluded cabin at the end of that weed-covered driveway, he could take his time with her. He stared at the wide-eyed woman with the ball gag in her mouth. The frightened expression she wore excited him. He found it enticing—it stirred him deep in his belly. He approached her, and she squirmed. Her eyes darted back and forth across the room. The ropes that secured her to the old stove prevented her from escaping.

He chuckled. "Think you can get away? It's unlikely—I'm good at tying knots. Didn't your folks ever teach you not to hitchhike, especially alone?" He slapped her cheek. "Idiot, now look at the mess you got yourself in. You deserve everything I'm going to give you. I'll let you stew on that for a while."

Max peeled the tin lid off the can of pork and beans with

the hand-crank can opener he'd bought at the hardware store. With the plastic silverware he'd saved from the fast-food restaurant, he scooped out a heaping mouthful and ate it.

"I'd share, but there's no need. You won't live long enough to die of starvation." Max laughed. "That was kind of funny, right? No—can't take a joke? Whatever, you probably aren't hungry, anyway."

A mouse scurried across the scuffed, rotting floorboards. Max watched it for a minute, amused at its ability to frighten the young woman. He scraped the remaining beans out of the can then whipped it across the room. The mouse squeaked and disappeared under the couch.

He smirked at the look of relief written across the woman's face. "That little mouse was the least of your problems. Wait until you see what I have in store for you." He rose from the wooden stool and stretched his back, then guzzled the rest of his beer. "Stay put. I've got a hole to dig."

Max exited through the creaky door and slammed it at his back. He grabbed the shovel from the van and headed into the woods.

Chapter 18

"Clark better retire soon," Jack said as we crossed the parking lot and headed to the sheriff's department's front door.

I jerked my head back. "Why would you say that? He's only in his mid-fifties."

"Look at the guy. He probably has a gut full of ulcers. Haven't you seen the amount of antacids he wolfs down every day? First, there's the problem with the megastore and the deadlines, and now another snag in the progress? It's going to send him over the edge."

I shrugged. "I don't know if I agree with that. Clark is a tough old codger and a seasoned cop."

We entered the bull pen after offering a short update to Jan and Peggy. I glanced across the room and saw Clark sitting at his desk, shaking antacids into his hand. Jack elbowed me. I gave him the upper left lip snarl.

Clark waved us into his office when he saw us. "Have a seat. What's the latest?"

I let Jack take the lead. I wanted to watch the lieutenant a little closer.

"Well, boss, the mayor and the developer came out to voice their opinions. Needless to say, they're not very happy."

Clark waved away Jack's comment. "You know what they can do, right?"

"Yeah, boss. This is an investigation, and that comes first."

"Exactly. Jim Gleason enjoys the limelight and prestige of being the mayor. Once in a while, he can get dished up a pile of shit just like the rest of us. Plus, I've had enough cursing in my ear for one day. What did Dan and Kyle say?"

"Dan said on initial exam, he doesn't believe it's an Indian burial site. The bones don't appear that old."

I waited my turn then spoke up. "Boss, we need forensic archaeologists at the site now. We have no idea how many bodies are out there, and something the size of that bulldozer just makes a huge mess. Luckily, there were five intact female pelvic bones the guys found so far. At least we know there are that many bodies out in the field."

Clark shook his head. "And that's a good thing?"

"Sorry, I didn't mean it that way. It's just that we don't want bits and pieces of bone scattered here and there. We'd never know how many people were buried out there if that were the case."

Clark rubbed his temples. "I'll call in the experts. They're in a holding pattern right now waiting for the okay to get out there. Remains of five bodies are a significant find."

"Can I make a suggestion?" I asked as I picked up the

container and shook out three antacids for myself.

Clark nodded.

"Let's get some cadaver dogs out there, like right now. It's going to take at least a few hours before the forensic archaeologists show up."

"Good idea, Jade. I'll call Tom Sanders. He and Lieutenant Colbert can get the dogs and their handler out to the site. We need the city's help on this one if they can spare the officers. I'll make the calls, then I better get out there myself. I want you to help Clayton and Billings here for a while. Let's start locally. Pull up all the missing women cases in Washburn County starting from the mid-eighties. I actually remember working on a few of them with your old man, Jade. The ladies were never found."

Clark made his calls and left. I started a fresh pot of coffee and took my seat. I pulled up the missing persons database and leaned in.

"What have you guys found so far?" Jack asked as he pulled out his office chair and sat down.

"We have all the missing women between 1987 and 1993. That was a statewide search, though, and totaled 387 women, mostly from Milwaukee County. After you guys called, we narrowed it down to southeast Wisconsin. Now the boss only wants us to check Washburn County?"

"Print out what you have and then go back and change your parameters for those same years but only locally. Jack and I will do 1994, 1995, and 1996."

"Got it, Jade. Who wants coffee? I need to get up and stretch."

Each of us needed coffee—badly. Chad filled our cups, passed them out, and then took his seat again. We missed lunch, but there wasn't time for it, anyway. I got up and grabbed the tea basket from the beverage station and shook out the contents. I slipped out of the bull pen and followed the hallway to the lunchroom where I filled the basket with snacks from the vending machine. Back in the bull pen, I passed the basket and let everyone take something to sustain them until dinner. What we had to do was much more important than going out for lunch.

When we finished the local search, those nine years from the time Darryl bought the property until he went to prison had produced fourteen women.

I leaned back and rotated my shoulders—they were cramped and achy.

"Okay, we can handle fourteen. I wonder, then, if the rest of those women in the photos, assuming they are the buried women, were from other counties."

"Probably," Jack said. "Now, we have to find out, after all these years, if there's still next of kin living locally. We're going to need family DNA, or we'll never identify the remains."

Billings piped up. "Yeah, because there won't be hairbrushes or toothbrushes to go off of all these years later."

"Give me a minute. I have to call my dad." I walked down the hall and entered the conference room. I needed to quiet my brain for a second before I made the call. I took a deep breath then dialed his number.

Dad answered on the second ring. "Hey, honey. Calling me during your workday? That can't be good."

"Hi, Dad. Actually I need your expert opinion on a case."

"Sure, go ahead."

I told my dad everything we knew so far.

"Sounds like you guys are on the right track. It takes a long time to identify unknown victims by skeletal remains, Jade."

"I know, and we don't have the luxury of years to work this case. I remember you talking about an event you guys held a few years back. What was that called?"

"Yep, good memory, honey. That was the 'ID the Missing' event. We had over forty-seven people with missing family members come in to give us DNA samples right at the sheriff's department. The DNA didn't help us solve the cases, but we did identify some unknown victims and give several families closure. It's a good program. I think you guys should do it."

"I do too. Thanks, Dad. I'll call you tonight when I get a minute to breathe. I want to hear what the doctor said about your knee problem."

"Okay, honey. Talk to you tonight."

I clicked off and returned to the bull pen.

"All right, listen up. My dad said they've held an event at the sheriff's department in San Bernardino called 'ID the Missing.' He said they had good success with it. We'll have family members of missing people come in and provide DNA samples, then we'll try to match the samples with the deceased women's DNA. Let's contact anyone in the county who may be related to the women on the missing persons list."

Clayton shook his head. "But there were more than fourteen ladies in those photos. Should we include Milwaukee County?"

"That's going to bog us down. Let's start small and see if we get any hits first."

Jack piped in. "We need to narrow it down even more to fit this case. We'll say we're doing the first event with women that went missing between 1987 and 1996. We don't want people to think their missing loved ones, male or female, aren't important, but we have to keep this first event limited to fit our parameters of Darryl Sims's time at the farm."

"I agree. Let's get something out to the press and on TV. Maybe if we move on it, the segment will hit the six o'clock news. I'll call Clark and tell him what we're doing." I picked up my desk phone and dialed.

Chapter 19

He wiped the dirt from his hands onto his pant legs then speared the ground with the shovel head—he'd need it again soon. Mosquito bite welts reddened his neck and arms. He scratched where they itched, then rubbed that annoying tic above his left eye. He pushed young tree limbs aside as he exited the woods. A twig snapped back and hit him in the face. Max punched the nearest branch and bloodied his knuckles. That anger fueled his desire as he licked the blood from the back of his hand. He returned to the van and opened the toolbox he'd brought from the house. He rummaged through his choices.

This will do nicely.

He closed the toolbox and the van and crossed the unkempt driveway to the cabin, being mindful of those porch boards. The door creaked when he opened it—he ducked his head slightly and entered. The sight of him made her hyperventilate.

"Stop that! I don't want you to pass out. We're in this together, and I want you to enjoy it as much as I will. I need to know your name, so I'm going to remove the ball gag. If you do anything other than answer my questions, I'll kill you. Got it?"

She nodded her response.

"All right, stand up and lean your head forward so I can unbuckle the gag."

She did as she was told, and he removed it. She sucked in a deep breath through her mouth. Tears pooled in her eyes and slid down her cheeks.

"Is there something you want?" Max asked when he noticed she looked as though she was about to speak. "Caught yourself, didn't you?" He grinned at her obedience.

She nodded.

"Go ahead, what do you want?"

"Water, please."

"Sure thing." He pulled a bottle of water out of the plastic sleeve and turned the top counterclockwise. The cap broke free. "That's right, your hands are tied. Here we go." Max tipped the bottle into her slightly open mouth and poured. She gulped half of the bottle down before taking a breath.

"Pretty thirsty, weren't you? What's your name?"

"Haley Atwater."

"Where were you going, Haley? Why were you hitchhiking?"

"Because I don't have a car. I wasn't going far, just to my friend's house near the casino. I do it all the time."

"But today wasn't your lucky day, was it?"

"No."

"I want you to close your eyes, Haley, and think good thoughts."

She started crying harder.

"I'm only saying it once."

She reluctantly squeezed her eyes.

"Don't peek, either. I have a surprise for you." He swung the hammer fast and hard and imbedded the claw into her forehead. She slumped, and blood dripped to the floor. Max swiped her skin with his fingertip, coating it with blood, then brought it to his face. With a stroke on each side, he marked his cheeks with her blood then licked his finger. He pushed her head—it flopped. "Are you really dead?" He chuckled as he leaned down to look at her face. The gash across her forehead opened her skin and exposed her skull. "Damn, I guess you are dead. Okay, time to fill up that hole outside."

Max released the ropes that held her to the stove, and she dropped face-first to the floor. He crossed the main room, peered out the windows, and scanned the tree line and driveway, just to be cautious. With an arm in each hand, he dragged her outside and followed the deer trail into the woods.

Chapter 20

"Hey, boss, do you have a minute?"

"Yeah, hang on. I'm going into the farmhouse. Those damn dogs are so loud I can barely hear you."

I heard a door open and close. Muffled voices through the phone lines told me officers were still going through the house.

"There, it's a little quieter in here. The city boys are pitching in. Right now, their forensic team, along with Dan and Kyle, is in the field with shovels and rakes."

"That will take forever."

"Nah—the anthropologists should be here in an hour or so. They have the best equipment, but we might have the heavy machinery drivers come back if we need them. Right now, we had the workers leave the premises so the dogs can do their job."

"Have they hit on anything yet?"

"Oh yeah. That's why the guys are digging."

"Boss, the reason I called is because we'd like to try something that went really well for my dad and his team in

California. They had anyone with missing family members come in and give a DNA sample. Whenever they found an unidentified body, primarily just bones, they matched it against the samples they had gathered. They were able to identify a handful of victims that were John and Jane Does for years."

"Uh-huh. That sounds like a good program, Jade. Make it happen."

"Thanks, boss. Wow, what's with the racket?"

"Hang on a second, Monroe."

I heard Clark set his cell phone down, then a number of loud, anxious voices began yelling in the background.

"Boss, boss?"

Doors slammed, and commotion echoed through the phone line.

"Boss?"

Clark finally picked up the phone again. "Son of a bitch, Jade, I have to go."

"What happen, Lieutenant?"

"I was just told the dogs alerted on something in the woods. The handler and several officers followed. There are two dead women buried in shallow graves. The officers said it looks like they've only been there a few days. I have to check this out. Get that event started and send Billings and Clayton out here with the photo of Deborah French her folks gave us. Send Lena and Jason too. This is turning into a serious shit storm."

I hung up and yelled to Clayton and Billings. "The boss needs you guys now! Take that photo of Deborah French with you. The dogs just found two women in the woods that were buried within the last few days. Go, and get Lena and Jason out there too."

"Son of a bitch." Jack paced the bull pen. "Max Sims is following in his old man's footsteps."

"We've got to get word out about the DNA event. We have to identify those bodies as soon as we can. Unfortunately, the newest ones will be a lot easier."

Jack rubbed his eyebrows, as if in thought. "We need to focus on our task here. Let's get that ad for the 'ID the Missing' event in place and take it over to *City News* before they close."

"I'll put that together if you'll call the news stations. I think I'm better at getting my point across in writing rather than with spoken words."

Jack chuckled. "You finally realized that?"

I threw my pen at him and grabbed another one and got busy.

Jack sat at his desk and called all the local stations in the southeast Wisconsin viewing area.

I whispered to him, "Make sure they say Washburn County residents only for now with female family members that went missing between 1987 and 1996. Tell them to run that seg—"

Jack interrupted. "Yeah, yeah, Mom, I know—run the segment on Max again."

"You're lucky this is my last pen and I need it." I got up, poured a coffee for each of us, and got back to writing the ad.

"Okay, that's done," Jack said a few minutes later as he hung up the phone.

"My ad is done too. Want to ride with me to drop it off? After that, we should head over to the farm and see if anyone needs our help."

As we walked out, I told Jan where we were going. I called Jamison and Horbeck and asked them to come in early and cover the bull pen. I looked up at the sky as we walked to the cruiser. The wind was picking up, and a cold breeze swept across the parking lot. Ominous clouds were gathering and turning a threatening shade of gray.

"I hope to hell it isn't going to rain. That field finally dried out, and another night of rain and mud will just prolong the investigation. What we need to know first is who the recent victims are. The others probably don't have a loved one sitting on pins and needles, wondering where they went."

We dropped off the ad and asked them to put a rush on it. Mr. Emerson, the office manager, said he'd have it out in tomorrow morning's paper. We thanked him and left.

At the farm, the driveway had filled up with more vehicles. The coroner's van sat on the grass closest to the woods near the barn. Several city patrol officers were inside the house, with two of our deputies cataloging anything that seemed worthy of taking back to the station.

I jerked my head toward the woods. "Let's see what Jason and Lena can tell us. We may be going to the French home yet tonight." I looked off at the distant field. There had to be at least fifteen people out there with the dogs, digging and searching. I turned back to the sound of vehicles approaching. I sighed a breath of relief. "Finally, the forensic archaeologists are here. Maybe they can do something to keep this impending rain from slowing down the progress." I looked at the sky again. We didn't have a lot of time.

Jack and I entered the woods and found Lena and Jason within a taped-off area. The two victims had been uncovered and removed from their shallow graves. They lay on top of the soil with dirt coating their naked bodies.

Jack shook his head at the sight of them, opened up from sternum to pelvis.

"What can you tell us other than the obvious?" I asked as I knelt next to Lena.

"We don't know who that woman is yet"—she pointed ten feet from the victim we were next to—"but this one is most likely Deborah French. Her decomp isn't as extensive as the other woman's, meaning she's the most recent victim buried here. It looks like both of them were tied to something. They have ligature marks on their wrists and ankles."

Jason walked over and joined us. He nodded. "Jade, Jack."

"Jason. What a nightmare, right?"

"Most definitely. Since we had Deborah French's fingerprints on file, I compared them to hers." He pointed to the young woman lying in the dirt nearest us. "They're a match. We confirmed her features with the photograph Clayton brought along too. At least one victim has been identified."

"Has anyone searched the woods for anything else?" Jack asked.

"The two graves were the only things the dogs hit on, but you have to see this." Jason waved us along. "Follow me. Dan and Kyle have already done an initial search and photographed everything over here. The guys are spreading themselves thin. We're okay wandering around within the taped area, though." Jason led us through the woods to a tree not far away. "What do you make of this?"

Jack and I stared at the tree trunk in front of us. Dozens of hash marks were etched in the bark, as if made with a knife. Not far from that tree stood another with what looked to be dried blood covering a large portion of the trunk.

"Yeah, we tested it—it's human blood."

"So this is where he did the killing?" I asked.

"It appears so, Jade. Then he marked each person off on his scoreboard. I just wonder if that tree with all the marks went back to Darryl's reign. If not, Max has killed a serious amount of women."

I gave Jack a worried look. "We need to change our parameters again. We have to go from 1987 until now. We never took Max into consideration. All these years he's stayed under the radar. Chances are, he's worse than his own father. Thanks, Jason."

We headed out to the field to talk to Clark and the forensic archaeologists. As we made our way, we saw a group of new faces talking to the lieutenant. These people, ten of them, were the lead forensic archaeologists as well as helpers and apprentices in the field. I was happy to see that many experts show up. Jack and I reached them and exchanged handshakes with everyone as they were introduced. The person in charge, a tall, middle-aged gentleman with wire-rimmed glasses and thinning black hair, introduced himself as Dr. Phillip White.

"Let me explain how this process works," Dr. White said. "We can either excavate the entire field, find all the bones beneath the surface, and go on to identify and match the bones to complete an entire skeleton, or if we're trying to process the area as a crime scene, we'd be searching for other evidence that would lead us to the perpetrator as well."

"After all these years, I doubt if there's any forensic evidence," Clark said.

I added, "And we know, depending on how long the bones have been out here, who that perp already is. The owner of this property is serving a life sentence at WSPF in Boscobel. At this point, I'd say it's recovery and identification. We'll have confirmation of the responsible party once we know how long the bones have been out here. After that, we can focus on identifying the remains. Agreed?" I looked at Clark, Jack, Clayton, and Billings.

"Agreed," Clark said.

"Okay, that just made our job a little easier. We don't have to tread lightly. We'll have the bulldozer driver just skim the surface, taking off layers at a time. Pretty soon, we'll be able to see the majority of the burial field. I wouldn't imagine it farther than three to four feet deep."

"It looks like rain is coming," I said as I took another look upward.

"Not too much of a problem. It will initially slow us down, but it looks like the soil around here is pretty sandy. The rain water will filter through quickly."

The sprinkling began. I glanced toward the woods and was thankful to see Lena and Jason loading the bodies into the van.

Dr. White scrolled through his cell phone. "It says on the weather forecast that the rain should subside around two in the morning. The ground should be okay to work after daylight. Shall we start first thing in the morning?"

Clark nodded. "I'll make sure the bulldozer driver is here at daybreak."

"Sir?"

"Yes, Sergeant Monroe?"

"Are you equipped to take a bone with you and test how long it's been out here? It would speed up the process and tell us definitively who the responsible party is by the time your group is ready to begin in the morning."

"Sure, we can do that."

I nodded at Dan, who already had a number of bones bagged. He brought a bag over and handed it to an assistant. We said our goodbyes, and the group left for the evening.

"Boss, I think we ought to pay Mr. and Mrs. French a visit."

Clark waved us on. "Go ahead. Meet me back at the station afterward."

Jack and I walked through the field and passed the

house. Through the windows, I saw officers still milling around. We climbed into the cruiser and left. As Jack drove, I called the French home and told them we had news. We'd be there in twenty minutes.

Just outside the Slinger city limits, we made a few turns and ended up on Liberty Lane. Jack pulled into the familiar driveway. I let out a deep sigh before we exited the car. The procedure was always the same—tell the family what they needed to know with as few details as possible. Manner of death would be foul play, nothing more. Parents never needed to know the gruesome details of their children's demise—never.

We followed the sidewalk to the front door. The porch light was already illuminated, and evening was upon us. The skies darkened, and the slow drizzle turned into rain.

Lynn French opened the door when we knocked. Her eyes, swollen from crying, told us she had a mother's intuition—she'd already assumed the worst.

We stayed for thirty minutes and consoled the grieving parents. Deborah was their only child. They would need to make a positive ID even though her fingerprints had already confirmed her identity. I suggested they wait until tomorrow. I wanted to give Lena time to clean Deborah up so she'd look presentable for her parents. Their sorrow was already bad enough.

We returned to the station at seven o'clock. Inside, Clark waited our arrival with a cup of coffee and a bag of chips. He rose from his desk, walked fifteen feet, and plopped down on my guest chair.

"How did it go?"

"As sad as expected. They're coming in tomorrow to make the positive ID. Now we have to find out who the other woman was. We didn't get any missing persons call other than Deborah's. That's leading me to think she was from another county."

"Have Lena take some pictures after she's cleaned up. We'll look through the database in the morning and see if anything pops."

"Got it, boss. I'm out of here. I'll see you guys bright and early. I'll tell Lena what we need on my way out."

Chapter 21

I made a quick stop in the autopsy room before I left the building. Lena was busy washing down both women when I entered. I relayed the information from upstairs and told her I'd stop by first thing in the morning. The Frenchs said they'd call at nine a.m. to find out what time to come by. After a few minutes of updates between us, I said good night to Lena and Jason and closed the door at my back.

As I crossed the parking lot, I pressed the unlock button on my key fob. A short chirp sounded from my car. Now, at seven thirty, I was finally heading home. All I wanted was a glass of wine, snuggly sweats, and a bowl of popcorn. I needed to decompress.

Amber and Spaz greeted me when I walked in through the garage. My glass of wine and a bowl of freshly popped popcorn sat on the breakfast bar, waiting for me to dig in. I thanked my sister with a hug and told her I would be right out. I needed to get out of my work clothes and relax in something loose and comfy. I glanced at my bed as I passed by my bedroom. What I really wanted to do was put on those sweats and dive into bed. I'd drift off into slumberland without a care in the world and wake up to a sun-filled day without any mention of the name Sims. Of course, that wasn't reality. I still had to call my old man. I was thankful for the two-hour time difference between Wisconsin and California. I'd have time to drink my wine and eat my popcorn before I needed to make that call.

I updated Amber on my day and watched the news broadcast that she'd taped for me earlier. Max Sims appeared on the screen again in the breaking news segment.

"He's a scary looking dude, and now you're saying he's committed murder too?"

I paused the TV. "Yeah, at least two that we're pretty sure of. There's nobody else other than Max that would fit the profile. It was his property, he never had anyone visit him, and Deborah went to his house only a few days ago, hoping to be hired as his housekeeper and cook. Instead, the bastard murdered her."

I clicked the play button, and we continued watching the broadcast. We still hadn't gotten any calls for sightings of Max from when the first segment was aired a few days back. Now it made sense that we hadn't had sightings of Deborah—she was already dead and buried. The anchorman mentioned the Washburn County event we would run beginning tomorrow. I was optimistic that we'd be able to identify a few of the remains in the field.

I snuggled on the far left side of the couch. My wineglass with a coaster beneath it was within reach on the end table. I dialed my dad and put my cell on speakerphone as I placed it in my lap. Amber sat next to me, and Spaz found a way to squish himself between us. His purring told us he was comfortably positioned.

"Hi, Dad," Amber and I said at the same time when he answered.

He chuckled. "Hi, girls. Are you two behaving?"

"Absolutely not," Amber said. "That would be so boring, Daddy. I can't wait to begin at the police academy on Monday. That's when I'll start behaving."

"Damn straight. You better take that seriously, honey."

"I will, for sure."

I took my turn to ask the questions. "Okay, what did the doctor tell you about your knee?"

"Just what I expected—surgery. Guess I've chased too many crooks over my lifetime and jumped over a few too many fences."

"How much downtime is the doctor saying you'll have?" I asked.

"The guy is a quack. He said a month off of work and crutches, plus no driving for two weeks. That's impossible. I have to get around."

"I have the solution to everything. Since I can't come out there with this insane case going on, and Amber can't miss her police training, come here for the surgery. We can both take care of you."

"Nah—I was just there."

"Dad," I said sternly, "that was at Thanksgiving. This is May. Almost six months ago doesn't qualify as 'I was just there.' Your insurance is nationwide, isn't it? I'm sure it's the same as mine. The doctor that patched up my leg when the dog got ahold of me can do it. He's an orthopedic surgeon."

"I don't know. It sounds like a big hassle."

Amber piped in. "It sounds logical, Daddy. Just do it and quit complaining. If left to you, you'll never get that knee fixed. Plus, you want to hear all about the academy, don't you? I'm starting in a few days."

"So now it's come down to this—guilt trips?"

"Uh-huh. Please say yes. Jade didn't have a lot of time to spend with you over Thanksgiving. She can make up for it now."

My dad laughed, and I gave Amber the shit eye and smacked her arm.

"All right, I'll do it. I have to schedule things first at the sheriff's department for a medical leave of absence. I need that doctor's name too so I can have my own physician talk to him."

"No problem, Dad. I'm so happy you're doing this. Oh, by the way, we're starting one of those 'ID the Missing' events tomorrow."

"Good. I hope it will help bring closure to some of those families. Okay, good night, girls."

I set the popcorn bowl and my wineglass on the kitchen counter. "I'm turning in, Amber. I'm beat. See you in the morning."

She gave me a loving hug. "Good night, Jade."

Chapter 22

Max stepped off the curb and walked back to the van that was parked a half block from the coffee shop. After his haircut and shave, he sat at a small corner table in that espresso bar decorated with a definite hip vibe. A half hour was all he needed. With a cup of black coffee and free Wi-Fi, he conducted a thorough online search for Tom Monroe, his biography, and the personnel at the North Bend Sheriff's Department. Max snickered when he found exactly what he was looking for. Tom Monroe, now a captain at the San Bernardino County Sheriff's Department, had two daughters, Jade and Amber Monroe that resided in North Bend, Wisconsin. The search for Jade Monroe had brought up her photograph as well as a newspaper clipping from when she was promoted to sergeant at the sheriff's department just last year.

As he drove out of town and headed south to Boscobel, he scratched at the back of his neck where newly cut hairs had found their way beneath his T-shirt. He needed to update his father on what he had found out.

The two-hour drive from Green River Falls to WSPF was still a bit shorter than driving from North Bend. He pulled into the visitors' lot at eleven thirty. Max noticed a new gate guard on duty when he arrived.

"Where's Frank?" Max asked the young man that looked no older than twenty.

"He transferred to Waupun. I have the gate from now on. Sign in here, then take a seat."

Max snarled. "I know the drill, kid." He deliberately signed his name illegibly and took a seat.

"Prisoner number?" The youngster's name tag had Evan written across it.

"450-A72." Max grabbed a ticket for the locker room and a newspaper and got comfortable on a single cushioned chair opposite the other visitors. Five people were ahead of him, and he knew he'd be waiting at least thirty minutes. A small article on page three caught his attention. The headline read "Killing Field Discovered near North Bend, Wisconsin." Max looked at the other visitors waiting their turn to be called into the next room with lockers to store their belongings. His eyes darted from one person to the next. Nobody paid attention to him, and most were scrolling through their cell phones. He was glad he'd decided to clean up his appearance—he wouldn't stand out now that the unkempt hair and bushy beard were gone. Other than his height, he'd fit in with everyone else. His mind reeled, and he wasn't sure what his next move would be. The four-paragraph column stated that human bones had been discovered in a field, and cadaver dogs had found two bodies buried in shallow graves.

Damn it—the cops know those bodies had to be my work. They're too recent. That bitch Sergeant Monroe will be looking for me soon enough.

No names were mentioned in the article, which surprised Max. He was sure the cops had something up their sleeves.

"Number thirteen," Evan called out.

Max stood and was escorted into the next room beyond the security doors. There, he had to empty his pockets and put everything in a locker. He gripped the key in his curled fist and followed Evan into the visitation hall.

"You have an hour with the inmate."

"Yeah, I know." Max stuffed the locker key into his pocket and entered the large visiting room. He sat at a small table next to Darryl and leaned in close to his father. Every corner of the room had surveillance cameras with live audio and video feed. He knew the conversations could be heard unless he covered his mouth and whispered. "The cops already know about the others."

"I'll take the blame. There can't be anything but bones left, anyway."

Max shook his head. "They found the recent ones in the woods too."

"How the hell did they do that?"

"I saw a newspaper article out in the waiting area. They brought in cadaver dogs after the first bones were discovered yesterday morning. Somehow, they smelled the girls in the woods."

"Too fresh?"

"Who the hell knows? There's no getting out of this one. I've got to lie low, but I can't stay at the cabin forever."

Darryl looked Max over carefully. "Good thing you changed your appearance. You might be able to hide in plain sight."

"Yeah, but I can't hide my size." Max paused and stared down at the table when a guard walked by. "Anyway, I checked out that Sergeant Monroe woman. Apparently her name is Jade, she has a sister named Amber, they both live in North Bend, and Tom Monroe is their father."

Darryl slapped the table and laughed. "That's perfect. Where is the old man living, in North Bend too?"

"Nah—he's a big shot at the San Bernardino County Sheriff's Department in California. The article said he moved there ten years back."

"And the judge?"

"He's retired, but his son, Antonio, followed right in the old man's footsteps. He's a circuit court judge in North Bend with a wife and two kids. Get this, they have a vacation home north of Green River Falls. What are the odds?"

"Humph… I'm impressed. You sure know how to finagle that World Wide Web."

Max smirked. "I'll break in while I'm in the area and see if I can get more information on them. I'm sure vacation homes get vandalized all the time."

Darryl chuckled. "That's even better, but be careful. Looks like you're going to have several problem-solving opportunities, if you know what I mean." He winked at Max. "If the cops are looking for you, I don't know how smart it would be for you to keep visiting me. You'd be easy to nab here. Get a post office box in Green River Falls. I'll call your phone at four o'clock. All I need is the box number, nothing else. All of the calls are monitored, you know. We have to be extra careful."

Max fidgeted then cracked his knuckles.

Darryl flicked Max's hand.

The guard called out, "No touching."

Darryl went on. "Focus, son. After I get the box number, I'll send you a letter with instructions as soon as I come up with something. I'm going to think up a code to use so when we write to each other, even if the letters are opened, nobody will know what we're saying. I'll make up a code for phone calls too. Understand?"

"Yeah, I got it."

"Okay, don't come back here. It isn't safe. Only collect calls from me to you and coded responses. I'll call Mondays and Fridays at four o'clock. Now go and be safe. Stay under the radar."

Max stood and stared at his father for an extra minute. He knew that might be the last time they'd ever see each other in person. Touching the prisoners wasn't allowed, so he couldn't give Darryl a farewell hug or even a handshake. A look of acknowledgment was all they had. Max turned and walked out.

Chapter 23

My desk phone rang at eight o'clock—Lena was calling.

"Hey, Jade, I wanted to update you on the autopsies. Jane Doe looks to be in her early twenties. She's five foot four inches, and her remains weigh one hundred fifteen pounds. Her hair is dark blond, and she has hazel eyes."

"Would she have weighed more, say, a week ago?"

"Yes, maybe as much as ten pounds. Less water content, blood loss, no nourishment, and of course, the bugs—well, they've done extensive damage. Once there's an opening in the body, as in a situation like this, the bugs move in quickly. Also, her face is smashed in badly. It looks like she was hit hard with something wide enough to do damage to the width of her face."

"Like a shovel?"

"Yeah, a shovel would make sense given the fact that she was buried. Her teeth, nose, and jawbones are all broken."

"Poor thing. I hope that didn't happen while she was alive. What about Deborah?"

"She's ready for her official ID. I cleaned her up the best

I could. I sent out blood work on both ladies. Max Sims definitely sedated them, or there would have been more signs of a struggle. I know there were traces of Rohypnol in Deborah's soda, but I have to do it the official way with blood tests for the records. Plus, we don't know anything about Jane Doe. I'm guessing she probably has traces of Rohypnol in her body too."

"Okay, I'll let you know when to expect Deborah French's parents. Thanks, Lena."

"Sure thing."

I hung up the desk phone and looked at Jack. "Are you ready to set up the conference room for the 'ID the Missing' event?"

"Yeah. How is that going to work?"

I got up and filled our coffee cups. "It's going to be pretty basic, I guess. We didn't have time to print out official looking paperwork. I put in the ad for people to call the nonemergency department number and set up a time to come in. We'll get all the pertinent information we need on the missing person, take a DNA swab from the relative, and go from there."

Jack stood. "I'll get the DNA swab kits from the cabinet downstairs. We could probably put together makeshift questionnaires and print them off. We actually have no idea how many people will show up now that we had to add missing women after 1996. What's the total between 1987 and the current day?"

I checked the numbers in the folder. "As of the day Deborah went missing, our total since 1987 is fifty-one. Of course, that doesn't mean they all went missing under suspicious circumstances. Some women left on vacation and never returned, others were runaways, and then separations or divorces were thrown in the mix, where the woman didn't want to be found."

Jack shrugged. "Yeah, abusive boyfriends or husbands, I guess."

"Uh-huh. Okay, I'll put something together, and you get the test kits. After I print everything off and set up the conference room, let's go through the statewide missing persons database for the last month. Somebody has to know who our Jane Doe is. After lunch we can head out to the farm. I'll have Jan call us if anyone sets up an appointment to give their DNA."

We each got a fresh cup of coffee and sat at our desks. All of the parameters fitting Jane Doe's description were checked off, and the statewide search began. Sending sheets to the police and sheriff's departments in each county might have gone faster, but we didn't have a useable photograph of Jane Doe to provide them. According to Lena, the poor girl's face was crushed.

"I'm leaning toward the counties surrounding Washburn County," Jack said. "Whatever ruse Max used to get a woman to his house wouldn't have worked unless the woman lived within a half hour of the farm."

"You could be right." I grabbed my desk phone and dialed *City News*.

"What are you thinking?" Jack asked.

"This may speed things up. The housekeeping ad may

have run a few times. That could be Max's ruse. It will rule out him picking up someone walking along the road or snatching them from a parking lot like Robert Lynch did to Deidra Nelson last fall." That case of a killer from last year was still fresh in my mind.

"Yeah, don't forget Jeremy and Matt and their human trafficking enterprise too." Jack pressed his temples. "That's exactly what they did all over Washburn and Milwaukee County."

I pressed my hand to the air for Jack to hold that thought. *City News* was picking up.

"*City News*, how may I direct your call?"

I set the receiver down and clicked over to speakerphone. "Hello, this is Sergeant Monroe from the sheriff's department."

"Yes, of course, I remember you."

I smiled at Jack.

"That's nice. I'm wondering if you'd be kind enough to check how many times Max Sims ran his 'Housekeeper Wanted' ad."

"But—"

"But, the warrant is still in effect. Do I need to come down there in person?"

"No, ma'am. One moment please."

She clicked over to elevator music.

Jack chuckled. "You're a hardass, Jade."

"It gets the job done, doesn't it?" I pulled a five-dollar bill out of my wallet while I waited and passed it across the desk to Jack. "Will you be a sweetheart and get me a chocolate bar? Grab whatever you want too."

"Yep, no problem." Jack pushed back his chair and went down the hall to the lunchroom.

"Are you still there, Sergeant?"

"I sure am. What have you got?"

"It looks like Mr. Sims ran that ad four times, each a week apart, beginning the last week of March."

"Okay, thanks a lot. Goodbye."

"What did you find out?" Jack asked as he came around the corner and handed me the chocolate bar and a fistful of change. He sat at his desk and tore open a bag of chips.

"I agree with your theory. Max has run that ad four times. Coincidentally, he started them the last week of March. That's about the time when the ground is thawed enough to dig a hole. Let's start close and expand out."

"You take Waukesha County, and I'll take Ozaukee," Jack said as he tapped his computer keys and changed the locations for the search.

I did the same and munched on my candy bar as I continued through the list of missing women.

I checked the time on the lower right corner of my computer. We were closing in on ten thirty. I'd called Lena forty-five minutes ago and told her to expect Mr. and Mrs. French. They called as they were leaving their house. I'm sure by now they had come, made the devastating identification of Deborah, and had left to go home and mourn. I leaned back in my chair and stretched.

"Anything look promising?"

Jack took a break and rubbed his eyes. "I think I'm

getting double vision. I've saved a few listings that we can go over closer when we finish this. I have sixteen left to go. How about you?"

"I've saved three. Some descriptions sound right until I see the age. I have six left. Let's finish these and compare our findings." The next image on the screen made me sit up and take notice. I leaned in closer, my face resting in my open hands. "I might have something here, Jack."

"Really?" Jack pushed back his roller chair, stood, and walked around his desk. He took a seat in my guest chair.

I pointed at the listing on the screen. "That one, right there. Compare it to Lena's notes. It's dead nuts on. Says she disappeared from Sussex ten days ago. That distance and time frame fits the parameters perfectly."

"I agree. Print it out. Let's take it downstairs and show it to Lena."

I hit the print icon on my computer, and we heard the printer come to life. Two pages slid out, one with the young woman's picture and the other, her statistics.

"Come on. Let's go."

I was anxious to call Clark out in the field, but I wanted to be sure first. Jack and I peeked into the autopsy room—nobody was there. We went to the next room, the coroner's office, and I knocked. Lena called out for us to come in.

"Hi, guys, what's up?" She set down the recorder she had been talking into and gave us her full attention.

I handed her the pieces of paper. "What do you think the chances are of this woman being our Jane Doe?"

She motioned for us to take a seat as she read over the

statistics and studied the face in the photograph.

"I need to check on something. I'll be right back." Lena rose and exited the office.

I turned and looked at Jason. "What is she doing?"

"May I?"

I handed Jason the sheets of paper. "Yep—she's checking for identifying features. It says there's a small beauty mark behind this woman's left knee. That's most likely what Lena's doing—checking."

We waited. I drummed my fingers on Lena's desk, and Jack talked to Jason about the basketball playoffs. The door finally opened, and Lena entered.

"It's her."

I stood. "Seriously—it really is?"

"I'm ninety-nine percent sure. There's always a tiny smidge for error. I'm thinking it's a safe bet to contact her parents. At this point, I'd only ask for a DNA sample from each parent. Once it's a confirmed match, you can give them the definitive news."

"Thanks, Lena. The death of a loved one is never good news, but at least the family can move forward and give their daughter a proper funeral." I glanced at the papers again. "Her name was Amy Patterson, and she was only twenty-two. We've got to find Max Sims and bring him to justice."

Chapter 24

The field was full of people when Jack and I arrived at the Sims farm. Yellow police tape was secured across the driveway near the house. An officer directed law enforcement and forensic experts around the taped-off area. People that didn't belong at the site weren't allowed through.

We were stopped where the tape crossed the driveway. Jack and I showed our badges and were motioned to pass through at the opening. We parked fifty feet beyond the tape in a grassy area behind the milk house and I caught a glimpse of Clark as we exited the cruiser. He, the mayor, and Mr. Chesak stood on the porch, arguing with each other. I elbowed Jack and jerked my chin toward the men. Clark saw me and gave me a scowl.

A processing area comprised of five large canopied tents had been erected just south of the field between the barn and the woods. Two portable toilets stood to the left of them, and at the far right another tent looked to be the food and beverage area. They had come well prepared. A gas generator provided power for the large coffee urn, stainless steel warming bins for food, and the computers and phone-charging stations.

Jack and I passed the makeshift all-inclusive tent city on our way to the field. "Can you believe this? These guys are no joke."

Clayton saw us and waved us over. "Hey, guys, quite the setup, right?"

Jack nodded. "I'd say. What have they found so far?"

"The bulldozer started early this morning, scraping off layers of dirt with the blade. On the third round, bones started showing up. That's when the crew began. They have sifters, shovels, rakes, hoes, you name it. They photograph and catalog their finds right at the site, then take the bones over to the lab they have set up that does radiocarbon dating." Clayton pointed at the third tent. "They do all their magic right in there. It's pretty sophisticated stuff."

"Sounds like it. Did Dr. White get back to you guys on the age of those bones we gave him last night?"

Dan crossed the field and joined in on our conversation. "He told me this morning they have been buried more than twenty years but less than forty."

"That's good enough for me. We can add all of these victims to Darryl Sims's murder count. Unfortunately, with Darryl serving a life sentence with no chance at parole, it's like these women, whoever they were, didn't count for anything. We have no leverage whatsoever over the man to find out the names and how many women he actually killed."

"Unless—"

I interrupted Billings. "Unless what?"

"Unless we get creative and think of a way to use Max as leverage."

My excitement faded quickly. "Yeah, that's another problem all its own. We'd have to find him first."

"Maybe not. Cops have the right to get 'very creative' in order to gather information."

Jack chuckled. "Code for lying, but it might work. We'll have to put our heads together and think of something that could actually get Darryl to start talking."

I craned my neck and shielded my eyes. The sun, straight above, shadowed the porch area. "What's the deal with Clark and the guys? They know this is a crime scene, so why are they busting his chops?"

"Schedules and deadlines. The Swedish company is on the edge of pulling out," Clayton said.

"But they already own the land."

He shrugged. "They haven't put any work into it yet. They can put it up for sale and look for a spot somewhere else."

"Yeah, and I bet they're threatening to build the store in another county. That's the only pressure they can put on the mayor, which somehow becomes Clark's problem."

Billings nodded. "True, but think of all the lost revenue that would mean for Washburn County. The lieutenant is under the gun to get this nightmare wrapped up."

The thought of Max placing four ads weighed heavily on my mind. I had no idea if there were two more women somewhere in the woods or in the field with the others. The best-case scenario would be if nobody had responded to the first two ads at all.

Clark finally stepped off the porch and headed our way. I saw him grumbling and shaking his head.

I whispered to the rest of the group, "He doesn't look happy. Maybe telling him we have an ID on Jane Doe will help."

"Damn city officials and corporate red tape. They're grinding on me every chance they can." Clark planted his feet next to the rest of us and huffed his irritation, then jammed his fists into his jacket pockets defiantly.

"We found out who Jane Doe is, boss. That's something positive," I said.

He perked up. "Yeah? Let's hear it."

"Her name is Amy Patterson. She was twenty-two years old and from Sussex. Lena suggested we collect DNA samples from the parents as a confirmation before we tell them definitively that it's her."

Clark nodded. "Yeah, go ahead and get that done. There really isn't anything here for you guys to do." He jerked his chin toward the field. "Those people are more than capable of handling this. As a matter of fact, we can all go back to the station and check in with Dr. White over the phone. He said they'd have the field cleared within two days."

"Boss?"

Clark raised his eyebrow at me. "Why does that always mean something bad is going to come out of your mouth?"

"Because that's usually the case."

“Go ahead. What is it?”

I turned to Jack. “It’s your turn to deliver the bad news.”

“Thanks, partner. We checked at *City News*, and apparently Max ran four ads within four weeks. The dogs found two women. It seems like the ruse Max used to get women out here was the ad for housekeeping. There could possibly be two more women buried in the woods.”

Clark kicked a few rocks near his foot. “Then we have to get the dogs back out here. Clayton, go ask Dr. White if they found anything that appears more recent than the rest. If it’s only been four weeks, the remains would be more than just bones.”

“Got it, boss.” Clayton jogged off to the middle of the field where Dr. White stood.

“All right, you two head to Amy Patterson’s house. Anything on the DNA event?”

“Haven’t heard from Jan. She said she’d call when someone set up an appointment.”

Jack and I walked back to the cruiser and left. Both sides of the driveway and most of the grassy area held parked vehicles.

“You want to drive?” Jack asked.

“Yeah, right. I’ll let you figure out how to maneuver out of this parking lot.”

After a bit of backing up and going forward, Jack managed to get to the driveway and exit onto Highway G. We headed south toward Sussex. I pulled the papers out of the door pocket and read the directions aloud.

“Take 45 south to Countyline Road, then turn west. Go

west a mile to Townline Road and turn left. Take that to Plainview, then turn right. Their house is about a half mile in on Plainview. I'll give you the details once we're closer."

"You called the folks earlier, right?"

"Yeah. Only the mom was home, but she said she'd call her husband and have him leave work early. Her name is Nancy, and the husband is Mark. They're expecting us."

Chapter 25

Max passed the *Green River Falls-population 3,618* sign at three thirty. He drove through the touristy downtown area to the post office on Fillmore Street. He parked the van and took the sidewalk to the twelve steps that led to the glass-doored entrance of the nondescript brick building. Inside, there were three counters to the right through another glass door, and to the left were the shipping supplies as well as the post office boxes.

He opened the door to the right and took his spot behind a young woman already at the first counter.

"Next in line," the clerk said.

Max approached and stood at the second counter.

The clerk looked him up and down then smiled. "Ever play basketball?"

"If I had a nickel for every time I've been asked that, but no, I've never played basketball."

"Sorry. What can I help you with?"

"I need a small post office box."

"Sure, no problem." She pointed at the counter at Max's

back where all of the forms were stacked side by side. "There are pens in the cup. Just fill out the form for renting a box then bring it back to me when you're done. You'll need your ID."

Max turned and took four steps back. He stood against the counter and filled out the single-page form. He was finished minutes later.

"Sir, over here." The same clerk called him to her counter. She took the form and looked it over. "Long way from home."

"Just staying with a friend for a bit."

"Would you like to pay monthly, semi-annually, or yearly? You get a two-dollar discount for yearly."

Max sighed a deep breath. "Let's make it monthly. I'd hate to wear out my welcome."

She chuckled. "I'll need to see your ID."

Max pulled the wallet out of his back pocket and flipped it open. His driver's license was behind the plastic sleeve.

"Can you take it out, sir?"

He removed it from the wallet and slid it across the counter to her.

"Okay, that's twelve dollars for the month."

Max handed her fifteen. She gave him his change, the receipt, and the keys for box number fourteen.

"Have a nice day, sir."

Max walked out without looking back. He reached the cabin ten minutes later and parked the vehicle as deep in the woods as he could. The day before, Max had purchased a padlock for the door, along with a sheet of plywood and a box of nails—he already had the hammer. Now that the plywood was firmly nailed over the loose, rotten boards, the porch was safe to cross. Max stuck the key in the padlock and turned it. He lifted the padlock off the latch and gave the door a shove. It opened grudgingly. The shutters were kept closed.

Finding a decent spot to sit on the sofa proved difficult. The damage from mice was extensive. Max sat there, anyway, with a can of beer in his hand and waited for the call from Darryl. He stared at the woman splayed out on the floor. Her arms and legs were stretched to her sides, each limb tied to a heavy object so she couldn't get away. The ball gag, his favorite device for silencing cries, was jammed firmly in her mouth, and dried blood matted her hair. Max set the beer can on the floor and stood. He walked over to the woman and noticed the area beneath her was wet.

"Pissed yourself? Guess I *was* gone a long time." He tapped his forehead. "I bet you have a headache. You were pretty wasted last night. Grabbing you was as easy as pie." He picked up the purse that was knocked over a few feet away and sat back down. "Feels heavy. Why do women keep so much shit in their purses?"

She writhed and pulled at the ropes.

"Don't waste your energy. You aren't going anywhere." Max unzipped the purse and dumped its contents on the floor in front of him. A cell phone, wallet, makeup case, a small notepad, and several pens fell out. A plastic container of mints, lip balm, and an emery board were inside the zipped inner pocket.

Max popped two mints into his mouth and sucked on them while he browsed through her wallet. He nearly choked on the mints when the name on her driver's license caught his eye. He looked at her closely and remembered the newspaper article he'd read online. The age was right, and she was from North Bend! She had to be the younger judge's wife. "Theresa Gardino, huh? Sounds Italian." He kept his identity and excitement to himself. Max checked for money and found sixty-seven dollars in cash. "This will come in handy, and you won't be needing it, anyway."

She squirmed and moaned even harder.

"Zip it!" He continued where he'd left off and pulled out her credit cards and library card. With them fanned out, Max noticed one in particular had a photo of her on it. He pulled it from the bunch. "Holy shit, Theresa, you didn't tell me you were a doctor. I finally found somebody with an occupation that might come in handy."

Max's phone rang just as he guzzled the last of his beer. He picked up and listened to the automated voice asking if he would accept a collect call from WSPF.

"Yes."

A short pause and a click later, Max heard Darryl on the other end. "What's the number?"

"Fourteen."

The phone clicked off.

Max's attention went back to Theresa Gardino. He snapped open another can of beer and sat on the floor next to her head. He stroked her long dark hair, then grabbed a handful and yanked it. She screeched through the ball gag.

Tears rolled down the sides of her face and pooled in her ears.

"What do you think I should do with you, Dr. Gardino, and why were you sitting in that bar alone late last night? Don't you know it's dangerous for women to go to bars without a strong man along to keep you safe? You were quite the social butterfly, but look what you got yourself into. You intrigued me so much I had to know more, and then you passed me on the sidewalk." Max laughed. "You had no idea you were about to get cracked in the head." He grinned and flicked his tongue as he knelt over her, just inches from her face.

With a quick jerk upward, Theresa head butted Max. Blood ran from his nose to his upper lip where it pooled. He laughed and wiped the blood with the back of his hand.

"Guess I should have seen that coming." He balled up his fist and punched her in the right eye.

She groaned in agony.

Max stood and walked over to her left arm, stretched straight out and secured by a double-knotted rope under a closed door. "Hmmm—the wedding ring explains everything. You and hubby have a fight last night?"

Max opened the cooler and pulled out a green apple. He bit into it with a loud crunch. "Hungry?"

She nodded.

"Okay, don't do anything stupid. We're very secluded out here, so nobody will hear you yell for help, except me. You don't want to make me angry, do you?"

Theresa shook her head. Max released the ball gag, and

she let out a long moan as she relaxed her cramped jaw. "Water, please."

"You want water?"

"Please."

"After you tell me what I want to know. Why are you in Green River Falls?"

"We have a vacation home north of town near the river. We're here for a week."

"Who's we?"

"Me and my family. Please let me go."

Max reached back, and with a violent swing, slapped her hard enough to split her lip. "You're only supposed to answer my questions. I don't want to hear anything else. Got it?"

She groaned again and licked her bloody lip.

"I asked you if you got it?"

"Yes."

"What does your husband do?"

"He's a judge."

A deep barrel laugh echoed in the room. Max imagined Darryl's expression when he told him who he was sharing the cabin with. Max cracked open another beer and thought about his options. "I can see it now. Your smug judge husband will be expecting a ransom call. Of course, the cops will try to trace it, but they won't have any luck—I'm not stupid. Your old man will beg me to release you and return you safely back to him. See, Theresa, people like you think money is the answer to life's problems. I don't want millions of dollars."

"Then what do you want?"

Max shot her a threatening look. "Revenge is what he wants. Justice is twenty years overdue."

"He?"

"Don't make me slap you again."

She lay still and whimpered quietly.

Max scrolled through Theresa's cell phone. "What's your old man's name?"

"My husband's?"

"No shit, Theresa. Don't play stupid with me because I'm not amused. Yes, your husband's."

"Antonio."

"See, that wasn't so hard. Here we go—Antonio." He smirked. "It's the first one on your contact list."

Max sat on the couch and tapped the call icon next to Antonio's name.

"What are you doing?"

"Calling the hubby. What do you think I'm doing?"

"I'm sure he's contacted the police by now."

"That's nice. Now shut the hell up."

A man picked up on the third ring.

"Hey, Antonio, this is Theresa's killer. Just calling to say how much we're enjoying each other's company—for now."

Theresa began screaming. Max rose and kicked her in the stomach.

"Anyway, Theresa says goodbye. She hopes you have a nice life without her." Max hit the red end call button and threw the phone on the couch. "Want some water?"

Theresa went silent.

"Suit yourself. Anyway, I was just kidding when I was talking to Antonio—I'm not going to kill you unless you give me good reason. I might need your skills sooner or later, who knows?"

Chapter 26

"I think we're getting close. Plainview should be the next right," I said as I guided Jack to Amy Patterson's house.

My cell phone rang just as Jack turned.

I looked at the caller ID. "It's the station. Hello, Jade here."

"Jade, it's Jan. I have two families that want to come in to give their DNA sample. Can you get back here by five o'clock?"

"Doubt it. We're almost to the house of the other young woman that was found in the woods. Call Clayton and Billings. Clark said they were all going to head back, anyway. The forms for the families to fill out and the DNA test kits are in the conference room. Everything is self-explanatory."

"Got it. I'll let them know."

"Thanks, Jan." I clicked off just as Jack slowed in front of a two-story contemporary home in a country subdivision.

"Is this it?" I craned my neck to see the house number then double-checked the address on the sheet. "The address is 3861 Plainview."

"Yeah, this is the right house." Jack sighed. "Let's go deliver the bad news."

"Hang on, I'm getting a text from Clayton." I read the message silently while Jack waited. "Okay, he said they'll take care of the DNA samples and that the dogs are working another scene. The handler will bring them back out in the morning and go over everything again."

"Yeah, unfortunately that's a hundred-acre parcel. Max could have buried those other two women anywhere. Shall we?"

"Yeah, let's get this over with."

Jack parked in the driveway next to a late-model Ford sedan. We exited the cruiser and walked up the wide flagstone sidewalk that was flanked by rows of early blooming flowers. The large porch looked welcoming with two wicker rockers and a small glass table nestled between them. A plant stand holding a potted Boston fern sat in a shaded corner. I rang the doorbell. An extremely young looking woman, who I assumed to be the mother, answered the door and opened it widely.

I smiled. "Ma'am, we're detectives from the sheriff's department. You must be Nancy?"

"Yes, please come in. My husband, Mark, is in the kitchen. Let's have a seat in there."

We followed Nancy through the stone-floored foyer, past a short hallway, and into the kitchen. Her husband stood, introduced himself, and shook our hands. I was surprised to see how young Mark looked too.

"Mr. and Mrs. Patterson, we have reason to believe we've found Amy."

"Meaning she's dead? She'd be with you if she was alive." Tears welled up in Nancy's eyes.

We waited as Mark comforted his wife.

"We're very sorry for your loss." I looked from one to the other. "What we're going to need is DNA samples from both of you to confirm Amy's identity."

Mark spoke up. "That's impossible."

Jack frowned. "Sir?"

"Amy is adopted. She was almost ten when we finally brought her home. She was originally from Poland."

I nodded. Now I understood why they seemed too young to have a twenty-two-year-old daughter. "I'll need something of Amy's to confirm a DNA match."

"We can get you her dental records."

The conversation I had with Lena popped back into my mind. "How about something I can take with me now like her hairbrush and toothbrush?"

Mark nodded, and Nancy stood. "Excuse me. I'll get those items."

"Thank you, ma'am."

Nancy returned a few minutes later with a plastic grocery bag in hand. "I put them in the same bag. I hope that's okay."

"It's fine, thank you." Jack and I got up to leave.

"Detectives?"

"Yes, ma'am."

"How did Amy die?"

I stared at the floor and tried to think of the most sensitive words to use. "Mrs. Patterson, I don't—"

"Please, Sergeant Monroe. You can sugarcoat it to a degree if you need to."

"Amy was assaulted with some type of knife. That's what killed her."

Mark and Nancy gripped each other and sobbed. I reached out and held Nancy's hand. "You have my word, we'll find the man that did this."

"Thank you, detectives." Mark took the cards we handed him.

Jack and I shook their hands and extended our apologies again. "We'll show ourselves out."

"That was tough," I said and let out a sigh as I took my place in the passenger seat. "Don't you think it's weird that no calls have come in from the news segment? There haven't been any hits on the BOLO, either."

"It's what snakes do, Jade."

"Yeah, what's that?" I turned to Jack.

"They hunker down out of sight until it's time to strike. They catch people off guard—it's when they're the deadliest."

"We have to come up with something to say to Darryl. Do you have any idea how long it's going to take to extract DNA from the bones and match it to the samples people bring in? We may only get a handful of volunteers. It was twenty years ago, for Pete's sake. I think we need to make a trip to Boscobel."

We pulled into the station and went inside. Clayton was escorting a couple to the door, and Billings was placing the paperwork and DNA sample in an evidence bag to take downstairs. The samples would be stored until we had enough DNA from bones to start testing for matches.

"How many people have come in?"

"Four families," Billings said. "Not bad for day one, but this may have to be ongoing for a while."

Clark exited his office and grabbed a roller chair to sit on. "How did it go at the Patterson house?"

"About as bad as you'd expect." I poured myself a cup of stale coffee and slurped it down.

"Did they give you a DNA sample?"

"They aren't her biological parents. Nancy, the adoptive mom, gave me Amy's hairbrush and toothbrush. I already took them downstairs to forensics."

Clark rolled his neck, and it crackled. "Okay, here's the latest. The mayor called about thirty minutes ago. He said we have a week to get our work done at the farm or the megastore is pulling up stakes."

"What about the other two possible victims? There's a lot of ground to cover, boss."

"I know, Jade. That's why we're getting more dogs. I made a call to Milwaukee County Sheriff's Department after talking to the mayor. They're loaning us nine canine units. They'll be at the site at eight tomorrow morning. I want everyone to go home and get some sleep. We're heading to the farm at seven thirty sharp."

I glanced down at the list of unfinished business on my desk. "Crap."

"What's wrong?" Jack asked.

"Judge Gardino was supposed to let the Clerk of Courts

know when he was scheduling a pretrial hearing for our punk car thieves. They were going to call me today and tell me when it's supposed to go on the docket." I looked at the clock. "The courthouse offices are closed—guess I'll call them tomorrow." I pulled out my cell phone and set a reminder for myself.

"I thought he was on vacation," Billings said.

"Great. Nobody told me about it." I grabbed my purse, sweater, and gun, then crossed the bull pen to the door. "Good night, guys."

"Night, Jade."

Just as I climbed into my car, Amber texted me. I turned the key in the ignition and read her message.

Pot roast will be done in fifteen minutes, and Dad said he's calling at eight.

I texted her back. *Yum—see you in a few.*

I pulled out of the parking lot, made a quick detour to Pit-Stop, filled up my car, and bought a four-pack of Scottish Ale.

At home, we had a delicious meal of pot roast, carrots, potatoes, and gravy, compliments of my amazing sister. She must have gotten her cooking skills from Mom since I knew I was seriously lacking in that department. I felt overly stuffed and deliriously tired after dinner. With the kitchen clean and the plates stacked in the dishwasher, I waited on the couch for my dad's phone call.

"Wake me up when Dad calls. I'm going to rest my eyes for a few minutes."

"Sure, no problem. Do you mind if I watch the news? I'll keep the volume down."

"Go ahead. It's okay."

The voice of the news anchor faded as I felt myself drifting off.

"This is Angela Miles reporting live with breaking news from Jackson County. Well-known circuit court judge of Washburn County—"

Amber paused the TV. "Jade, wake up. Watch this." Amber shook my knee. "Wake up."

"What?"

"Pay attention. This is important."

I rolled over to face the TV and rubbed my eyes. Amber clicked the play button.

"Antonio Gardino, a longtime resident of North Bend, reported earlier today that his wife of twelve years, Theresa Gardino, has been kidnapped. She was last seen around two a.m. this morning at the bar behind me, The Last Stop. The family owns a vacation home on the banks of the river in Green River Falls."

"What!" I sat straight up on the couch, now fully awake.

Angela Miles went on to say, "Local police located Mrs. Gardino's white Mercedes sedan parked a few blocks from the bar, but there have been no sightings of the woman. Theresa Gardino is a thirty-seven-year-old mother of two and a well-respected doctor at St. Joseph's Community Hospital south of North Bend. According to Judge Gardino, a call came in at four thirty this afternoon from his wife's cell phone. The caller, a male, didn't identify himself but said he was Mrs. Gardino's killer. The call ended before it could be traced. Contact the Green River

Falls Police Department at the number seen at the bottom of the screen if you have any information about Theresa Gardino's whereabouts. Stay tuned for more as information comes in on this disturbing situation."

"Holy crap, I need a drink."

Amber jumped off the couch. "Stay put, Jade. What do you want—wine or beer?"

"Wine, please. I don't know what to do. The family lives here, but the crime has been committed in another county. It's no wonder the judge didn't update the Clerk of Courts today."

Amber handed me a glass of wine as I picked up my phone. "What are you doing?"

"I have to call Jack and run this past him in case he didn't see the broadcast. I need his opinion. We may or may not be heading to Green River Falls tomorrow."

Amber's phone rang as I talked to Jack. "It's Daddy. What do you want me to do?"

"Hang on a second, Jack. This call is on you, sis. If Dad has information about the surgery and when he thinks he'll be here, write everything down. Apologize for me." I got up and walked down the hall to my bedroom. I sat at the small desk facing the window and pulled out a notepad and pen in case I needed it. "What should we do?"

"We'll ask Clark about it first thing in the morning and see what he suggests. I'm sure Green River Falls PD has interviewed half the town already. If I were them, I would have talked to everyone at that bar too."

"Why do you think she was alone at that time of night, Jack?"

"Good question. I'm sure they've interviewed the judge and asked him the same thing. It makes me wonder if there was trouble in paradise."

Chapter 27

Threatening rain clouds loomed. My wipers were set at intermittent, but I still had to turn them manually every minute or two. It sprinkled, then it didn't, then it did. I checked the time as I passed the bank—7:22 a.m. I made sure to wear all-terrain shoes every day this week since I never knew what I'd be doing. I kept a pair of low heels on the floor of my car just in case I needed to look presentable.

Jack, Clayton, Billings and I arrived at the sheriff's department at the same time and parked side by side. We exited our cars and walked to the entrance together.

"Did you guys see the breaking news last night about the judge's wife?" I asked.

Clayton whistled and raked his hands through his hair. "Sure did. What a nightmare. Don't they have young kids?"

"Yeah, they aren't even in middle school yet."

"Is it supposed to rain all day?" Billings looked at the sky and pulled the hood of his rain slicker over his head.

"Don't know, but the field has to be getting close to

complete, doesn't it? You guys were out there every day. How's it going?"

"Slowly, but that's just my opinion," Clayton said.

Jack held the door open for us.

"Can dogs still smell a human scent through rain?" I asked as I peeled off my own rain slicker.

Everyone shrugged.

Clark paced the bull pen, his hands clasped behind his back. He looked at us, then the wall clock, as we entered through the security door.

"We're on time, boss," I said. I noticed the anxiety written across his face.

He nodded and continued pacing. "Did everyone see the news? I swear this month just keeps getting worse."

"Remember, one day at a time? You've always told us that, sir." I poured each of us a cup of coffee. Clark needed to sit and take a breath. "All you have to do is delegate. We've got this, boss."

Clark sucked in a deep gulp of air and let it out slowly. "Yeah, I know. I shouldn't let the mayor stress me out like he has. Okay"—Clark pointed at Jack and me—"you two are taking a day trip. First stop is Green River Falls. Find out everything you can there. Talk to the local PD and tell them you're in town. We don't want them to think we're meddling in their case. Let them know Judge Gardino is a personal friend from our county and you're just there to lend support. Talk to the judge, his kids, the bartender, the neighbors, you get the idea. The judge has been a good friend over the years. We need to help out if we can."

"Understood. What else, boss?" Jack asked.

"You're paying Darryl Sims a visit after that. I'm tired of the mess he and his son have created. Lie to him, give him a line of crap. I don't care what you say, but make him think it's in Max's best interest to turn himself in. At this point, Max is a fugitive from justice. He could be armed and extremely dangerous. We'll shoot to kill if we find him and deem it necessary. Make sure Darryl knows that."

I poured coffee in my travel mug as Clark rattled off instructions. I knew we were in for a long day.

"Clayton and Billings, you're going out to the farm with me. The handlers and dogs will be there soon. We need to wrap up this case. Find out from Dr. White if there's anything we can do to expedite the discovery. Catalog samples, bag bones, act as a go-between, etcetera. Any questions?" Clark looked from one face to the next.

"No, boss, everything is perfectly clear," I said.

"Good." The lieutenant slugged back his coffee, and then with a *crack*, he slapped his hands together. "Let's move, people."

Jack and I headed to one cruiser and got in. Clayton, Billings, and the lieutenant climbed into another.

"Keep me updated on anything you get," Clark said through his open passenger side window.

"Will do, boss." I rolled up my window as Jack pulled out of the parking lot. We had a long drive ahead of us—nearly three hours. I pulled out my notepad.

"Whatcha doing?"

"Trying to think of a line of crap to hand Darryl when

we see him. We didn't really get a chance to brainstorm like I had hoped."

"Let's just tell him we have Max in custody. We'll say we only have circumstantial evidence, but we're looking to convict him of first-degree murder unless Darryl wants to cough up the number of women he buried in the field. We need names too."

"I doubt if he'll buy it," I said. "He'll just confess to all of them."

"Not the recent ones. He can't explain those away."

I stared out the side window and watched the scenery turn from city streets and stoplights to country farmland as we left North Bend in the rearview mirror. Fields planted in corn and soybeans were beginning to show shades of green. The winter wheat was almost ready to harvest. In a half hour, the scenery would change again. Interstate 94 would take us most of the way.

Thoughts of the agony Judge Gardino must have been going through brought me back to the moment.

"I hope the judge is still in Green River Falls. Nobody at the station has his personal cell phone number. I'm not even sure where his vacation home is."

Jack turned the radio off. "The police department will know all of that. They can put us in touch with him."

"Where do you think Max went, Jack?"

"No idea. There haven't been any sightings of him or his van, and the BOLO hasn't had any hits. It's like he's disappeared."

The sky cleared as Jack drove west. I checked the time.

We had been on the road for two hours already.

"Let's get some coffee at the next exit. I want to call Clayton too and see if the dogs hit on anything else in the woods."

"Sure thing."

"I forgot to tell you, Amber talked to our dad last night while I was on the phone with you. He's going to come here for his knee surgery. I guess it's serious enough that he scheduled it for next week already. He's flying in on Sunday, and the surgery is Tuesday."

"No kidding? That makes a lot of sense. It's tough enough getting around on crutches, but without help? No, thanks."

"Was that a subtle reminder aimed directly at me about the dog bite last summer?"

"Uh-huh, but apparently it wasn't very subtle." Jack grinned as he clicked his blinker and got into the far right lane. The exit was a quarter mile ahead, where we could fill up the cruiser, grab hot coffee, and stretch.

Jack turned into the truck stop and pulled up to pump nine. "Want to grab a bite too? Truck stop food is usually good. We can get a couple of sandwiches and take them with us."

"Yeah, sure. I'm going to give Clayton a quick call." I got out and walked over to a decorative bench under an awning near the entrance to the diner. I scrolled to Clayton's name and stared at the busy oversized lot adjacent to the restaurant. Semis entered and exited, while others sat idling in a long row of parked trucks. The drivers were probably sleeping in the bunks or inside the diner, enjoying a hearty meal and strong coffee. I waited for Clayton to answer. "Hey, Chad, how's it going with the canine units?"

"Hi, Jade. Luckily the sky has cleared up, and the dogs are busy with their noses to the ground. No hits yet, so that's a good sign. The handlers sectioned off quadrants of the woods so the dogs aren't overlapping each other. It would be great to catch a break on this one. I think Clark really needs it."

"Yeah, I hear that. Okay, we just stopped to fill the gas tank and grab some coffee. Call us if anything shakes loose."

"Roger that."

I hung up right as Jack moved the cruiser to a parking spot.

"What did Clayton have to say?"

"So far the dogs haven't alerted on anything."

"That's good news." He cocked his head toward the door and pulled it open. "I'll pay for the gas, then we can check out the menu."

We were on the road again thirty minutes later, each of us with a greasy burger in hand and a cup of strong coffee to go. I glanced at the time on the cruiser's dashboard.

"We should be there just before noon. Let's head to the police department first, talk to them, and then see what the judge can tell us."

Chapter 28

Max slapped at the mosquito on his neck as he stood on that precariously crumbling pier. He threw a line out and hoped to catch a few bluegills for dinner. With his hand on his forehead, he shielded his eyes every so often and peered across the lake. The sun's rays bounced off the ripples, making it difficult to see without glare. Trout Lake was small and surrounded by private property. Only seven cabins sat on the banks of that beautiful "No Motors" body of water. Anyone that might be fishing would likely be doing it off their own pier or in a rowboat. With most of the cabins being on the west side of the lake, the likelihood of Max being seen was slim, and that was exactly how he wanted it.

The float jiggled, and the line went taut. He waited, his finger gently touching the line. The bobber sank under the surface and disappeared. Max flicked the pole and hooked his dinner. He pulled back with just the right amount of pressure as he cranked the reel and pulled in the first fish of the day. Three more times before noon, he reeled in fish.

Max watched them flop in that old bucket he'd found behind the cabin. They amused him as they flailed, their mouths gaping and gasping, their gills opening and closing. They suffocated and died slowly. It gave him an idea.

He carried the bucket with that day's catch inside. Max watched his footing as he walked the pier back to solid ground and followed the deer path to the cabin. Every so often the bucket would jiggle, and a fish inside took its last breath of deadly air.

Max entered the cabin and approached Theresa. She sat on the couch with her arms outstretched. The rope tied around her wrists secured her to the doorknob on her right and the kitchen cabinet handle on the left. She had nowhere to go. The ball gag jammed in her mouth kept her quiet.

"Look what I caught for dinner. You get to eat something other than potato chips. Those fish gave me an idea I've never tried out. Are you game?"

She squirmed and thrashed her head back and forth. Max grabbed her legs and yanked her to the floor. Using his enormous size and weight, he easily pinned her down. He pressed her arms flat with his knees and gripped her face tightly in his left hand. With his right thumb and index finger, he pinched her nose closed.

Theresa bucked and thrashed even harder than before as she tried to get air. He let go. Her nostrils flared as she sucked in oxygen.

He laughed loudly. Max enjoyed this new game he'd discovered thanks to watching the fish die. "How was that?" He gave her a few seconds of air then did it again—four more times. He slapped her cheek after the last round of near-death suffocation. He could barely revive her. "Hey, wake up. You aren't going out this easily." He yanked the ball gag out of her mouth.

Theresa's chest lurched as she gasped for air. She caught her breath and burst into tears. "Just kill me, you son of a bitch! You're going to do it eventually, aren't you?"

Max's knees popped when he stood. "Yeah, just not yet. I'm having way too much fun. I like your company." He shoved the ball gag back in her mouth and untied her hands, then retied them behind her back. He tied her ankles together, giving her a foot of rope so she could walk. "Get outside and do your business. I'm sick of cleaning up after you." Max pushed her out the door and followed her into the woods. Mosquitos swarmed his face, and he swatted them while he waited. "Hurry the hell up." A few minutes later and back in the cabin, he tied her to the bedposts. He unfastened the ball gag and poured water into her mouth, then put it back in place.

"I'll be back soon—we have more games to play." Max walked out and slammed the door behind him. With the padlock clasped and secure, he gave it a tug to make sure, then climbed into the van, backed it out of its hiding spot under tree cover, and drove away. He needed to check the post office box.

Chapter 29

Jack exited the interstate at the Green River Falls ramp and turned left onto Main Street. I pulled up the police department's address on my phone then checked the time—11:45. I enlarged the map as Jack drove.

"That's easy enough. Just go west on Main Street for a few blocks then turn left on Second Street. It's right there."

Within a few minutes, we were in front of a block of newer looking, nicely designed redbrick buildings. City Hall, the police department, and the library were among a group of connected buildings on one side of the street, and the fire department, wearing a matching facade, was located across from them.

Jack parked, then we crossed the lot and headed to the double glass doors. Inside, the marble floors glistened, and the walls wore a rich birch paneling. A long reception counter faced us, and two friendly looking middle-aged women sat behind it.

We approached them, and I spoke as we pulled out our badges. "Hello, ladies, we're from the Washburn County

Sheriff's Department. My name is Sergeant Jade Monroe, and this"—I touched Jack's shoulder—"is my partner, Detective Jack Steele. We'd like to speak to the officer who's handling the case about Judge Gardino's wife."

The blond woman wearing glasses spoke. "Oh, my word, the town feels so bad for that family. They've been coming here every summer for years now. Give me one moment, please." She rose, opened a door at her back, and disappeared around it.

"What was her name?" I whispered to Jack.

"Don't know. She didn't say."

The other woman behind the counter smiled. "Sorry, I wasn't trying to eavesdrop, but you are only five feet from me. Her name is Barb."

"Thank you," I said as I motioned for Jack to come with me. "Let's wait in the guest area."

"In case someone is listening?" He chuckled.

"No, because we might have something private to discuss." We sat on a pair of matching upholstered chairs. I felt like napping and yawned. "Man, could I use some coffee."

Jack looked around and pointed. There's a coffee station right over there. Sit tight. I'll grab a cup for each of us."

"Thanks, Jack."

Jack returned a minute later and took his seat. He handed me a coffee.

"Do you think the judge will be candid with us?" I asked. "I mean there had to be a reason why his wife was out alone that night."

"Yeah, you're right, but that might backfire—he may want to keep that side of his life private. Don't forget, we all know the same people and we work in the same city. I'm sure he wouldn't want a scandal."

I perked up. "What if this isn't an abduction at all? Maybe she ran off with a boyfriend."

"Yeah, but you're forgetting about the man that called the judge and said he was her killer."

I waved that comment away with a swipe at the air. "That could have been to throw the judge off. She and a boyfriend could be in another state by now for all we know."

Jack shrugged. "Let's stick to the facts as we know them—which isn't much yet." He jerked his chin to the right. "It looks like the contact person is heading our way."

I glanced over my shoulder and instantly felt deflated. The man approaching us wore an officer's uniform and didn't look old enough to shave. He reached out to shake our hands.

"Deputies."

I cringed. "It's *Sergeant* Monroe and *Detective* Steele. We're from the Washburn County Sheriff's Department."

"Yeah, Barb told me that. What can I do for you?"

"Are you the person in charge of Judge Gardino's case?"

"That's correct, I'm Officer Duke—Martin Duke."

"Is there a private place where we can talk, Officer Duke?" Jack asked.

He looked around. "Um—how about an interrogation room?"

I raised a questioning brow. "You don't have a conference room or a guest lounge?"

"Oh, okay. I just thought the interrogation room would be different."

"Yeah, I'm not all that excited about different. I kind of enjoy being comfortable."

"Sure, follow me."

I turned toward Jack and rolled my eyes as we followed the youngster.

"Come on in and have a seat. My lieutenant and a few officers are out doing interviews. They left me in charge. Our police force is small, and Lieutenant Connors is the boss for six officers. I'm curious as to why you're here."

I spoke up. "We have another place to be somewhat close by and wondered if we could help out in any way as long as we were in the area. The judge is a personal acquaintance of ours, you know. We often sit in on his cases as material witnesses and so forth. He knows us well."

"I see."

Officer Duke stared at us while an awkward silence filled the air.

Jack took over. "Okay, what can you tell us, Martin? Where has this investigation led you so far, and who have you spoken with?"

"Oh. Well, obviously we talked to the judge and the bartender."

"And?" I asked.

"And what?"

"And what did they tell you?" I was ready to strangle this

boy, and I knew he was deliberately withholding information from us.

"The judge said he got a phone call from a man using his wife's phone. The bartender said it was a busy night. The locals were all in, and more tourists were arriving every day. He had one helper and didn't remember much. He said Mrs. Gardino talked to a lot of people, and she was kind of drunk. That's all he remembered."

"Does that bar have surveillance?" Jack asked.

"Yeah, but it doesn't store information—it tapes over itself daily." He grinned. "Nothing exciting happens in our neck of the woods."

I groaned. "Except when it does. Where is the judge's vacation home?"

"A couple miles out of town going north. His place is a big log lodge on Cinnamon Lane. You can't miss it."

We got up and thanked him. I knew there wasn't much more we'd get from Martin Duke. We were outsiders, and we'd have better luck talking directly to the judge. At least the coffee had perked me up. We walked back to the cruiser and headed north out of town.

The judge's home was easy to find. Calling that monstrosity a vacation home was like Cornelius Vanderbilt II calling The Breakers, his seventy-room mansion in Newport, Rhode Island, his summer cottage. The home was ostentatious.

Jack parked the cruiser, and we got out. Several cars sat on the driveway, a good sign saying that the judge was likely home. We took the four steps up to the enormous veranda, and the view from that spot was beautiful. In another life, if I was ever rich, a place like this would fulfill all my dreams. Jack clanked the knocker on the massive eight-foot-tall door. We waited, but nobody answered. He clanked again, a bit harder, but there was still no response.

"Come on. Let's check the back," Jack said. He led, and I followed down the railroad tie steps and around to the back of the house. Voices sounded as we turned the corner. We looked up to see an enormous upper deck that faced nothing but wilderness. In the distance, I was sure I spotted a beautiful blue lake nestled among the fir trees.

"Judge Gardino, is that you?" I shielded my eyes and looked upward toward the noontime sun.

"Who's down there?" The judge came to the railing and peered down. "What the—" He caught himself before he finished the sentence. Two young children came and stood by his side. "Jade Monroe and Jack Steele?"

"Yes, sir, it's us. We knocked, but I guess you couldn't hear it from back here."

"Come on up. The stairs are over there." He pointed beyond his shoulder.

Jack and I climbed the two full sets of stairs to get up to his deck. He shook our hands with a confused expression.

"What are you doing here?"

"We're on our way to Boscobel, sir, to see Darryl Sims."

"Ah, yes, the infamous Darryl Sims. It was my father that sentenced that lunatic to prison. I remember the stories well."

"That's right. I forgot your father was a judge back

then." I gave Jack a concerned look.

"The last I heard, Max was causing problems with vacating the homestead."

"That's correct, Judge, but that's the least of his problems."

"What has he done now? I've been out of town for a week, you know."

"The property is littered with human bones, sir, and some of them are recent."

"You think he's responsible?"

"It sure looks that way, but we didn't find out about this until he left the property. We have no idea where he went."

"Wow"—the judge pressed his temples—"what a nightmare."

I glanced at the kids sitting on several lounge chairs. They looked to be preoccupied with their devices. "Do they know anything?"

He whispered his response. "No. I don't have the heart to tell them their mom is missing. I said she left for a few days. We don't know if that caller was a quack or if he actually has her. Where are my manners? Let's go inside where we can talk privately. How about some coffee?"

"That would be nice." Jack and I followed as he slid the large glass door to the side and entered the great room.

Judge Gardino turned back before closing the slider. "Kids, my guests and I are going to talk inside for a while. Stay on the deck where I can see you."

They mumbled an okay without looking up.

"Have a seat, and I'll tell you what I know." The judge

placed the coffee carafe and three cups on the coffee table. "I imagine you want full disclosure?"

I smiled. "It would be helpful."

He took a deep breath. "First off, Theresa has been seeing somebody for the last six months. I'm not sure if this threat is real or a sick joke at my expense. It doesn't seem like something she would do, though—at least not to the kids. We haven't slept together in months." He looked around. "I'm thankful for our large homes. We can keep our distance and stay out of each other's hair. The kids don't notice anything unusual."

"Sir, what about the man that called?"

"Well, the Green River Falls Police Department is doing everything they can, but they're a small unit. Yet—" He paused.

Jack spoke up. "You were about to say?"

The judge shook his head, and his eyes clouded with tears. "First off, they told me to stay put. You know, the whole 'husband did it' theory. I told them everything I know personally, which isn't much. All I know is the situation before Theresa left here. I can't tell them anything beyond that. I wasn't with her."

"Why don't we start there, before she left?" I said.

He nodded and took a sip of coffee. "We were arguing, as usual. She wants to move to Madison—I don't. I have a good career in North Bend—hell, we both do. I don't want to uproot the kids, either. They have a lot of friends and after-school activities. I know it's because her boyfriend lives somewhere near Madison. They met at a medical convention, but that's all I know."

I wrote as he talked. "Why doesn't she just get a divorce?"

"A public figure in the community like a doctor? She doesn't have the nerve, and she wouldn't want the kids to know about her affair. I hate to admit it, but I'm just not sure if this abduction actually happened or not."

"Do you have any idea what the PD has done yet? Have they looked over surveillance cameras near that bar?"

"The only thing I know for sure is that they interviewed me and the bartender. They haven't updated me since."

"Well, in my opinion, surveillance cameras would be the fastest way to rule out, or confirm, foul play. Theresa has to be on video somewhere in town. Main Street isn't that big. Would you mind if we looked into it?"

"I don't mind, but good luck getting the Green River Falls PD to share their spotlight with you." He smirked and got up to look out the patio door. The kids were in the same spots as before. Judge Gardino turned back toward us. "They haven't had a situation like this in forever."

"Wouldn't this news hurt tourism?" Jack asked.

"Not necessarily. Most of the tourists are longtime cabin owners that spend their summers here, or weekenders that play blackjack at the casino."

I nodded and wrote that down. "Where exactly is that bar Theresa went to?"

"It's called the Last Stop, and it's right downtown."

We stood and thanked him for the coffee. "We'll update you before we leave town. May I have your cell phone number?" I handed him my notepad.

"Sure, here you go. The phone reception and Internet service out here are sketchy. I usually go into town when I need to make calls or use the Internet. There's a cute espresso bar downtown called the Black Elixir. Their Wi-Fi is strong, and so is their coffee."

"Thanks, we just might stop in and check it out."

I nonchalantly glanced in each room as we made our way to the front door. The home was rustic and beautiful. I sighed with envy. After we were back in the cruiser and alone, I asked Jack's opinion.

"Well, at least he's being as transparent as possible. We have to assume the threat is real, though. It seems too farfetched to be a ploy to run off with a boyfriend."

"I agree. So how are we going to find out if the PD has checked surveillance tapes? We don't have the authority to override them, and this isn't our jurisdiction."

"We'll talk to the store owners directly. We have every right to ask that much. Let's do a walk through the downtown area and check to see who actually has cameras outside their establishments. We'll go in, tell them who we are, and ask if the police checked out the tapes. That's all we have to do. We'll go over our information with the PD and see what they intend to do about it."

I nodded. "Okay, and we have to keep good notes."

Jack parked the cruiser in the first open spot he saw on Main Street.

"We'll walk the length on this side"—he pointed—"then turn back and hit the other side of the street."

"Yep, sounds good. Remind me to call Clayton again later. Maybe after we hit the stores on this side we can go to that espresso bar and have lunch. I'll call from there and check emails too."

Jack and I began the process of walking Main Street with our heads looking upward. We checked every door, rooftop, and corners of buildings for mounted cameras.

"Here we go," Jack said. "Store number one is Andrew's Resale. Write it down."

"Got it."

We walked into the old-time, odd-smelling secondhand store. Shelves and counters were filled with trinkets, knickknacks, and junk. Racks of "gently" used clothing lined the walls at the back of the store.

A woman, leaning toward the heavy side and with short gray hair, came out from another room. "Hello there, folks. Have a look around and let me know if you have any questions."

I smiled. "Actually, ma'am, we do have questions." I showed her my badge, introduced Jack and myself, and told her what we wanted.

"Well, I did hear about the abduction. Everyone in town is talking about it, but nobody came in and asked to see our camera footage."

"May I have your name, please?"

"It's Betty Lou Jones."

"Thank you, Betty. How long do you save the video feed?" Jack asked.

"It saves a week's worth of tape, then it deletes that footage and starts over."

"When does the tape begin?"

"It starts over with a clean slate at 12:01 a.m. every Monday morning."

I mentally calculated how much time was left before the footage was deleted. We only had a few days left. "Okay, I think that's all we need to know. Thank you, ma'am."

Jack and I left, and I wrote down what Betty had told us.

"Okay, next."

Chapter 30

He parked at the front of the building and walked inside. Max turned to the left where the post office boxes were located. He scanned left to right and looked for box number fourteen.

"There you are."

Max knelt down. Box fourteen was on the second row from the bottom, the fifth box in. He pulled the key from his pocket, stuck it in the keyhole, and turned it. The door opened, and Max peered in. One lone envelope sat inside. He reached in, pulled it out, and checked the return address—WSPF, Boscobel, Wisconsin. Max stuffed it in his pocket, locked the box, and left. Fillmore Street, where the post office was located, was only a block off Main Street. He glanced at the sunny sky and decided to walk. When he reached Main Street, he turned left. An unmarked black cruiser sat in a parking space directly ahead of him. The tall antennas, side-mounted spotlights, and municipal plates gave it away. Max's eyes darted from one side of the street to the other, then he saw them. Black Elixir was just ahead on his side of the street. He stepped up his pace and ducked inside, hopefully unseen. Max grabbed a newspaper off the coffee counter as he passed and kept going. He found a small table for two at the back of the café and sat. He had an unobstructed view of the window from his location. The waitress took his order for a tall black coffee and a ham sandwich then walked away. He kept his eyes on the window as he pulled the envelope out of his pocket and tore it open. Inside was the letter he expected from Darryl. Every communication between them in letter form was identified with codes. Phone conversations would be kept to a minimum with only yes or no responses to what Darryl had written down. Each statement had a number written next to it. If Darryl said 'three,' that would be the statement Max would look at. His responses would be yes or no. Darryl reminded Max that he'd call on Friday at four o'clock and to keep the sheet of paper with him at all times.

The waitress brought the sandwich and coffee to Max's table. He thanked her and watched out the window as he ate. There they were again, walking out of Pete's Appliances.

What the hell are they doing in Green River Falls? How would they know I'm here? I've got to get back to the van and leave the area. They're getting too close.

Max watched and waited. As soon as they walked into another store, he'd make his move and sneak out.

Shit, they're heading this way.

The newspaper sat on the table for a reason. Max didn't care what the latest headline said unless it had something to do with the abducted doctor. It was a good prop in case he needed one, and right now, as they walked toward Black Elixir, it looked as though he did.

The bell clanked above the door as Jade and Jack walked in. Max sank back in the chair so he wouldn't seem so tall and hid his face behind the newspaper. He listened as they approached the counter to order. He heard that bitch sergeant place an order for two coffees and two banana nut muffins. He perked up when their conversation went to Jade's father, Tom Monroe.

"Well, this door-to-door thing is telling us a lot."

"Yeah, like *you know who* isn't checking camera feeds along Main Street. We need to get this case figured out with or without the support of the Green River Falls PD. I have to be at the airport to pick up my dad at ten o'clock Sunday morning, and I'd like to spend some quality time with him before he goes under the knife on Tuesday. That doesn't give us a lot of time to find Theresa and wrap up things at the farm. That reminds me, I have to call Clayton."

Max heard the counter person tell Sergeant Monroe their order would be ready in a minute.

"Let's grab a table."

Max recognized the male detective's voice, but he didn't remember his name.

"I'll call Clayton now while I have a minute."

Max listened to Sergeant Monroe talk on her cell phone while he remained well hidden behind the newspaper.

"Hey, Chad, what's the word? Uh-huh, okay, that's good news. Really? I guess it's doing its intended job.

Thanks, we'll keep you posted, and tell Clark I'll update him later on Judge Gardino and his missing wife."

"What did Clayton say?" Jack asked after she hung up.

Her voice lowered to a whisper, but Max could still make out the words.

"The canine unit didn't find anything else, so I guess it was only Amy and Deborah in the woods. Now they can focus on finishing up in the field. He also said five more people came in to give DNA samples. Are you ready to continue on?"

"Yep, let's do it."

Max heard the chairs being pushed back and cautiously peered around the newspaper. The two detectives were heading toward the exit. When the door closed behind them, Max stood and moved to a stool near the front window. He saw them enter another building.

Good—time to get out of here and plan my next move.

Chapter 31

"Damn it." I jammed my hands into each pocket and dug through my purse.

"What's wrong?" Jack asked.

"I think I left my cell phone on the table at Black Elixir. I'll be right back."

I walked out of Katie's Closet and looked both ways before crossing the street. Someone caught my eye near the corner of Fillmore and Main Street. I stopped dead in my tracks and shaded my eyes. His height and gait looked right.

There's no way. His hair is different, but how many people are that tall?

Instinctively, I reached into my pocket to grab my phone and call Jack then remembered I didn't have it. "Crap!" I looked back at Katie's Closet, then down the block at Black Elixir. If I went to either place, I'd lose him for sure.

Just before he rounded the corner, the man glanced back. There was no mistaking it. Max Sims looked me dead in the eyes.

"Son of a bitch." I quickly looked up and down the street. I had to make a split-second assessment. Luckily at this time of day, most people were indoors enjoying lunch. I yelled out, "Max Sims, stop right now."

He disappeared around the corner without looking back.

"Shit." I ran across the street while trying to secure the strap of my purse over my head and under my arm. I reached inside my blazer and pulled out my service weapon. With my back pressed against the side of the last building before Fillmore Street, I peeked around the corner—nobody there. I hoped he hadn't found a house to duck into. Dealing with a hostage situation wasn't high on my bucket list. The sound of an engine turning over caught my attention. I scanned the street and looked at every parked vehicle. There he was—a block up. Max backed his van away from the curb and headed toward me.

"Gotcha." I ran into the street and took my stance. My grip was steady, and my weapon was pointed at his windshield, ready to fire. I yelled out, "Stop your vehicle right now, or I'll shoot!"

He stepped on the gas and floored it. I got off two rounds, and his windshield exploded with a spray of glass before he swerved and hit me with the side mirror of the van and sped away. The force threw me to the pavement. I braced myself and cradled my head when I hit the curb with a hard thud. Everything spun around me. A voice got louder and louder until it was right above me.

"Jade, Jade, can you hear me? Somebody call an

ambulance! Jade, it's Jack. Open your eyes. Tell me you can hear me. Where does it hurt?"

I groaned and squinted.

"Jade, what happened? I thought I heard gunfire."

"What? Jack?"

"Your jacket is ripped, and your shoulder and head are bleeding. Lie still, the ambulance is on its way. What can you tell me? Do you remember what happened? Your service weapon is on the curb. What were you doing?"

I reached up and touched my forehead. It was wet and sticky.

"Yeah, partner, that's blood. What happened?"

I heard sirens getting closer. "Jack," I moaned, "Max Sims is here. Put my gun back in my holster—hurry."

"What?" Jack did as I asked then looked around. People began to gather. He leaned over me. "Jade, are you sure it was him?"

"I'm positive. Don't say a word to anyone and go get my cell phone."

The ambulance and a squad car arrived at the same time. The patrol officer got out of his cruiser and approached Jack. "What happened here?"

"I don't have a clue. She said something about tripping over the curb when a car sped by too close to her. We're detectives from North Bend and just in town for the day." Jack flashed his badge.

I added my two cents as I lay looking upward at the officer. "I'm fine, just banged up a bit. It was my own clumsiness."

"You don't look fine, ma'am. The EMTs will assess your injuries."

The officer pulled Jack aside. "Somebody reported gunshots."

Jack nodded. "Yeah, the sound fooled me too. Sergeant Monroe told me the old clunker that sped past her backfired twice and startled her. That's probably why she tripped and fell."

"Ma'am, we're going to help you up gently and put a collar on you. Tell us if it hurts too much."

I groaned again as they sat me up on the curb and wrapped the foam collar around my neck.

"Let's take a look at your head wound." The EMT carefully wiped the blood from my head and looked it over. "Head injuries bleed profusely even if they aren't that bad. You'll probably get by with butterfly stitches, but you're going to have a goose egg for sure. I think you ought to be admitted overnight for observation. It doesn't take a lot of force to cause a concussion."

"Is that really necessary?" I asked.

"It's in your best interest, ma'am. Let me see that shoulder." He cut the sleeve of my blouse open and took a look. My entire shoulder was road rashed and dotted with blood spots. "Can you lift your arm and rotate it?"

I did and it hurt, but nothing was broken or dislocated. I nodded. "It's okay."

"All right, let's get her into the ambulance. You need to stay the night for your own good."

"Can you give me a second?" I tipped my head at Jack.

I needed to talk to him. "I don't mind staying overnight at the hospital. Better safe than sorry, I guess. I was going to call Clark, anyway, and ask if we could stick around after seeing how the PD isn't doing quite as much as they should. Now, after seeing Max, my hunches are telling me that he is somehow connected to Theresa's disappearance. Maybe he's been stalking the Gardinos all along and knew they were here."

Jack whispered. "But why?"

"Remember? It was Antonio's father that put Darryl in prison. Get my phone and come to the hospital. We have to figure out where Max is holed up." I took a deep breath. "Holy crap, my head is throbbing. Make sure to call Clark and tell him what's going on."

"Will do." Jack stood and waved the EMTs over. "She's all yours. Where's the hospital?"

The EMT pointed. "Three blocks up on Division."

They helped me up to the gurney and loaded me into the ambulance. Jack gave me a thumbs-up and disappeared around the corner.

Chapter 32

He looked at his right shoulder in the visor mirror. Blood covered his shirt. "Stupid bitch shot me. This better be a flesh wound and nothing else."

Max had to think this through. Now that the sergeant had recognized him, he had to get out of the area before he was found. He needed a different vehicle. The van's windshield was blown out, making it far too visible and nearly impossible to drive. His eyes watered from the wind coming in at fifty miles an hour. The throb from the bullet wound didn't help. He'd have to go through the totes in the back of the van and find the first aid kit that had been in the bathroom of the farm. He thought about the sergeant's comments he'd overheard earlier and smirked.

She isn't as smart as she thinks she is. Just because they didn't find any more bodies in the woods doesn't mean they aren't out there.

He turned into the driveway and drove the van deep under the tree cover. Max climbed out and grimaced as he slammed the door behind him and went to the back of the van. There were boxes, totes, and bags full of things he took from the house at the last minute.

Where the hell is that first aid kit?

"Ah, there you are." He pulled the entire tote out of the van and dragged it to the porch. There were other items inside he might need. He fumbled for the padlock key buried somewhere deep in his pocket. His arm was quickly going numb from blood loss. His hand shook as he slipped the key into the lock and opened it. He kicked the door open. She woke with a start and slunk back against the wall when he entered.

"I need your help, doc. I've been shot. I'm going to release your hands but not your feet. I swear if you try anything, I'll gut you on the spot. Understand?"

She nodded.

He kicked the first aid kit toward her, and it slid across the floor.

"Bend your head down so I can take the ball gag off you."

She complied, then he untied her hands too.

She rubbed her rope-burned wrists. "How did you get shot?"

He gave her a threatening look. "With a gun, how do you think? Just fix my shoulder and shut up."

"If you want to know how bad the wound is and what I can do for you, I have to talk."

"Fine, but keep it to medical talk only. Open that kit and see what you can use in there. I have a knife on my hip that I'll use without hesitation. Keep that in mind."

"You have to take off your shirt. Open the shutters so it isn't so dark in here, and bring the lantern closer. I'll need cold and hot water and a rag."

"Why both?"

"Because I'm thirsty." She rummaged through the first aid kit as she spoke. "I'll have to make do with the items in here. I'll know more after the wound is washed."

Max did everything Theresa requested, then sat on the floor and removed his shirt. He turned toward the light. Theresa took several gulps of water to revive herself. She dipped a rag in the bucket of hot water, washed her own face, and then dipped it again.

"This is going to hurt, but don't take it out on me." She wiped his shoulder with the hot, wet rag. He flinched but sat still. Theresa looked at the back of his arm. "It's a through and through."

He gave her a quizzical stare. "Meaning?"

"Meaning, I don't have to dig a bullet out. Consider yourself lucky to be alive. Now I have to clean it good and stitch it somehow. I don't see anything in this first aid kit to do that with, though. The best you have in here is gauze and medical tape. It will help but not enough to stop the bleeding."

"I have fish hooks and line."

"Are you serious?"

"I'm not going back into town. The windshield of my van is shot out. That would be a bit noticeable, don't you think? Are you going to do it or not?"

Theresa growled. "I doubt if I have a choice in the

matter. Go get your tackle box, and I'll see what I can use."

Max stared at her suspiciously. "Give me your hands. You're getting tied back up while I'm outside."

She stretched her arms out in front of her.

Max smirked. "Nice try. From behind."

Chapter 33

Jack sat in the chair next to my bed and waited for the nurse to leave. Other than my pounding head sporting a lump the size of a golf ball, I felt okay. My shoulder was sore, but the X-rays confirmed nothing was broken.

After I downed a few aspirin, the door closed at the nurse's back, and we were finally alone.

"Did you call Clark?"

"Yeah, after the cursing and hearing that Max tried to run you down, he said it was good that we were staying the night. He wants us to find Max no matter what it takes. The man is a wanted fugitive." Jack gave me a thoughtful smile. "I don't know about you, Monroe. Always the rogue cop looking for attention."

I smacked him on the arm. "I am not. I'm just always in the right place at the wrong time—or is it the wrong place at the right time?"

"Yeah, right. Anyway, Clark said the search at the farm was almost complete. They think they have all the bones they're going to find."

I pressed the button to raise the back of the bed. "That's good to hear. Now they just need to extract the DNA and see if there are any matches to the samples brought in. Did Clark say anything about the Swedish store pulling out?"

"Yeah, he told the mayor the forensic team would release the farm in five days. Now it's up to the mayor to act as a go-between with the developer and the store. Clark can wash his hands of the stress that created."

I reached for the cup on my tray table and took a sip of water through the straw. "So why do you think the police department here is dragging their feet on the Gardino case?"

"To be honest, Jade, I don't think they are. I'd say they're a little overwhelmed and aren't sure what to do."

"Come on. We all went to the police academy and learned How to be a Good Cop 101. There's no way they can be that ignorant."

Jack shrugged. "I'd really like to help out but—"

"Yeah, I know, it isn't our jurisdiction. What if Judge Gardino insisted on our help?"

"I'll talk to him about it. So tell me everything that happened after you realized you left your phone at Black Elixir. Oh, by the way, here you go." Jack stood and reached in his jacket pocket and pulled out my cell phone. "They already had it behind the counter so nobody would snatch it. They made me show my badge to prove I was an honest cop."

I laughed. "As opposed to a dishonest cop?"

"I guess. Okay, go ahead."

"Well, I left you at Katie's Closet and waited for traffic

before crossing the street. That's when I saw him at the corner of Main Street and Fillmore. I knew I'd lose him if I did anything other than chase him down. He looked over his shoulder before turning the corner and saw me. We locked eyes, Jack, and by the way, he's changed his appearance. He knows we're after him."

"What did he change?"

"His hair is shorter and he shaved off his beard, but I'm one hundred percent sure it was him, and I know he recognized me. At that point, I didn't have a choice. I had to go after him."

Jack nodded. "Hard decision, but I probably would have done the same thing. Then what?"

"Then I rounded the corner and didn't see him. I glanced down both sides of the street for his vehicle. Then I saw him backing out of a parking spot. I ran into the street with my gun drawn and called out for him to stop. He floored it and headed right for me. I got off two rounds before he hit me with his side mirror and threw me for a loop."

"You could have been killed, Jade."

"I'm a cop, for Pete's sake. Cops put themselves at risk every single day. It's what we signed up for, Jack."

He nodded. "Yeah, I know, but this past year you've taken a few hard knocks."

I smiled. "Are you worried about me? You're so sweet."

He chuckled. "Get a grip. You're probably tougher than I am. Anyway, give me the judge's cell number. I'm going to call him. Maybe he'll stop in."

"You want him to come here?"

"Yeah, if we're both going to talk to him. Or would you rather go play Uno with the elderly patients?"

"Smart-ass." I tossed my purse to his side of my bed. "His number is written in my notepad." Jack made the call, and the judge agreed to stop by the hospital. He told Jack he'd be here in a half hour.

"I'm going to grab a bite to eat in the cafeteria. That muffin didn't hold me over for long. Want something?"

"I'm sure I'll get dinner later, but yeah, bring me something crunchy."

"You got it. I'll be back in a flash."

The nurse returned while Jack was gone. She checked my pupils, took my blood pressure and pulse, asked me who the president and vice president were, then left. I turned on the TV that was mounted to the wall on the opposite side of the room, then remembered I had to call Amber and tell her what had happened. She picked up on the third ring.

"Hey, Jade, how's Darryl Sims doing?" She chuckled into the phone.

"We haven't made it there yet. We're staying overnight in Green River Falls."

"Really, is there something you want to tell me about you and Jack?"

"Cute. Actually I'm spending the night in the hospital, and Jack will probably find a cheap motel in town." I heard Amber's voice tighten and go up a few octaves.

"Why the hell are you in the hospital? You obviously aren't dying, otherwise you couldn't call me."

"No, I'm not dying, but Max Sims is in town, and he tried to run over me. He hit me with the side mirror of his van and threw me to the curb. The EMTs that took me to the hospital suggested I stay overnight for observation." I had to hold my cell phone a foot from my ear or my eardrum would have been blown out by Amber's yelling. "Sis, I'm okay, really. Just sore and a little banged up. Gotta go, Jack is back in the room. We have a lot of planning to do. I'll keep in touch, I promise." I said good night to Amber and clicked off. "What did you bring me?" I asked.

"A bag of pretzels, two dill pickles, and a gooey chocolate bar."

I chuckled. "What kind of place sells two dill pickles separately?"

"None that I know of. They were from my burger plate."

"Well, keep them. You know I don't like dill pickles."

"But they're crunchy."

"So is tree bark, but that doesn't mean I want to eat it. The pretzels and chocolate bar are perfect. Thanks."

"Sure, no sweat. The judge should be here any minute. Is there anything you want to go over before he arrives?"

"Not really. I want to be totally transparent with him. He'll have to insist on the police department looking at every video the stores in town have. If Max Sims abducted Theresa somewhere on Main Street, it's on somebody's surveillance system. I really believe he thinks Theresa ran off with her boyfriend, but I don't. Why would Max coincidentally be here the same time the Gardinos are?"

"Maybe he has a place of his own. He did need to hide out somewhere."

"Hmmm… not bad, Jack. Let's check that out tomorrow."

A knock sounded on my half-opened door, and the judge peeked in.

"Come on in, Judge Gardino," Jack said. "Where are the kids?"

"I asked the neighbor to watch them for a few hours." He turned to me. "I heard about your accident this afternoon, Jade. Are you okay?"

"Yeah, just a bruised head, shoulder, and ego. I'll be fine. Judge—"

"Please call me Antonio. Let's save the formalities for the courtroom."

"Sounds good. Antonio, how certain are you that Theresa left with her boyfriend? I want your true gut feeling."

He stared off into space for a few seconds. "I guess it was just an assumption since this is a safe area of the state and we've been coming here for years. And of course, we fought that night before she stormed out. I figured she was teaching me a lesson. I can't imagine someone actually abducting her."

"Antonio, have you noticed a black van near either of your homes?"

"No, not that I can remember. Why a black van?" He looked from me to Jack, then back to me.

"Max Sims has a black van, and he's holed up somewhere in Green River Falls. He's the reason I'm here. He tried to run over me."

"You can't be serious. What would he want with me?"

Jack spoke up. "You said your dad put Darryl in prison."

"He was the acting judge in the case, but the jury made the call."

"Criminals don't look at it that way. They like to blame someone they can pinpoint. We think Max has Theresa," Jack said.

Antonio held his face in his hands and slumped. He was inconsolable. "And I've been doing nothing about her disappearance. I thought she left on her own."

"Would she really do that to her kids?" I asked.

"No, no she wouldn't. I can see that now in hindsight. What do we do? We have to find her!"

"Come with me. We need to pressure the police to check every security camera in town. You have to make that call. After that, we'll go to City Hall. It's in the same building. We have to check the property tax records to see if any parcel of land in the area is owned by a Sims." Jack turned to me. "Are you going to be okay? We really need to go now before everything closes for the day."

I waved them on. "Yeah, go ahead but update me later."

Jack gave me a wink. "Behave."

Chapter 34

"This is really going to hurt. Don't you have any booze lying around?"

"Just do it. You'd like it if I passed out, wouldn't you?"

"Whatever. I'm going to use the thinnest line you had and the smallest hook." Theresa held the hook up to the light. "I'd suggest cutting that barb off unless you really enjoy pain."

Max dug through the tackle box and found a clipper. He snipped the barb off the end of the hook and pulled the hook straight with a needle-nose pliers, then checked it under the light.

"It isn't going to get any better than this. Go ahead and stitch me up before I bleed out."

"Maybe you should put the ball gag in your mouth so nobody hears you scream."

"Yeah, you're real funny, doc. Get busy."

She wiped the needle with an alcohol pad to sterilize it, then wiped Max's shoulder with another one. He grimaced and moaned with pain.

"Hurts, doesn't it?"

Max punched the side of Theresa's head. "That hurts too, right? I don't want to hear your smart mouth again."

She groaned. Tears stung her eyes as she began stitching Max's wound. She wiped the blood every few minutes so she could see the injury better.

"There, the entry side is done. Turn around so I can do the back."

"Hold on, I need a beer." Max rose, then slumped to the couch. "I'm getting dizzy."

She saw an opportunity and frantically tried to untie the knotted rope around her ankles. Her anxiety was audible—sobs of frustration came from deep within.

"What do you think you're doing?"

She looked up to see Max standing above her. He kicked her hard in the face, and she toppled over. Theresa lay on the floor, writhing in pain, blood running from her nose. Max walked across the room and pulled a beer out of the cooler. He dropped to the couch and snapped off the pull tab while he stared at her. She held her face and cried.

"Are you done acting up?"

"I think my nose is broken."

"Serves you right. Now finish my shoulder. Next time it won't just be a broken nose."

Theresa sat up and wiped her nose with the back of her hand, then jammed gauze into each nostril to stop the bleeding. She finished stitching the back side of Max's shoulder, put gauze on each side, and wrapped tape around her work.

"You're done, and I need ice."

"For what?"

"For my broken nose. If you put that ball gag back on me, I'll suffocate. My nose is swelling closed, and so are my eyes. I can feel how puffy they are."

"Yeah, you do look like shit." Max rose and pulled a handful of ice cubes out of the cooler. He put them in a bowl and handed it to her. "You have an hour to do what you need to do. I'll get you some food, but after that, you're getting tied up again."

"No ball gag, right?"

He shrugged and walked away.

Chapter 35

"Don't beat yourself up, Antonio. You didn't really think Theresa was abducted."

"I know—but that phone call. Why didn't I take it as a serious threat?"

Jack shook his head without answering that question. "What I do know is the timing is critical. There hasn't been a ransom demand or any other call since the first one?"

"No, Jack, nothing."

"Okay, we have to make the police tell us what they know so far. Do you know who the chief is?"

"There isn't one in Green River Falls, just the lieutenant."

"That's right. A Lieutenant Connors and six officers at this location, correct?"

"Yes, but we'll insist on talking to him."

Jack drove to the police station on Second Street and pulled into the lot. He and Antonio walked in together. The same two women were behind the counter as earlier that day. Jack addressed Barb because he didn't know the other woman's name.

"Barb, we have to speak with the lieutenant. It's urgent, and please don't send Officer Duke in his place—no offense, but we need to speak to the top dog."

"Certainly. Please have a seat." Barb got up and disappeared around the same door as before.

Jack and Antonio waited on the guest chairs for five minutes. They looked up when the door opened. A portly older man, likely in his fifties, approached them.

Antonio whispered, "It's him, Lieutenant Connors."

He nodded at Antonio and looked at Jack. "I don't believe I've had the pleasure." He stuck out his hand, and Jack shook it.

Jack stood. "I'm Detective Jack Steele from Washburn County Sheriff's Department. Judge Gardino and I are personal friends."

Antonio spoke up. "Lieutenant Connors, I have to know what progress you've made on this case."

"Please, gentlemen, let's go in my office."

Jack and Antonio followed the lieutenant to a decent-sized office. Two green guest chairs faced the large oak desk. The lieutenant's name was engraved on a nameplate facing the guest chairs. Family photos in matching silver frames lined the walls on shelves to their right, and the American flag stood on a flagpole behind the lieutenant's desk.

"Have a seat." The lieutenant seated himself behind the desk in an oversized roller chair. "I'm sure you understand our position." He stared at Antonio as if he were waiting for a confirmation.

"Actually, I don't. I want to know what you've done so far to find my wife."

"Mr. Gardino, to be honest, you're our only suspect. We've spoken with the bartender from the Last Stop and a few other people that were at the bar that night. They said your wife was whooping it up with everyone in the bar."

"I don't like your tone, Lieutenant." Antonio pushed back his chair, but Jack grabbed him by the arm.

"Sit down and relax." Jack gave Antonio a stern look. "Lieutenant Connors, I'd like to talk to a few people myself if you don't mind. I have Judge Gardino's permission to act on his behalf."

Lieutenant Connors raised his eyebrow and tugged on his earlobe. "Oh yeah? What is it you want to do?"

"I want to check all the businesses downtown that have surveillance cameras. That should narrow things down immediately. If somebody is seen on tape abducting Theresa Gardino, and it wasn't her husband—well, you see where I'm going with this, right?"

The lieutenant rubbed his chin, as if in thought. He looked at Antonio. "There hasn't been any ransom call. You understand why we'd suspect you."

"I don't have time to hash this out with you right now. We have to find my wife."

"All right. Go ahead, but don't step on any of my officers' toes. They're still interviewing other people around town."

Jack and Antonio rose and thanked the lieutenant. They walked the back hallway that led to the municipal offices, the Clerk of Courts office being among them.

"We have to take care of this first. The municipal offices are going to close soon."

Antonio shook his head. "I swear that lieutenant was getting under my skin."

Jack patted him on the back. "I understand, but cockiness isn't going to get you anywhere with these boys. Let's see what the Clerk of Courts has on file for property tax payments. With any luck, they'll find the last name Sims in the record books somewhere."

They entered through the glass door and approached the counter.

"May I help you?" a competent looking young woman asked.

"Yes, you can. I'm Detective Jack Steele from the Washburn County Sheriff's Department. This fine gentleman next to me is Judge Antonio Gardino."

Her expression saddened. "I'm sorry to hear about your wife, sir."

"Thank you. We really need your help."

"Sure, what can I do?"

"We need to know if there's a property tax bill in Jackson County for anyone with the last name Sims."

"No first name?"

Jack spoke up. "I don't think it matters. Any Sims will do."

"Okay, hang on." She tapped the computer keys and waited. "Nothing comes up."

"In the entire county?"

"No, sir."

"How far can you go back?" Antonio asked.

"Our system saves files for seven years. Would you like me to go back that far?"

"Please," Antonio said.

She tapped again. "Sorry, still nothing."

Jack sighed. "I was sure I was on the right track. Do you have a plat book of the county?"

"Yes we do."

Antonio drummed his fingertips on the counter as he leaned in.

She gave him a sour look.

"Sorry." He crossed his arms in front of him. "How far back do you have?"

"Downstairs in our archives file we have back to 1851, but up here we have books back to 1920."

"May we see them?" Jack asked.

"Sure, follow me to our information data room. They're on a bookshelf in there. Would either of you like coffee?"

"That would be wonderful," Jack said. "Thank you, miss."

She smiled. "The name is Tara."

Jack and Antonio sat at a long table in the data room and began going through the plat books for Jackson County. Tara entered a few minutes later with a carafe of coffee and two cups. They thanked her, and she left them to themselves to continue their search through the property records.

"How far do you want to look back, Jack?"

"I'd say thirty years. Darryl was locked up twenty years ago. There wouldn't be a reason to buy property here after he was locked up. I doubt if Max would have bothered."

They searched the county properties book by book.

They began eight years back since the computer stored information for seven years. At the twelve-year mark, Antonio stood and stretched. He rolled his neck and popped the kinks out. Jack glanced at the clock.

"They're going to be closing in fifteen minutes. We're going to have to pick this up tomorrow. How are you on time?"

"What did you have in mind?"

"How about a quick bite, then we'll hit the stores with camera surveillance."

"Yeah, let me call my neighbor first and see if she can watch the kids a little longer."

After Antonio got the green light, he and Jack grabbed a couple of sandwiches and ate them as they walked Main Street.

"There are a few stores that Jade and I checked out already. Let's go there first. After that, since the bar will be open later than any stores, I want to see if they have video from that night. Oh, never mind—I forgot their video system tapes over itself every day. They won't have anything that can help us."

Antonio nodded and entered Andrew's Resale Shop with Jack. Betty Lou Jones sat behind the counter and smiled.

"I remember you. Where's your partner?"

Jack responded, "She's preoccupied right now. How about letting us look at your tapes from two nights ago?"

"Who is your friend? Is he a cop too?"

"Hello, ma'am, I'm Judge Gardino. It's my wife that

went missing. Please, can you let us take a look?"

"Oh, I'm sorry. Come on back."

Jack and Antonio followed Betty to a room the size of a broom closet. The computer, camera equipment, and the safe were well hidden behind a heavy curtain near the back wall.

"Here you go, gentlemen. I hope you know how to use this stuff because I can't help you. As far as I know, it's automated, and nobody has ever asked to view anything."

"Yeah, we can figure it out. Thank you, Betty."

Jack looked over his shoulder to see Betty disappear when the door chime sounded.

"What time did Theresa leave the house the other night?"

Antonio rubbed his temples. "I'd say it was close to ten o'clock. I remember the kids were already asleep."

"Okay, let's go back to nine thirty. Which car in your driveway was hers?"

"The white Mercedes."

"Good. The light color will make it easier to notice."

They started the video feed from Wednesday night at nine thirty. Andrew's Resale was across the street and four stores down from the Last Stop. The bar was out of camera view, but if Theresa had happened to drive by, they'd see the car. She'd be difficult to identify if she were walking. The nearest street lamp was two stores away, and other than ambient light from advertising signs, the sidewalk was dark.

"Do you remember what she wore that night?"

"No. She took off for the bedroom, where I thought she

went to sulk. I grabbed a drink and sat down in front of the TV. Next thing I knew, the front door slammed. I went to the window and saw her drive away. I'm guessing she went upstairs to change clothes or pack a bag."

"Okay, let's focus on the video. If you see anything questionable, I'll rewind the tape."

They watched the footage from nine thirty until three in the morning. They didn't see Theresa anywhere. Jack thanked Betty Lou, and they left.

"Now where?"

"Let's try Katie's Closet," Jack said.

They arrived at the door and stepped over the threshold.

A voice from the back called out, "We're closed, come back tomorrow." A young woman with a broom in hand popped her head around the corner. "Hi, Detective Steele."

"Hi, Katie. Any chance you'll give us thirty minutes to look at your video feed from Wednesday night?"

Her eyebrows furrowed. "I was ready to shut things down."

Antonio spoke up. "Don't you have to close out the till and sweep the floors?"

"Yeah, I guess."

"Then can't we stay until you lock the doors and leave? My wife is the missing woman everyone in town is talking about."

"Wow, that sucks. All right, go ahead. Do you know how to use the equipment?"

"We sure do," Antonio said. "Just lead the way."

Katie showed them into her office. "I'll be here at my

desk, but I won't bother you. I have to count out today's receipts."

"Sure, no problem." Jack prompted the camera feed to roll in reverse. They watched the time stamp in the lower right corner as the minutes, hours, and days went backward. "Here we go, nine thirty on Wednesday night." He set the footage to run at normal speed.

They both leaned in closely and watched as activity on the sidewalk slowed as the evening progressed. Stores closed and lights went off as proprietors left for the night.

"There! Back it up. I recognize that jacket—it's Theresa."

Jack backed up the feed just a smidge and played it again. The woman walked past the camera, crossed the street, passed by a few buildings, and disappeared out of the frame.

"She must have parked on Water Street, which makes sense. She would have been coming from the north—from our house. She crossed at the four-way stop and turned right. She's heading in the direction of the Last Stop."

"Okay, that means we should see her pass by the camera again at a little after two in the morning if the bartender's recollection is correct."

Antonio's face wrinkled with distress. "Unless she was abducted between the bar and this camera."

Jack checked the time and nudged Antonio. "We're going to get kicked out pretty soon. I'll fast forward to one fifty-five."

The feed slowed at one fifty-three, then one fifty-four, and at one fifty-five, Jack set it to normal speed. They stared at the screen closely and watched for that leopard-print jacket.

"Okay, guys, I'm closing up." Katie stood and watched over their shoulders.

Antonio glanced back at her. "Just five more minutes, please."

She let out a sigh. "Five minutes. I'm beat."

They watched until ten after two. Theresa never appeared on film again.

Jack shut the system down. "Come on. Let's go. We'll look at this tape in more detail tomorrow. Maybe the bartender got the timing wrong. Katie, we'll be back tomorrow, and I promise it will be earlier."

"Now what?" Antonio asked. His voice had become frantic.

"Let's stop at the police station one more time before we call it a night. I want to hear what those officers that were conducting the interviews have to say."

It was closing in on eight o'clock when Jack and Antonio walked through the doors of the Green River Falls Police Department. Barb and the other woman that were behind the counter had been replaced with two night shift officers in uniform.

The man wearing a name patch with Reynolds embroidered on the breast pocket spoke up. "How can I help you gentlemen?"

Jack pulled out his badge and responded, "Are there any officers around that conducted interviews in the Theresa Gardino case?"

"Give me a second."

He checked the board at his back. "Looks like Officer Miller is still here. Our night shift guys are out on patrol."

"May we speak to him?"

"Yep, give me a minute." Officer Reynolds stood and left the area.

Antonio paced. "What are the odds of Theresa being alive?"

"It depends on who has her and what they want. We're going to do our best to get her back safely."

Officer Miller walked out to greet Jack and Antonio.

Jack whispered, "Let me do the talking."

"Gentlemen, what can I do for you?"

"We'd like an update on the case of Judge Gardino's missing wife. We know there have been interviews with some of the people in town. What can you tell us?"

"You're correct, Mr.—"

"It's Detective Jack Steele. I'm from North Bend, the judge's hometown."

"I see, but there isn't a lot to report." He turned toward Antonio. "People from the bar said they saw your wife and spoke to her, but nobody noticed her leave with anyone. The bartender said she looked to be having a good time and drinking quite a bit. I'm sure you've already heard that by your expression, Judge Gardino."

"Yes and it's disturbing. Why would anyone let her leave alone if she was drunk?"

"Seriously? A bar isn't a church social. Everyone drinks at bars, and it isn't anyone's responsibility to watch your wife. Where were you, sir?"

"Okay, that's enough," Jack said when tempers began to flare. "Was anyone else interviewed?"

"Maybe, but not by me. At that time of night, most people are in bed asleep or at the bar. That's all I can tell you."

Antonio stormed out the door with Jack on his heels. "This is getting us nowhere," he said.

"Pick up your kids, go home, and get some rest. Have a stiff drink before bed. I want to get back at that video feed and the plat books first thing in the morning. Jade will be able to help us. They're going to release her right after breakfast."

Chapter 36

"How's your shoulder?" Theresa asked when the sound of Max walking through the cabin woke her. She squinted through her puffy eyes and saw daylight between the cracks in the shutters.

"I'll live." He did a double take when he looked at her. "Nice face. See what happens when you try to pull shit. Hanging around like this isn't working for me—I feel like a sitting duck. I've got to steal a car so we can get the hell out of here. I'm going into town."

"How?"

"I'll walk. It's only a few miles." He regretted making that statement once the words left his mouth. He cringed but couldn't take back what was said. Max hadn't told Theresa where they were. She was out cold when he drove back to the cabin that night. For all she knew, they could have been twenty miles from civilization.

"Can I have some water and use the bathroom before you leave?"

"Yeah, let's go." Max led her outside and helped her

down the steps. She walked slowly and craned her neck in every direction. "Don't get any ideas. You don't think I can read your mind?"

"I'm just enjoying a few minutes of fresh air, that's all."

"Right—make it fast."

Theresa stumbled, her legs tied together with just enough rope for her to shuffle awkwardly through the brush. Her hands remained tied behind her back. She came out of the woods a few minutes later and returned to the cabin. Max helped her up the steps.

"May I have some water now?"

"Yeah, I'll get you something to eat too. I may be gone for a while."

Max sliced an apple into bite-sized pieces and placed them in a bowl. He set it on the couch next to her with a bottle of water. Theresa stared at him.

He groaned. "I'm not feeding you."

"Then I guess you'll have to untie my hands."

"You've got five minutes, so chow down."

Theresa bit into the crunchy apple pieces once her hands were loose. "It was nice not having that ball gag in my mouth for one night. Can we just forget about that thing? I promise not to scream."

"No way. The minute I leave, you'll be screaming your head off."

"I won't be able to breathe with it on. My nostrils are swollen closed."

"You'll figure it out—or not. It makes no difference to me."

"Why did you abduct me the other night? You didn't demand a ransom from my husband."

"Don't worry about it."

"I want to know. What's the end game here?"

"You'll find out the end game when it happens."

"So, that means I'm going to die? My death by suffocation doesn't sound that exciting. You won't even be here to witness it."

"Fine, I'll leave the damn gag off, but your hands and feet are getting tied, and I'm closing the shutters."

Max secured Theresa to the stove and couch with ropes. He locked the cabin door and closed all the outer shutters. With the knife on his hip and a baseball cap on his head, he followed the deer path through the woods in the direction of town.

After an hour through brambles, vines that tangled and tripped him more than once, and marshy wetlands, Max came across a clearing where a cottage stood. A pickup and a station wagon, with rust eating through the wheel wells, sat parked on the dirt driveway. He assessed the area and didn't see anyone. Smoke from the chimney hung in the air like a gray cloud above the roofline. Somebody was home. He pulled his cell phone out of his back pocket and checked the time—barely seven o'clock. Coals at the fire pit still smoldered, and with the quantity of beer bottles scattered about, Max figured whoever was inside could very well be sleeping off a late-night party. He crept to the station wagon and peered in. Nothing of value caught his eye. He moved on to the truck and cupped his hands around his face against the glass. The gun rack mounted above the back window held a shotgun and a rifle, making Max grin. He checked his surroundings again—all clear, and nothing blocked the driveway. If he could get the truck started, he'd be long gone in seconds. As quietly as possible, Max lifted the door handle, and the driver's door creaked open. He climbed in and sat behind the wheel. He checked the center console, door pockets, and under the seat but found no keys. He pulled the visor down, and they fell into his lap.

This day is improving already, and it's barely seven o'clock.

He found the right key and slid it into the ignition. With the window rolled down, he looked back to make sure everything was clear, turned the key over, and slipped away unnoticed. He was at the safety of the cabin ten minutes later. Max turned the truck around on the road and backed in. With the nose facing out and the box of the truck against the back of the van, he'd transfer all of his belongings to the truck and leave the area for good.

He heard screams for help coming from inside the cabin.

Stupid bitch has no idea it's me. She's in for a world of hurt.

Max quietly slinked up the steps and turned the key in the padlock. He gently lifted it off the door latch and, with the full force of his enormous frame, kicked the door open. It bounced off the opposite wall, almost breaking it off the hinges. Like the giant he was, Max stomped into the room and looked into her terror-filled eyes.

"I guess I'll be here when you die after all."

Chapter 37

"You can pick me up. The doctor just released me." I closed my hospital room door and stripped off the gown patterned with tiny flowers while I had Jack on speakerphone. "You'll have to come to my room and get me. They won't release me on my own."

"Yeah, I know the drill. I believe we've done this before." Jack chuckled. "I'll be there in ten minutes. We have a full day ahead of us. Are you up for it?"

"Definitely, and you can tell me everything when we're driving. I have to get dressed." I clicked off.

Ten minutes later, Jack gave my door a knock and said he was coming in. He pushed a wheelchair into the room while I was brushing my teeth. "You have to leave via the wheelchair, like always."

"Okay, I'll be ready in a second." I came out of the bathroom, gathered my belongings, and took a seat in the wheelchair. At the nurses' station, I was given instructions to watch for headaches, dizziness, or blurred vision and to call the hospital immediately if any of those symptoms occurred. I signed the papers and was released into the sunny morning. Jack opened the cruiser, and I climbed into the passenger side while he returned the wheelchair to the vestibule. "What's the plan?" I asked when he took his seat behind the steering wheel.

"We're meeting Antonio at the Clerk of Courts office. We checked yesterday, and there weren't any property tax bills that went to the Sims name."

I raised my brow in question. "Then why are we going back?"

"They may have had property years ago that was sold to someone else. Max could be hiding out in an area that's familiar to him. He wouldn't risk staying in town for any length of time with a van that has a BOLO out on it."

I nodded. "Okay, so we're going through old records?"

"Yep. Antonio and I started late yesterday with old plat books. The computers store seven years of tax records. No Sims came up in those seven years, so we started on year eight and got through year twelve before they kicked us out for the night. I figured thirty years would be a safe bet."

"Good idea. Between the three of us, we should be able to knock that out in a few hours. What's after that?"

Jack turned out of the hospital parking lot and headed toward Main Street. "After that, we're going to Katie's Closet. We looked at the surveillance tape last night and actually saw Theresa cross the street and walk down the sidewalk. The tape didn't show her starting position, but we assumed it was where the car was found parked. She turned in the direction of the Last Stop, but the camera didn't cover that wide of an area."

I perked up. "That's a good start, though."

Jack agreed. "We need to check the alleged time she left the bar more thoroughly. We looked at fifteen minutes of tape around the two a.m. mark and never saw her. I want to widen those parameters. The bartender could have been wrong on the time." Jack pulled into the parking lot at City Hall. "There's Antonio."

A black Cadillac Escalade was parked near the entrance. Antonio climbed out when he saw us park two vehicles away.

"Jade, good to see you're up and around. How do you feel?"

"I'm okay and anxious to get busy. I hear we have clearance and your permission to help search for Theresa."

Antonio looked relieved. "I don't want to dismiss the effort Green River Falls is putting forth, but it seems like they're over their heads on this one. Nobody has a clue as to what happened to Theresa, and time is ticking away. I've heard they've searched along the riverbanks and through some of the county-owned wooded areas, but there's an awful lot of land to cover and not many people helping out. We aren't locals, so to speak, so not very many people know us personally. To me, it sounds like they're looking for a body, not Theresa being held captive."

I patted Antonio's shoulder. "I think they're looking for anything that might help. They could find her purse or cell phone lying in a ditch, that sort of thing. Don't assume they're only looking for a body. We have to stay positive."

Jack jerked his head toward the door. "Shall we?"

We walked into City Hall's main entrance. Marble floors, guest chairs, and a large reception counter filled that space. A directory showed all of the offices within the building. Jack and Antonio knew where to go.

"This way," Jack said as he turned right at the sign that listed the municipal offices in that wing. We walked the hallway to the fourth office on the left, where the Clerk of Courts sign hung above the door. We passed through the glass doors, and a young woman glanced up from behind the counter. She smiled at Jack and Antonio. "Hello, Tara," Jack said. "Is it okay if we continue where we left off last night?"

"Certainly."

"Tara, this is my partner, Sergeant Jade Monroe. Jade, this is Tara. She was very helpful last night."

I extended my hand. "Nice to meet you."

"Would you like coffee?"

"That would be wonderful, thanks," I said.

"Go ahead back to the information data room. I'll bring in a carafe for you."

I followed Jack and Antonio down the hall, and we entered a large room. Shelves covered most of the four walls, and file cabinets flanked each end of the long table.

"The plat books are over here." Jack pointed at a shelf to his right. "Let's grab years thirteen, fourteen, and fifteen. We'll do three year increments, then search the next three years, and so on."

"So, these are only Jackson County plat books, we're looking for any parcel with the name Sims on it, and we'll end at 1986, correct?"

"You got it," Antonio said.

"Okay, let's dig in."

Tara showed up with three cups, a carafe of coffee, and condiments. We thanked her, and she left the room.

We worked in silence as we each dug in and searched names in the plat books for the year in front of us. On average, each book took us nearly forty-five minutes to scan every parcel for the name Sims. The writing was small, and the entries were crowded.

"I swear I'm going to have another headache, have blurred vision, and need reading glasses by the time we're finished here."

"Yeah, and that's only if we don't go blind first," Jack said.

We were each on our second book when Antonio called out anxiously, "You guys, check this parcel. Does that read Sims or Slins? Everything is in cursive and jammed together."

Jack and I leaned in and took a closer look.

"It's almost impossible to tell. I'll ask Tara if there's a magnifying glass here somewhere." I exited the room and walked to the main counter. Tara was on the phone. She put up her finger as if to say *one minute*. I waited.

"Sergeant Monroe, what can I help you with?" she asked when she hung up.

"Would anyone have a magnifying glass we could use? Some of that writing is hard to make out, but we might be on to something."

"That's good news, and yes, there's a magnifying glass

just for that purpose in the top drawer of the filing cabinet on the right side of the room."

"Thanks."

I returned to the data room and told the guys where the magnifying glass was. Jack found it immediately. We took turns peering over the writing on the parcel and still couldn't come to a definitive conclusion.

"Which year is that book?" I asked.

Antonio turned it over and checked the spine. "It's 1999."

"Okay, let's see if Tara can search the records for ownership of lot number 143 in 1999."

We returned to the main desk and gave Tara the information we'd gathered. We held our breath while she entered the data into the system.

With a few taps of the keys, a long list of parcels for 1999 showed up. With her finger, she went down the list in numerical order until she reached lot number 143. She looked up at each of us and grinned.

"Bingo! The owner at the time was Lee Sims. It shows he owned the twenty-acre parcel on Trout Lake from 1983 until 2000 when he let the county reclaim the land for back property taxes. Now I know why the name Sims didn't come up in the tax records for privately owned property."

Jack huffed. "Back taxes, huh? It must run in the family. So does the county still own that land?"

"Yes, it appears so. Usually when the county gets land back, they hang onto it. There are too many subdivisions going up in other parts of the county the way it is. We need to keep some land pristine, especially around pretty little lakes like Trout Lake."

"So you know where it is?" I asked.

"Sure. It's only a few miles out of town."

"Thanks, Tara," Jack said. "You've been a big help."

"Good luck."

We walked out and gathered near Antonio's Escalade. The concern on his face was evident. He knew what the Sims family was capable of. "Are we going out there?"

I glanced at Jack and gave him a nod. He had spent more time with Antonio, and I felt he should explain the situation to him. Max Sims was a dangerous man, and if he was at that property, he'd likely fight his way out. If Theresa was indeed with him, she'd either end up as a hostage or he'd kill her if she wasn't already dead. Our plan was to go in with the entire police force from Green River Falls assisting us. Antonio, as a civilian, had to stay away from the area. It could quickly escalate into a very dangerous situation. My cell phone rang just as Jack began explaining the process to Antonio. I excused myself and crossed the parking lot to stand by the cruiser.

"Hello, Sergeant Jade Monroe speaking."

"Jade, it's Lieutenant Clark."

"Boss, whose phone are you using?"

"The battery on mine died. I'm using Dr. White's phone. It looks like they're wrapping up everything at the farm. They've retrieved all of the bones they can find in the field. We had the canine unit do one last sweep of the area, and they haven't alerted on anything else."

"That's good news."

"I'd say. Now we just need to match DNA results with the families that volunteered samples. We've had a pretty good turnout so far. Eleven families have come in. Lena and Jason have recorded all of the DNA from the families, and Dr. White's team is going to start extracting samples from the bones. It will be a slow process, but we've actually released the property back to the developer. The Swedish megastore agreed to forge ahead at the Sims property site."

I breathed a deep sigh. "I'm relieved to hear that. There are quite a few North Bend residents looking for work, and that place could create a lot of employment opportunities. Plus, now we can move on with identifying some of those remains. Anyway, boss, we may have a lead in finding Max Sims's whereabouts. I don't want to get Judge Gardino's hopes up, and we don't know what we're heading into. It could be a twenty-acre parcel of empty land. Apparently, there used to be a Sims that owned property here in Green River Falls. I don't know if there is a connection or not, but we'll coordinate everything with the PD first and go in together. If Max is actually there and if he has Mrs. Gardino, it could get hairy."

"Watch your back, Jade, and tell Jack the same thing. Call me later. I don't care what time it is."

"Will do, boss. I better go."

"Be safe." Clark clicked off, and I joined Jack and Antonio.

Jack addressed me. "I was telling Antonio that he ought to go home and be with his kids. We'll let the PD know we're going to check out the property and we need their assistance. I don't think it's smart to go into an area that large when it's only you and me."

"I agree."

Seeing the anguish and guilt on Antonio's face broke my heart. In the next hour, he might find out his wife is dead, a hostage, or nowhere in the area.

"We've got to go. Antonio, we'll call you as soon as we know something—I promise. Go take care of your kids. Jack and I are good at our jobs. We've got this."

I gave him a nod and left. Jack and I headed back into the building and followed the hallway to the police department. I was sure Barb was getting tired of seeing us.

Barb looked up from the counter when we walked in. "I know," she said as she pushed back her chair and opened the door at her back, "you need to see the lieutenant."

I held my tongue momentarily. "Yes, and right away. It's important."

A few minutes later, Lieutenant Connors walked out to greet us. "This isn't a good time, detectives. A report of a missing girl just came in. We're up to our eyeballs with missing women this week. What's going on? And please make it quick. Barb said you had something important to tell me."

"We do, sir. We have reason to believe the person likely responsible for Theresa Gardino's abduction is nearby. We're going to check out the location, but we need your help. We have to go as soon as you can gather officers. She's been missing for several days, and we can't prolong this anymore. This new information of another missing woman could be directly related to the person in question."

Lieutenant Connors squeezed his head between his hands and groaned. "Okay. I have four officers on duty right now—with me, it's five. How do you want to move forward?"

"We have to see a satellite image of the area first. We need to know what we'll be walking into. Can we check on your computer?"

"Yes, you can take care of that while I call in my officers. The few that are on duty are out on patrol. Follow me. We'll go into my office. Do you have the address?"

Jack spoke up. "I have it right here."

The lieutenant looked at the piece of paper. "That's county land, probably overgrown and wild."

"We need to see what the best way to enter the property is and if there's a structure on the land. We don't need any surprises."

Lieutenant Connors nodded. "Go ahead. See what you come up with. I'll round up my guys."

With everyone the lieutenant could spare in that short time frame gathered around his office computer, they studied the satellite imagery of the old Sims property.

I sat and listened as Jack led the conversation with the group of officers. Here, out of our jurisdiction, my rank didn't mean anything to them. They had their own commander. These were good ol' boys, and I thought it better to have a man go over the plan with everyone.

Jack pointed at the computer screen. "This satellite

imagery isn't going to help us. It was taken during the summer months, and all that shows up is the small lake to the south and a dense tree canopy. We'll be going in blind."

"If Max Sims is somewhere on the property, you may see an older black van. It could be what he's using to sleep in." I kept the fact that I'd shot out the windshield to myself. "The man is dangerous, has more than likely murdered several women already, and is a big guy. Max Sims stands six foot four and is close to three hundred pounds."

Jack continued, "Since the property is heavily wooded on three sides and one side is bordered by that lake, I'd say the safest way to go in is on foot. If anyone is there, they won't be alerted by the sound of us coming in. Surprise is key and our ally. We can stage the cruisers at the end of the property lines and at the intersections of these two roads." Jack pointed again. "Here and here. There are seven of us in total. We can spread out through the woods and make our way to the center, where we'll meet up. If he's there, he'll be surrounded. Any questions?"

Officer Duke spoke up. "Do we take him alive or shoot to kill?"

"Well, Martin, we usually try to take criminals into custody, if possible, especially if there's a hostage involved. The perpetrator may have stashed the victim somewhere that we'd never find out about otherwise. Let's go and organize our approach when we get close. Everyone definitely needs to be wearing a vest. Now isn't the time to take any chances."

Between Jack, myself, and the Green River Falls Police Department, we had four cruisers. The drive to the property took five minutes. We were in the lead and made one slow pass in front of the property. The only identifying feature was a stake in the ground with the road coordinates on it. A quarter mile up the road, Jack turned the cruiser around at the intersection and parked in the gravel next to the ditch. We waited for the other cars to fall in behind. Once everyone had arrived, we exited the cruisers and gathered in front of our car.

Lieutenant Connors spoke up. "A call came in to dispatch about a stolen truck about two miles north of here. According to the caller, it's an older red Ford F-150."

"Okay, let's keep our eyes peeled for that vehicle too. We'll leave two cars here pointing in opposite directions and a cruiser at the end of the property lines on both roads. Everyone take your place, have your radios on, and be on the alert for sounds and movement in the woods. Don't go off half-cocked and start shooting at noises. There are likely deer, squirrels, and plenty of wildlife back there, so keep your heads on a swivel. If you do see the vehicles or someone that isn't in law enforcement, hold your position, give the rest of us your coordinates, and wait for the group. Don't approach this man alone. He isn't likely to back off, and we want him brought in alive. Is everyone ready?" Jack looked from face to face. The officers nodded. "Secure your vests, get those radios on, and let's go."

Everyone left to stage their cars. Jack and I checked our service weapons, made sure the magazines were full, and began walking into the brush. Lieutenant Connors was fifteen yards away, entering in the same direction we were. The rest of the officers drove off to take their positions at the property lines and walk in too.

Chapter 38

"You lied to me," Max said, his head slightly cocked toward Theresa. "You promised you wouldn't scream for help, and what the hell do I hear the second I drive in? I don't like it when people lie to me, Theresa."

Terror spread across her face when she realized the person coming through the door was Max and not someone there to rescue her. "I'm sorry. I promise I won't do it again." Theresa slunk into the corner and tried to make herself look small and nonthreatening.

"It's too late for backpedaling. I'm leaving, and I don't need a travel companion. You've served your purpose. I think my shoulder will be fine now." Max headed to the door.

"Where are you going?"

"I have another hole to dig."

"Another hole?" She tried to hold back the sobs but couldn't.

He turned back and stared at her. "You had one chance and one chance only. You blew it." The ball gag lay on the couch. Max grabbed it then walked toward Theresa. "Open your mouth, and if you say one word, I'll kill you now."

She opened her mouth, and he jammed the ball in. Max pushed her head forward and secured the strap in the back. He turned and headed out the door.

Max grabbed the shovel off the porch then stopped at the truck. He pulled the rifle from the rack and checked the chamber—it was fully loaded. With the strap slung over his shoulder, he continued on. One could never be too careful, especially with a decomposing carcass buried nearby. Coyotes and wolves were plentiful in the area. Max followed the deer trail into the woods where he'd buried Haley Atwater several days earlier. Another shallow grave would serve the purpose. He was sure that within a few days, the animals would have their way with Theresa, anyway. He reached the spot where Haley was buried. The fresh mound of soil had been dug up, and half of her body was exposed. Thanks to wild animals, there were voids where skin and muscle used to be. He grimaced.

Max stabbed the ground with the shovel and threw dirt over her remains as he prepared a new hole next to hers.

Twenty minutes later, a sound caught his attention. Max scanned the area, his eyes searching for something that could have caused the rustling. The sound was too heavy to be a squirrel or raccoon. It lumbered through the woods as though it wasn't in its natural environment. With his back pressed against the large tree trunk and the shovel gripped tightly in his hand, Max waited as the sound grew closer. With barely a movement of his head, he peeked between a limb and the trunk base and saw an officer approaching through the woods. He was ready and waiting as the clueless man passed within feet of him.

Max whispered, "Hey."

The officer turned, and Max slammed him in the face with the shovel. Max knew his minutes were numbered. Where there was one cop, there were more. With the stealth of a bobcat, he quickened his pace and headed for the cabin. He watched for branches that might snap under his feet and give away his location. Once back at the van, Max quickly transferred everything he couldn't do without into the truck box, then went inside the cabin.

"Sorry, Theresa, but I don't have the luxury of time to drag this out. It's time to go." With a fast swing of the shovel, he cracked the spade across her face and sent her backward. Her head hit the stove, and blood spattered across the floor.

Chapter 39

"Shit!" My eyes darted over the surroundings, where I checked and double-checked every shadow and limb. "Jack, Lieutenant, over here," I called out under my breath.

"What's up?" Jack whispered as he neared my location.

"Adams is down." I leaned over the man whose face was crushed in from the blow of something. I checked his neck for a pulse and felt nothing. "And look over here." I pointed to my right where a shallow grave had been dug. Next to it was a partially exposed, decomposing woman. The smell was horrendous.

Jack reached me with Connors ten feet behind him.

"Holy shit, what's that smell?" Connors asked.

I pointed to my right.

"Son of a bitch, it's probably the missing girl that was reported. And Adams?"

I shook my head. "He's gone, sir."

Connors punched the trunk of the tree next to him. "That lunatic is out here somewhere, and he probably knows this woods better than we do."

"Lieutenant, call your men," I said, "and tell them to watch their backs. We've already got one casualty."

Before the lieutenant had a chance to use his radio, the crack of gunshots echoed through the woods. Return fire sounded.

"Damn it," Jack called out, "let's go. The sound is coming from the south. Watch yourself and use the trees for cover! Max knows we're here. Jade, take the right, Lieutenant, go left. I'll go straight."

I headed right and crouched low as I zigzagged through the woods. I used every wide tree trunk I could find as a barrier between my adversary and me, even though I had no idea where he was. More gunfire shot out, this time closer than before. My ears rang when a zing shot past my head, only inches away.

Son of a bitch, that was close.

"Jade, are you okay?" A voice sounded in my radio. It was Jack.

"Roger that. It was close, though. I see a cabin up ahead. He's probably holed up inside and picking us off one by one. Duke, can you hear me?" No response. "Reynolds?" Dead silence. "Jack, do you have eyes on anyone?"

"Only the lieutenant, and he's fifty feet to the left of me."

"Tell the lieutenant I can't get a response from Reynolds or Duke. I don't remember the last officer's name."

"It's Conway, Bob Conway. Hang on a second, Jade. Conway, is that you?"

"Jack, yeah, Conway here. I saw Reynolds go down

about forty feet to my right, and Duke doesn't answer my calls. I can't tell where the shots are coming from."

"We can't, either. Jade saw a cabin—do you have eyes on it?"

"No, I'm near the lake. I don't see a structure anywhere. I see the lieutenant, though. He's heading my way."

"Okay, stay low and don't take any chances."

"Roger that."

"Jade, what's your location?"

"I'm right behind the cabin."

"Son of a bitch. If he's inside, he may be watching your every move. Wait for me."

"No promises, Jack. If I see him, I'm moving in." I clicked off and crept closer while trying to stay beneath the windows. As I rounded the side of the cabin, I saw Duke in the distance. He was on the ground and moaning, but he was alive. I scurried toward him through the tree cover. Gunfire blasted at my back and turned the tree where I took cover into shrapnel. I had to regroup and catch my breath. "Duke, Duke, are you okay?"

"He only hit my vest, thank God. That shot knocked the wind out of me for a minute."

I crouched low. "Do you know where he's shooting from?"

"I think he's by the van in front of the cabin. It sounds like he has a rifle."

"Are you able to get behind something? You're too exposed right there." A sound behind me made me spin. Luckily, it was Jack. I raised my hand for him to stay put and clicked the radio to talk to him. "Duke is okay. He's only hit in the vest. Wherever Max is, he has eyes on me. Don't approach. Duke says the van is in front of the cabin. He thinks the shots are coming from that direction."

"Okay, hang on. Lieutenant, Conway, do you have eyes on the vehicle or see any movement in the area?"

The radio crackled. I heard the lieutenant's response to Jack. "We see the van but no movement."

I lifted my arm to get Jack's attention. "I'm moving in from this side."

"Stay low, Jade, and behind cover. Don't let him get a bead on you. I'll check this side."

"Got it." I slid down the tree until I was near the ground, then ducked and ran for the west side of the cabin. So far so good. No rapid fire aimed in my direction. I carefully peeked around the corner and saw Max standing next to the driver's side door of the red truck. From what I could see through two rolled-up windows, it looked as though he was reloading his firearm. I had to take my chance while I had one. I stood and called out his name with my service weapon pointed at him, fifty feet away.

"Max Sims, throw down your weapon. You're surrounded!"

He disappeared below the truck door and began firing in every direction. I had to retreat and take cover.

"Jack, Lieutenant, Conway, do you have eyes on him?"

Max fired off another few rounds and dove into the truck.

I yelled out through my radio, "He's getting away."

Max shot out the passenger window and continued firing in my direction as he floored the accelerator and disappeared into the brush. I emptied my magazine in the direction the truck went but had no idea if I hit anything.

Jack ran through the woods toward me. "Conway was hit in the leg. The lieutenant went to check on Reynolds. Are you okay?"

"Yeah, but Max got away. I have no idea if I hit him, the truck, or anything at all, damn it! There must be a path to the road. The truck wasn't pointed in that direction by accident. Call on your radio for ambulances, Jack. I'm going to follow his trail."

"Got it. Be careful."

The grasses and tall weeds were flattened by the tire tracks. That made following his escape route much easier. I knelt and checked the ground—gravel. A driveway lay hidden beneath years of overgrowth and likely made his escape to the road faster. I followed the trail, close to three hundred feet, and ended up at the road. I looked left and saw one of the cruisers parked farther down. To the right stood our cruiser and the lieutenant's, both parked and facing different directions at the intersection, just how we left them. I jogged down the road to take a look, even though Jack had the keys.

I shook my head. "Damn him!" The tires in both cruisers were slashed, and I was sure Max Sims was long gone. I heard the sound of sirens getting closer and waited on the road for the ambulances. In the distance, I saw flashing lights heading my way. I flagged them down when they reached me, then climbed into the first ambulance.

"Turn in right here," I said. "There are remnants of an old driveway under the matted grass. We need to go back about a hundred yards. There are two casualties and several injured officers."

We reached Jack and the lieutenant at the cabin. The lieutenant led the EMTs into the woods to the injured officers. There was nothing they could do for Adams or the half-buried woman.

Jack jerked his chin toward the cabin door. "Jade, come inside. I have to show you something."

I followed Jack, knowing full well I wouldn't be seeing anything I wanted to. It took a few seconds for my eyes to adjust to the darkened room, then I saw her splayed out in the corner near the stove. Blood covered her face, and a drying pool lay beneath her head. The ball gag in her mouth infuriated me. Now, I was even more determined to take Max Sims down at any cost. "We have to tell Antonio," Jack said. "Then we have to find that bastard."

"The tires are flat on our and the lieutenant's cruisers. I don't know about the other ones."

"Okay, I'll call the PD's dispatch on the radio. Maybe she can get in touch with an auto repair company for us." Jack got through to dispatch and spoke to Barb. "Barb, it's Detective Steele. I'm sure the lieutenant will update you soon, but for now, we need someone out to our location right away. We have two cruisers down with slashed tires. Call whoever the PD uses and get them out here with eight tires. We're at the intersection of Trout Lake Road and

Fairmont Drive. We need a forensic team and your coroner too."

"Oh my God. I'm on it right now."

Jack clicked off and plopped down on the tattered sofa with his head pressed between his hands. I paced the cabin and relived the carnage that had just taken place over the last hour.

"As soon as the tires are replaced, I'm heading to Boscobel. I'll leave talking to Antonio and dealing with this nightmare to you. There has to be something I can leverage to get information from Darryl. I'll have almost two hours of driving time to figure it out."

Chapter 40

After hours of waiting for the tires to be changed and going over the scene with the forensic team, we ended up with three dead bodies, two officers with gunshot wounds, and one with bruised ribs. Jack, the lieutenant, and I were lucky to come out unscathed.

I stood by the cruiser with Jack as the last tire was changed, and the auto technician said the cars were good to go.

"I'll take the lieutenant's car and pick up him and Duke," Jack said. "The ambulances and coroner are taking the others."

I patted Jack's shoulder. "I sure wish this would have gone down differently. I can't believe what Max did to Theresa, that dead girl in the woods, and Adams." I sucked in a deep breath. "Okay, I'm taking off. I need to get to Boscobel. The only way to get information on Max is through Darryl. I'm sure it wasn't a coincidence that Max was hiding at the old Sims property. I'm thinking Darryl is, and always has been, the puppet master."

"Call Clark when you get reception and tell him what's going on."

"Will do," I said as I climbed in behind the wheel, clicked the seatbelt, and adjusted the mirrors.

"Be safe, Jade."

I closed the door and drove away from Green River Falls. As soon as I hit the freeway, my phone lit up with missed calls. I pulled off at the first exit and listened to the messages. Most were from Clark and Amber. They hadn't heard from Jack or me all day and were concerned. I checked the time—2:10 p.m. I called Clark first.

He sounded distressed when he picked up. "It's about damn time, Jade. What have you guys been doing all day?"

"The usual, boss—dodging bullets and trying to catch the bad guy."

"Is that a joke?"

"I'm afraid not." I sighed deeply. "We have casualties, and Max Sims got away." I held the phone away from my ear when Clark began to yell.

"I want to hear details, Monroe."

"Theresa Gardino and a young woman we found in the woods are dead."

Clark swore again—I waited.

"One of the officers from Green River Falls is dead, and two others have been shot, but they'll make it. One more was hit in the vest, and he'll be okay. Jack, the lieutenant, and I are fine. I'm on my way to Boscobel. Darryl better start talking. I'll make sure his ass is thrown in solitary so he can't communicate with Max. Was it a coincidence that

Max was in Green River Falls the same time the Gardinos' were, or was it a planned attack on the family? Max has been a pretty angry guy since he started getting the eviction notices."

"True enough, Jade. Maybe it was a coincidence, unless he's been stalking the family. Either way, I'm sure that's where Darryl told Max to hide out."

"I don't know and probably won't ever find out. What I do know is that Darryl Sims will feel my wrath since I can't do anything about Max yet."

"Keep it within the law, Jade. Are you coming back to North Bend tonight?"

"Yeah, after I go back to Green River Falls later and pick up Jack. It's going to be a long night, boss." I merged back on the freeway and put Clark on speakerphone.

"I've got a quick update for you. Amy Patterson was positively identified with the DNA from her toothbrush. Lena has already released her body to the family. The same goes for Deborah French. Her family is making funeral arrangements. Two of the bone samples have been identified from matches with the volunteer samples. Apparently, one of the women only went missing eight years ago."

I hit the steering wheel with my open hand. "That son of a bitch has been at this a lot longer than we thought."

"Yeah, he's a carbon copy of his old man."

"Okay, boss, I'll update you after I speak with Darryl. I've got to make a quick call to Amber then focus on the road." I clicked off and felt angrier than I had in a long time.

I got Amber's voicemail and left her a message that I was fine and would explain everything tonight. I told her to stay happy and positive—our dad would arrive in a few days.

I devised a plan as I drove. It made perfect sense to me, and with any luck, Darryl would fall for it.

Chapter 41

Luckily for Max, the police in Green River Falls apparently had too much on their hands to think of putting a BOLO out for the red pickup truck. The day had started like any other, but by midafternoon, they had three dead people, two seriously injured officers, and another that likely had bruised ribs.

Max skated out of town in the stolen truck and took to the freeway with nobody on his tail. He needed a place to go—somewhere to hide that wasn't easily tracked. There would be too many people looking for him in a matter of hours. He'd find another vehicle and stay invisible. Darryl would tell him exactly what to do.

Max checked the time—3:45. Darryl would be calling at four o'clock sharp. In an almost panic, Max grabbed at his shirt pockets and then his jeans. With a sigh of relief, he felt it—the folded, coded paper Darryl had told him to keep close at all times. Max was sure his father had received the letter he sent a few days back. Written in the specified code, it had taken much longer to compose than necessary. Max kept it short and to the point. He reported that one of Darryl's two requests had been fulfilled. Theresa Gardino, the daughter-in-law of the judge that had put Darryl away, was in Max's custody. Max told Darryl he would address the second request very soon.

Now, two days later, Max couldn't wait to tell his father the latest news—Theresa had met a violent death. Max smiled at the thought, knowing Darryl would be beaming with pride.

He exited the freeway at the next ramp and turned into the truck stop a half mile to his west. Big rigs idled in a long row of semis. The constant rumble of so many engines sounded like thunder in the distance. Max checked the sky to be sure—clear and blue. Hunger pangs groaned in his gut. Food would wait until after the phone call with Darryl. Max couldn't afford a noisy background or perked ears listening in on their conversation. It would take place in the privacy of the truck with the coded response sheet spread out on the passenger seat.

With the volume turned low, Max listened to country music on the radio. His cell phone sat in the cup holder with the screen facing his way. He checked the time again—3:58. Any minute now his phone would ring. He tapped his fingers on the steering wheel with the beat of the song until the phone rang, then Max turned the volume knob to Off. He picked up and listened to the automated attendant asking if he would accept a collect call from WSPF inmate number 450-A72.

Max responded yes, and Darryl was put through.

"Hello, son, how is everything going?"

"I'll manage."

"Good to know. How about that number three?"

Max glanced at the sheet. Number three asked if he was safe. "Yes, for right now," he responded.

"I like number seven."

Max scrolled down with his finger to number seven. It asked if he'd completed any of Darryl's requests. Max smirked. "Sure did, and her hubby isn't going to be very happy about it."

Darryl chuckled. "That sounds real good, son. My friend mentioned number two."

Max jumped up the sheet to number two. It asked if the cops were after him. "Yep, but I haven't found the right vacation spot yet."

"I hear number four is a good option."

Max checked number four. It said the best place to hide was Milwaukee.

"Understood, and I'll take care of the other project soon."

"Very good, son. I'm proud of you. I'll call you Monday at four."

The phone call ended abruptly. Max crossed the parking lot and pulled open the fingerprint-smudged glass door of the diner. The hostess seated him at a vacant stool along the counter with seven haggard looking men. Max assumed they were truckers.

He ate until his stomach felt like lead. The meal was filling, and the coffee was strong. Max paid his bill, tossed the five-buck tip on the counter, and left the diner.

Back in the truck, he exited the enormous truck stop parking lot and hit the ramp to get back on the freeway. This time, he'd turn north instead of south and work his way to Milwaukee, but he needed a different vehicle soon.

Chapter 42

It was nearly four thirty when I entered the city limits of Boscobel. I took the street into town and turned at the sign with an arrow showing the direction of the penitentiary. I turned and backtracked until I saw the enormous facility standing in what appeared to be a clear-cut forest. The prison looked solemn, stark, and depressing. The concrete-colored buildings stood within a row of razor-wired fencing. Double outer walls standing ten feet high had razor wire between them and topping them. WSPF, which was formally called the Supermax Correctional Facility, held the worst offenders and was the most secure men's prison in the state. The place was no joke. Regular visiting hours had ended, but I called in advance and permission was granted. I would be expedited through to have a private meeting with inmate 450-A72—Darryl Sims.

The arrow led to a parking lot on my right. I pulled in, parked, and followed the sidewalk to the visitors' entrance. After passing through several heavy steel doors, I finally arrived at a counter where I signed in and showed my credentials. The guard led me into a room where I had to empty my pockets and leave my purse and sidearm in a locker. I dropped the locker key into my pocket.

The guard addressed me. "It will be a few minutes, ma'am. We have to prepare the prisoner."

I nodded a thank-you.

I thought over my speech again for the tenth time. I'd tell Darryl we had Max in custody after a gun battle earlier that day. We had him on numerous murder charges, which included killing a police officer, and that in itself was a death penalty sentence. Max would be sent directly to Terre Haute's federal prison for death row inmates. I'd make sure Max spent the rest of what life he had left in the worst area of the prison with the worst criminals housed there. With any luck, somebody would stick a shiv in his gut and kill him. The story was true, all except for the part that we had Max in custody. I'd take Darryl's temperature on the story and tell him there could be a slim chance that Max could be held at Boscobel until the final sentencing, if and only if Darryl told us who the women were in the field at the farm.

"Ma'am, the prisoner is ready for your visit."

My heart pounded with anger at the Sims name, but I couldn't let Darryl Sims get under my skin. I had never met the man, but according to Clark, he was devious and clever. I had to be careful, watch my words, and show no emotion. I couldn't let my guard down.

I entered a private interrogation room. Green cinder block walls and cold steel furniture engulfed the space and made the hair stand up on my arms. In front of me sat a haggard looking man with disheveled long hair and a thin frame. He was nothing like I had imagined. Those faded photos at the farm showed someone tougher, younger, and stronger looking. Darryl was just a frail old man, maybe a mean, nasty one, but frail and old nonetheless. He stared at me, his legs shackled and his hands cuffed to the table. Hate filled his eyes even though he had no idea who I was. I took a seat across from him and stared at his beady eyes that gleamed with malice. I felt the thickness of his breath as he sized me up. I wanted to look away but couldn't—I had to stare him down. He wouldn't win.

"Darryl Sims, we finally meet."

"Yeah, and who the hell are you?"

"Somebody that's going to offer you a deal."

He laughed. "I don't deal with smart-ass bitches unless I know their names."

"Why would my name matter?"

"Guard," he yelled, "take me back to my cell." He stood with his hands still secured to the table. "I don't have time for the likes of you."

"Is that what you said to all of the women you killed?" I cocked my head. Two could play this game.

"Tell me your name, and we might have a conversation." He sat back on the chair and waited.

"My name is Jade Monroe—Sergeant Jade Monroe, with the Washburn County Sheriff's Department."

His eyes lit up, unnerving me for a second, then a wide grin spread across his face.

"Well, I'll be damned. Looky, looky at who came to visit

me. You couldn't possibly be the daughter of a Detective Monroe from days gone by—could you?" He licked his lips then puckered them.

I felt like vomiting or punching his face in—maybe both. I took a silent deep breath. "I told you my name. You don't need to concern yourself with my family tree."

Darryl laughed. "So, he is your old man."

That bastard was sly and had already scored one point—I had zip.

"I'm here to discuss Max and a possible deal."

"Max?" He chuckled again and cracked his knuckles. "What has that boy been up to lately? I haven't seen him in ages."

"Really? According to prison records and the sign-in sheet, he's visited you twice in the last ten days."

"Damn, you're good, and pretty, Jade Monroe."

Darryl looked me up and down. I felt my face flush with anger.

"You can call me Sergeant Monroe or nothing at all. We have Max in custody, Darryl. I felt you should know that, since you're his closest next of kin. To our surprise, it appears that Max has been busy murdering people, likely ever since you went to prison. Or was it before? Were you two partners in crime?"

"Why would I tell you anything, bitch? I'm a lifer here. I've got nothing to gain by talking to you."

My hands instinctively balled up into fists.

He looked at them and smiled. "Getting under your skin, am I?"

"The thing is, Darryl, Max killed a police officer. That automatically puts him on death row. He'll be going to Terre Haute, where they house the worst murderers in the country. They have a special unit, a cozy place just for death row inmates. I'm going to make sure that's where Max is housed—in the worst wing, with the worst roommate. Unless—"

He interrupted. "Unless what?" Darryl leaned across the table, his eyes full of curiosity.

"Unless you bargain with me. I want the names of all the girls you two killed."

"And then?"

"Then Max might be able to spend some time here with you until his final sentencing. Sometimes that takes years. You and Max can spend quality time together—just father and son."

"You do realize how big my boy is, don't you, Jade? I'm sure he could handle himself at Terre Haute if he was ever sent there."

"Trust me, he'll be sent there, but when is up to you. Do we have a deal or not?"

He laughed loudly, then shook the chains that secured his arms to the table. "Damn cops. Doesn't the lying ever eat at you?"

"Meaning?"

"Meaning, I just talked to Max less than an hour ago. The way I see it, unless that was the one phone call he's allowed—oh, but wait, that's right. We prisoners don't get incoming calls. Short story is, Jade, Max is fine, and on a road trip. I forgot to ask him where he was heading, though. Stupid bitch—lie, lie, lie, just like your old man."

I stood and slammed my hand on the table. "I hope you rot in hell. Guard, open the door!"

Darryl's laugh echoed down the hallway as that steel door slammed at my back. I walked out and left WSPF with nothing except hatred for the Sims family.

Chapter 43

I was still fuming when I called Amber. Darryl Sims had played me and caught me off guard. I had used the made-up story about Max being captured, and inside, he was laughing at me the entire time. I needed to get back to North Bend, regroup, and move forward in capturing that second-generation Sims family lunatic.

Guilt washed over me about being away during Amber's first week in the police academy. I knew she was over the moon, but other than our few short phone calls, I hadn't given her the proper congratulations or encouragement. I checked the time as I drove back toward Green River Falls—5:40. It would be a long night of driving, and Amber might be in bed by the time I arrived home.

She picked up on the third ring. "Hey, Jade, please tell me you're coming home tonight. I miss you."

I chuckled wearily. "Yes, I'm coming home, and I'm sorry I haven't been there for your first week of training. I feel awful about it."

"I'll live, and soon enough I'll understand even more

what you're going through."

"Are you enjoying your classes?"

"Absolutely, and so is Kate. We're really hitting it off as study mates and friends. I like her a lot."

"I do too, hon. Hopefully things will quiet down once Dad arrives. I bet he's excited to hear about the academy."

"I've talked to Dad a few times this week, so he's up to date on everything."

"Good to hear. Okay, sis, I'm going to pull off the freeway and grab a coffee for the road. I'll be home late, so don't wait up. I'd say you need your beauty sleep, but I don't think you could get more beautiful."

Amber laughed. "You crack me up. Love you, Jade."

"Love you too. Good night." I clicked off and pulled into the truck stop along the freeway. There was a large cup of coffee with my name on it waiting inside.

Back in the cruiser with the coffee in a Styrofoam cup and safely nestled in the cup holder, I called Jack to tell him my ETA. "Hey, partner, I'm on my way back."

"Good to hear. What time should I expect you?"

"I'd say seven thirtyish. How did it go with Antonio?"

"Pretty bad—he blames himself, of course. He feels he and the PD dropped the ball in the search for Theresa. Max had her for several days before he killed her. I can't even imagine what she went through. How did it go with Darryl?"

I huffed instead of swearing.

"That bad?"

"You could say that. He played me big-time, and I

didn't even see it coming. My speech about having Max in custody went nowhere. Apparently they had talked a short time before I arrived. He already knew Max was fine and on the road. I'm sure my bullshit story amused him."

"What a jerk. Don't worry, Jade. We'll eventually have the last laugh."

"I know, but it's the eventually part that worries me. A lot can happen between now and then."

I drove in silence the rest of the way to Green River Falls. My mind was filled with doubt that we'd ever catch Max Sims. He was good at his craft, especially since he had skated by for twenty years and never created a blip on our radar. Darryl had taught him well.

I was happy to see Jack when I pulled into the police station parking lot at 7:45. He had checked out of the motel earlier, gathered all of our belongings, and was sitting on the brick ledge at the building's entrance.

I popped the trunk then exited the cruiser. I needed to stretch, and I was handing off the driving duties to Jack. He could enjoy the three-hour drive back to North Bend while I reclined the seat and relaxed.

He patted my shoulder, threw our duffel bags in the trunk, and climbed in behind the steering wheel. "What a day, right?"

"Yeah, with no resolution."

"Tomorrow is another day, Jade. We'll get Max and bring him to justice."

Chapter 44

With a different set of wheels and the cops long in his dust, Max checked into the dumpy, weekly rental unit at the Northside Motel. Certain pockets of Milwaukee's northwest side left a lot to be desired. Nobody in the area cared who you were, what you did, or what you were about to do, as long as it didn't involve them. If they didn't see it—it didn't happen.

Although the room disgusted Max, Northside Motel was the perfect place to hide in plain sight, and at ninety bucks a week, he would stay as long as he had to. As bad as the place was, it was still better than the cabin. He paid in advance—cash only, no ID necessary, and no questions asked.

The twenty-year-old blue Chevy Cavalier wagon was safely tucked behind the motel in front of room three. The plates had been swapped out twice before he reached Milwaukee, and the current plates were stolen off a rusty old minivan when he passed through Madison.

Max pulled a few small totes out of the back of the

vehicle and brought them inside the room. He needed a shower, a fresh change of clothes, his phone charger, and a notepad and paper. Surprisingly, the room had reliable Wi-Fi service.

The soap and hot shower stung that makeshift stitch job Theresa had done on his shoulder several days back. He winced but continued scrubbing. Max hadn't bathed since he left the farm last week. Feeling somewhat human again, he dressed in a clean set of clothes and ordered a medium-sized pizza for delivery. Max sat at the table near the window and wrote a letter to Darryl. He needed to know what his next move should be, and when. He mentioned his new "vacation" spot on the northwest side of Brew City and how he'd just scored a different vehicle. Everything was under control. He'd stay put and wait for Darryl's phone call on Monday before proceeding with request number two.

Chapter 45

"Hey, partner, wake up. We're in North Bend."

"Huh? What did you say?" I rubbed my eyes and looked around, then pulled the lever on the seatback.

"We're at the sheriff's department. Go home and get a good night's sleep. We'll be hitting the conference room in the morning. We've got a lot of brainstorming to do."

"Yeah, awesome. What happened to those days where we had the weekends off?" I yawned then rolled my neck to get the kinks out.

"I don't remember those days. Surely you're hallucinating." Jack chuckled and killed the engine.

We both exited the cruiser and crossed the parking lot to our own cars.

"I'd suggest going in and seeing what Jamison and Horbeck know, but then we'd be in there for an hour. A good night's sleep sounds more appealing right now."

"I agree. Night, Jack." I headed to my car and clicked the key fob. The lights blinked twice, and the door locks popped up.

"Night, Jade."

I exited the parking lot and was thankful for the short drive home—I was exhausted. With a tap of the remote, the garage door lifted, and I pulled in. Inside the house, the lights were dimmed, and a note penned by my sweet little sister lay on the breakfast bar for me.

I'm glad you're home, sis! Be prepared for a delicious breakfast of pancakes, bacon, and freshly brewed coffee. We have a lot of catching up to do.

Amber's note made my heart ache. I loved her dearly, but I'd be lucky to enjoy breakfast and a cup of coffee with her before I bolted out the door and headed to work. Criminals didn't normally take the weekends off, but I wished they would.

I tiptoed down the hall with my duffel bag in hand and closed the bedroom door at my back. A hot shower would be relaxing and hopefully send me off to dreamland. While the water heated, I checked on my beloved birds. Polly and Porky were sound asleep and snuggled side by side on the perch. I left them alone and smoothed the cover over their cage.

I remembered very little after my shower other than scrunching my pillow and burrowing my head under the blankets. Now, the morning light streamed in between the slats on the window blinds. I saw light through my eyelids and forced my eyes open even though it took some effort. The clock was blurry. I swiped at the nightstand for my reading glasses and felt them. I slipped them on and looked at the clock again—6:30. I had plenty of sleep.

With my robe's belt cinched comfortably around my waist, I stumbled out to the kitchen. I hoped to beat Amber up and at least start the coffee. She sat at the breakfast bar with the morning newspaper, already sipping a cup of the brew.

"Who are you, the Energizer Bunny? Don't you ever sleep?"

"Yeah, but yoga helps."

I groaned and poured myself a cup of coffee. "No, thanks. Yoga isn't quite my thing. Sorry, hon, but I have to leave for work right after breakfast. This Max Sims case just keeps getting worse and worse." I saw the disappointment written across Amber's face even though she tried to hide it.

"No problem, I get it. It's all part of the job."

I kissed her cheek. "Unfortunately, that's true."

"Okay, then, I better start breakfast."

"And I'll get showered."

We enjoyed breakfast and conversation for thirty minutes before I had to leave. I pushed it as long as I could.

"Oh, by the way, Jade, I confirmed everything for Dad's knee surgery. The doctor wants him at the hospital at seven o'clock sharp Tuesday morning. His insurance cleared the procedure. It's a wrap."

I grinned. "I have to give Mom and Dad credit."

"Yeah, about what?"

"They gave me the best sister anyone could ask for. You're so responsible, and your cooking skills aren't half bad, either."

"That's all Mom."

I glanced at the clock on the stove and pushed back my chair.

"Yeah, I know, you have to leave."

I pulled a napkin out of the holder and wiped my mouth then hugged Amber. "Maybe tonight will be better. I'll do my best to eat dinner at home with you."

A half hour later, I was in the bull pen with the rest of the team. The only person not in attendance was Clayton, and he offered to pick up the doughnuts.

Clark paced. "There must have been a crowd at Pit-Stop this morning."

Billings smirked then fastened the shirt button he'd missed that morning. "He's probably waiting for the baker's dozen special to start."

"And that's when?" Clark asked, becoming impatient.

Billings checked the time. "Eight o'clock. He should be here any minute."

Jack and I cleared our desks and listened to voicemails as we waited.

We turned at the sound of the door opening. Clayton's grin preceded him. "I got the baker's dozen."

"Good, let's get down to business. Everyone, head to the conference room." Clark pulled the whiteboard out of the coat closet and led the way.

Each of us had our hands full as we followed.

Jack and I explained the chain of events that took place in Green River Falls.

"To be honest, boss, it was a mess, but in their defense, they don't know Max Sims and had no idea of the family history. His name likely wouldn't have come up at all if I hadn't been run down by the idiot and got a good look at him."

"That begs the question, was he there because of Judge Gardino or because he needed to hide somewhere and that cabin used to be his uncle's?"

Jack spoke up. "I'm leaning toward the latter. Does Max even know of the judge, or was Theresa a convenient victim? She was intoxicated, according to the bartender at the Last Stop."

"I have to agree with Jack. If we wouldn't have come up on the body of the girl in the woods, I might have thought differently. Max was only there a few days, and he had already committed one murder. It's an addiction with him. I think he was just trolling an easy mark, and unfortunately Theresa Gardino fit the bill."

"Okay, we can't change what has happened. What do we have on known associates?"

"He was a recluse, boss. Other than his weekly visits to Darryl, there wasn't anyone he hung out with," I said.

"So that's a dead end? Then go with bank records, credit card transactions, and phone calls."

Jack stopped writing and looked at Clark. "Max had a burner phone, remember?"

Clark groaned. "Didn't we get a court order for those records?"

"Nope," I said, "we went with the warrant for the newspaper ad instead. It was quicker."

"Fine. Clayton and Billings, you two get on the credit

card records and bank statements. Jade and Jack, call WSPF and get transcripts and video of the visits Max made to Darryl in the last month. I'll get the TV stations to post his picture again on every channel and every newscast."

"Hold off with that, boss. You're going to need Marie to do her magic first. I saw Max, and he's changed his appearance."

"Really, in what way?"

"He shaved off his beard and cut his long hair. Of course, the height and weight will be the same, but the picture will have to be updated before any news releases are aired."

"I'll get Marie on it. I may need you to sit with her and tweak the drawing, Jade."

"No problem."

Clark smacked his hands together. "Okay, everyone get busy. Let's meet back here at noon and compare notes. I'll foot the bill for lunch. Billings, pass the menu around for Omicron."

"You got it, boss."

Marie was gracious enough to come in on a Saturday, which happened to be the same day as her niece's high school graduation party. She hunkered down in the conference room with a cup of coffee and worked from the photo that was aired last week with no results. I hoped with Max's current look, he might be more easily recognized. I explained the changes, and Marie began working. She said she'd show me the updated drawing before it was finalized.

Back in the bull pen and at my desk, I waited until Jack

was off the phone to talk. He hung up seconds later.

I took a gulp of my cold coffee. "So, who was that?"

"That was the visitor clerk at WSPF. She went through the records for the last month and said Max had signed in twice. The signature on one was questionable, but the video confirmed it was Max. There was a new guard stationed that day that didn't know him personally. That visit was the last entry they have for Max there in person."

"That's odd. When was it?"

"Four days ago. Darryl made an outgoing call that same day at four o'clock that lasted ten seconds and then another one yesterday that lasted ten minutes."

"So he was telling the truth about talking to Max. Can they track the number he called?"

"Nope, inmates can only use pay phones, and they're collect calls. They record the conversations, though."

I rubbed the back of my achy neck. "Yep, that much I know. Are they sending us any audio transcripts?"

"Yeah, they said they'd send them over this afternoon."

"Good. Looks like Billings has the Omicron menu."

"Got a minute, Jade?" Marie came around the corner from the conference room.

"Sure, give me one second." I picked my lunch choice and told Jack to write it down, then I followed Marie.

The right side of the table was covered with drawing paper, facial templates, the original image of Max, several renditions of his style change, erasers, and a box of charcoal pencils. I sat next to Marie as she moved everything aside except the three drawings.

"Is there one that's closer to his current look than the rest?"

"These are great drawings, considering they're images of a lunatic murderer." I studied each closely, then compared them side by side. A few subtle differences showed up in his face shape, eye depth, and nose size from one drawing to the next. I tapped the middle one. "This one is dead nuts on. That's the current Max Sims."

"Okay, good to hear. I'll run a dozen copies off for your files, keep one for myself, and give this original one to the lieutenant."

"Thanks so much, Marie. You've been a great help. Want to stay for lunch?"

She smiled. "Thanks, but I'll take a rain check. I have a graduation party to get to." She gathered her drawing supplies and left to make copies.

A half hour later, we congregated in the conference room. White bags filled with partitioned Styrofoam meal containers sat on the center of the table. A stack of napkins three inches thick, along with five tall sodas, accompanied the bags. We sorted through the bags and checked the abbreviations scratched on each container, indicating the meal inside.

My steak sandwich and fries would hold me over until dinner, hopefully at home instead of the table in the conference room.

"Okay, ten minutes, guys," Clark said as he polished off his double cheeseburger. He still had an extra-large order of fries to finish. "We've got to get back at it."

I slid all the empty bags and containers into the garbage can in the corner. Our sodas and half the stack of napkins were all that remained on the table other than our notepads and pens.

Clark stood by the whiteboard. "Clayton, what did you come up with?"

"Max's credit card was used a few times at the hardware store in Green River Falls. It looks like he bought camping gear."

I nodded. "Those were the items found inside the cabin. There wasn't any electricity running into the property. He left behind a lantern, cooler, flashlight, rope, a shovel, and cleaning supplies."

"Okay, no help there. Billings?"

"I figured out how he's supporting himself, boss."

Clark perked up. "Don't keep us in suspense, just say it."

Billings took a long draw of his soda through the straw. "His bank records show a large withdrawal from a trust account."

"What do you call large?"

"Forty grand."

"Shit. That can hold him over for a long time. Who in the hell would have left him that much money?"

"Wasn't he living off his grandma's money?" Jack asked.

"He was for years, but the banker said that account was emptied out a while back. This trust was from his mother. Max wasn't supposed to have access to it until his fortieth birthday, unless it was an emergency. Either way, he still had to fork out a couple grand in early withdrawal fees."

"Good work, Billings. So it looks like all we're waiting on is the transcripts from the penitentiary?"

"That's right, Lieutenant, and they're supposed to show up in an hour or so."

Clark picked up the stack of papers in front of him and passed them out. "Here are the composite sketches Marie put together. Divide up the counties in the state while we're waiting for the transcripts from WSPF. Fax Max's face out to every sheriff's department in every county. They can forward them to their local police departments. This image is going wide to cover all of Wisconsin. If nothing hits, we'll spread the net out farther. He isn't going to be able to hide for long. With his face plastered in every county and on every news segment, it's just a matter of time."

I added, "Hopefully, a *short* matter of time."

Chapter 46

Jack plunked down. The chair's leather squeaked as he rearranged himself to find that perfect indented spot. He scooted in close to the desk and gave the mouse a jiggle to wake up the computer.

I glanced at the clock—2:00 p.m.

"I'll see if that email has come in yet," he said as he scrolled the roller wheel. "It's about damn time."

"It came?"

Jack nodded. "Let's see what WSPF sent us."

I rolled my chair around to his side and sat next to him at his desk.

"All right, it looks like they sent two audio files and two video files from the last ten days. I'll play the oldest phone call first, which coincides with an earlier visit from Max that same day." Jack opened the file and clicked the play arrow. We listened anxiously as the audio file began.

"What's the number?"

"Fourteen."

The call ended abruptly.

"What the hell was that?" I asked.

Jack hovered the mouse over the scrubber bar. "That's the ten second audio file."

"So we didn't miss anything? It was one exchange between them, and that's it?"

"Apparently so."

"How weird was that? 'What's the number?' in Darryl's voice and 'fourteen' in Max's? So that's definitely code for something, and fourteen is a relevant number."

"Maybe a room number, or the distance in miles to somewhere?"

I shrugged. "Weren't there fourteen local women that went missing the years Darryl owned the farm?"

"Yeah, but what does that have to do with anything?" Jack frowned at me.

"Whatever—set up the next audio file."

Jack closed out the first and opened the second. That file, a ten-minute one, made absolutely no sense to us.

I groaned my anger when I listened to their conversation. "They're being careful, those dirty dogs. They know the phone calls are recorded, and they're talking in code. None of that recording makes sense except the part where Max says, 'Sure did, and her hubby isn't going to be very happy about it.' That has to be referring to Theresa's murder."

"What do you think the part where Max said he hadn't 'found the right vacation spot' meant?"

"A new place to hide, I guess. Sounds like Darryl is going to call Max back at four o'clock on Monday. We'll have to get those tapes and every tape going forward until we capture that maniac. Let's get the lieutenant's take on this."

Clark joined us at Jack's desk, and we played the recordings for him. He agreed with our conclusions.

"They're definitely talking in code. Did you watch the video files of their visits yet?"

Jack spoke up. "Nope, but that's next." He clicked the thumbnail files on his desktop. "The first video was taped the day before Max vacated the farm."

We crowded in around Jack's computer monitor. Max and Darryl appeared on the screen in a segregated visitation booth that divided them with a Plexiglas wall. The video showed Max taking a quick glance at the cameras, then he cupped his hands around his mouth to talk through the six-inch screen.

I grumbled. "Nice—he's hiding his words, and we can't hear anything they're saying."

"Must have been a last-minute meeting," Clark said. "Those segregation booths are for special visits outside of the normal visiting hours. And that was the day before Max left the farm?"

Jack checked the file. "That's correct, boss."

Clark smirked. "He must have needed instructions from Daddy. Let's check the next one."

Jack clicked on the second video.

"Check that out!" I pointed at the screen. "He already has his hair cut and his beard shaved off."

"Good thing his height gives him away," Jack said. "Clean shaven like that, he could easily blend in with the crowd, otherwise."

The visit took place in the regular visiting room. Other inmates could be seen in the background with their families. This time Max sat next to Darryl, yet he still covered his mouth to talk.

Jack checked the dates on the audio files again. "Okay, this visit coincides with that ten-second phone call Darryl placed to Max later that day, and it's the last visit between them on record."

I added, "That last coded recording from yesterday is the end of it, but Darryl did say he'd call again on Monday."

Clark pushed the guest chair back to my desk. "Jack, get on the horn to WSPF and tell them we want every call and letter sent between them forwarded to us. Max Sims is a dangerous fugitive and needs to be apprehended quickly."

"You got it, boss." Jack picked up his desk phone and dialed.

The lieutenant turned to me as he headed back to his office. "Jade, does the clean-shaven, short-haired Max in the video look close enough to the drawing Marie rendered?"

"I'd say so, boss, and wouldn't hesitate to air that sketch."

"Good, because I'm going statewide on every news channel out there starting tonight. If everything is wrapped up for now, go home and get some rest. There's nothing we can do until the toll-free tip line calls start coming in. The first news segment will air at six o'clock. The Channel 58 news at nine will air his image and profile next, and then the last round will go out statewide at ten o'clock. I'm keeping my fingers crossed that somebody has seen him."

I noticed Clark studying the weekly calendar to see which desk deputies were working the evening shifts.

"Mary Davidson and Mitch Bryant can cover the phones tonight. The evening dispatch officers can pitch in too when they aren't busy. If any leads come in that sound reliable, you'll all be getting calls." Clark swatted the air. "Get out of here and go home while you still can."

Chapter 47

Max ignored the dumpy room and sparse amenities that Saturday evening. He had already been cooped up in the disgusting motel for a full day. In his opinion, the less he was seen, the better, and the room had been paid for in advance for an entire week, anyway. Like it or not, he had to hunker down, stay invisible, and go out only when he had to. For now, more important things filled his mind. He sat at the table with a cup of coffee in front of him, turned the locations tab off on his phone, and searched the Internet. He needed to find the home address for Sergeant Jade Monroe. Different scenarios played out in his mind, causing him to chuckle.

Max powered down his phone temporarily and turned on the TV. He pressed the channel selector on the remote until he found news broadcasts that came in clearly. He found two Milwaukee stations and went back and forth between them. The noose was tightening around his neck, and the recent changes he'd made to his appearance didn't help as he'd hoped they would. Both stations showed composite drawings of him with his face shaved and his hair cut shorter. His height, weight, and eye color were plastered across the screen too.

"Son of a bitch, she gave the news stations my new look."

Max clicked the off button on the TV and tossed the remote to the side. He got up and rifled through the totes he'd brought into the room yesterday. He looked over the handful of items carefully.

Yeah, these ought to do it.

He took the scissors, a bar of soap, and a bag of disposable razors into the bathroom with him. Max plugged the sink and cut his hair as short as possible with the scissors. He looked at himself in the mirror—only a few sprouts remained on his head. He scooped the hair out of the sink and flushed it down the toilet and began again. With the water running, Max lathered the soap between his hands and rubbed the suds all over his head. It took several cheap razor blades to turn his scalp into something as smooth as a cue ball. He checked his appearance again in the mirror, gave himself a nod, and threw the razors in the trash can.

With no other choice, Max paid the forty-nine bucks to an online phone and address search company. As soon as the verification screen came up and showed the transaction had cleared, Jade Monroe's address and phone number popped up.

Max laughed. "Bingo! The fun is about to begin."

The surveillance on Sergeant Jade Monroe would start tomorrow morning. Max knew it could be a risky move going out in daylight, but with a stolen car and plates, a hat pulled down low, sunglasses, and his lack of any hair at all, he felt he'd be just fine. Nobody had any idea what he was driving, and staying a safe distance behind her, he could follow Jade Monroe around for the next few days.

Chapter 48

I'll admit, it did feel nice to spend a leisurely Saturday night at home with Amber. She made a delicious enchilada dinner with Spanish rice and frijoles as side dishes. The meal was decadent, and she admitted that our dad would likely prefer something else while he was here for two weeks.

"Don't you remember at Thanksgiving he said how he ate Mexican food all the time? I want to serve him something else while he's here, so let's enjoy this food fiesta now."

"Sounds logical to me," I said with a mouthful of rice.

Why I felt guilty to be relaxing at home was beyond me—it had to be in my blood and likely something passed down from my dad. He was a workaholic, and I was glad he'd be having his surgery here, where Amber and I could keep our eyes on him and help out.

"It worries me that Dad will be spending most weekdays at home alone. I have the academy, you have criminals to catch and throw in prison, and Dad will be sitting here all by himself while he's recuperating."

I shrugged. "He'll be fine. He can watch TV, read crime fiction novels, play solitaire, and surf the Internet. All he needs to worry about is keeping his knee up and staying off that leg. He can relax on the recliner all day."

Amber laughed as she pulled the napkin off her lap and wiped her mouth. She got up and began clearing the table. "You are talking about our dad. He doesn't know how to relax." She gave me a sideways grin. "Sound familiar?"

"Humph—maybe."

"Yeah, I'm sure you have the bull pen on speed dial. How many times have you called in since the first news segment aired about Max Sims?"

I stuck out my lower lip. "Only three times."

"That's exactly my point."

"Fine—during the week, we'll come home at lunchtime and hang out with Dad."

That comment put a smile on Amber's face. She was such a daddy's girl.

My cell phone rang just as I sat down to watch my favorite crime series. Jack was calling. I held off on that much-anticipated glass of wine and answered.

"Hey, Jack, what's up?"

"Clark just called me with an update. He said he would call you, but I told him I'd take care of it."

"So something new?"

"You mean in the last half hour?" He chuckled. "I know you pretty well, Monroe. Deputy Davidson said you've called a handful of times already."

"Busted."

"Uh-huh. Anyway, a few people called in on the tip line from the Channel 58 news at nine."

"And?"

"And, they're all describing the same guy playing pool at a bar in Grafton."

"That doesn't sound right. Why would Max go out in public when every channel in the state is airing his face?"

"I thought the same thing, but since there were numerous calls, I didn't think it would hurt to check it out. I already called the Grafton Police Department. They have a copy of that faxed image from Ozaukee County Sheriff's Department. They said they'd check it out and get back to us."

"Yeah, okay, anything else?" I went ahead and picked up my glass of wine and took a sip.

"Nah—only crank calls and others where jilted women say the guy on the news is their estranged husband or boyfriend."

"Awesome. I wish people would realize that the tip line is for serious police work."

"True enough. So how is your relaxing Saturday night going?"

I heard the smirk in Jack's voice.

"I wish I could relax, but knowing that murderer has killing in his blood makes me nervous. Max is out there somewhere, planning his next move on a poor unsuspecting person."

Jack sighed. "Hopefully Darryl's call to Max Monday afternoon can shed some light."

"But if they're talking in code again, we're screwed."

"All right, get back to doing whatever it was you were doing. Tell Amber hi and have fun tomorrow with your old man."

"We might do a Sunday brunch after we pick him up. Do you want to join us?"

"Yeah, that sounds good. Your dad is a riot. Tom Monroe—the living legend."

I laughed. "Plus, he has plenty of awesome stories. Meet us at the Washington House at noon. I'll invite Kate too."

"Okay, see you then, and stop calling the bull pen. They'll let us know if something is urgent."

I clicked off the call, filled my wineglass, and went back to watching my TV show.

Chapter 49

Max left the motel early—better to err on the side of caution. He snugged the baseball cap down tight on his bald head and slipped on a pair of cheap sunglasses from Dollar-Mart. He remembered the conversation he'd overheard that day in Green River Falls. Jade was picking up her father at the airport at ten o'clock. Max would be waiting for her to leave the house.

Finding the information he needed on the Monroe woman was worth every penny he'd spent online. It saved him a lot of time searching. Darryl would be proud of his son when he heard the news tomorrow during their phone call.

Max stepped out into the foggy morning and took in his good luck. The weather couldn't have been better. The fog would help conceal him during his watch of the Monroe house. Max made sure he had everything he needed, then drove toward North Bend and used his GPS to pinpoint her address.

The Ashbury Woods condo neighborhood was located

on the south side of town. Max cautiously turned in at the main entrance and followed the route from the automated voice on his navigation system. He needed to find Sergeant Monroe's house quickly and position himself far enough away so he wouldn't be noticed, yet within view of her driveway. Max slowly passed her condo that stood at the end of a cul-de-sac with a woods behind it.

This could be a problem. Not an easy exit.

He double-checked the house number then followed the street back out. The clubhouse was just ahead and within view of her condo. Max turned in and faced the car toward the cul-de-sac. Early morning gym rats had already arrived. Max saw people working out through the large floor-to-ceiling windows. With his car tucked in between others, he wouldn't be noticed. Max parked, killed the engine, and waited. She'd have to pass the clubhouse to exit the complex.

Max pushed up his sleeve and checked the time, then peered at the sky. He figured she'd leave soon considering the fog hadn't lifted yet. The weather would slow her down a bit and give him plenty of time to do what he needed to do. He turned on the car radio while he focused on her condo. Movement ahead caught his eye. Her garage door lifted, and a black Mustang backed out. He checked the time again—8:40. He continued to watch, then brake lights flashed. The passenger door opened, and a young woman exited, ducked under the overhead, and disappeared. She returned a few minutes later, got in the car, then it backed out onto the street.

That has to be her younger sister, Amber, and apparently they live together. That's a bonus.

He slid lower in the seat, pulled the cap down even more, and watched as they passed the clubhouse and turned onto the street that took them out of Ashbury Woods. Max saw the car turn right and connect with the frontage road that led them south to the highway. He sat in the clubhouse parking lot until nine o'clock for good measure. When the time felt right, he crept out of the car and followed the path through the woods that led to the back of the condos. Max kept his head on a swivel as he passed other homes on his way to hers. He was thankful for the blossoming trees that gave him cover. Straight ahead, her condo stood at the end of the street, just before the cul-de-sac curved back around. Hers was the last residence on that side. With the dense woods and no other condos to concern himself with, Max was afforded privacy to go about his business. He stood behind a thicket of trees and bushes to surveil the home before stepping out of his cover. He faced a large deck with a set of sliding doors leading into the house. Two windows, possibly from bedrooms, faced the back as well. A covered pen with a pet door was situated on the left side of the deck. Max saw a cat sleeping on a cushion in the pen.

Good—one less thing to deal with.

He checked his surroundings once more, then slunk forward, took the four steps up, and crossed the deck. So far so good, and he didn't even wake the cat. Max removed his hat then cupped his hands around his face. He peered through the glass into what looked to be the family room.

He glanced down at the slider rail—no security bar.

What an idiot, and she's a cop?

Max slipped on the latex gloves and spread his hands out on the glass door. He lifted upward, disengaged the lock, and slid the door to the side. He waited—no alarm sounded. Max grinned and walked through.

Easy as pie.

He took in the layout of the condo and snapped pictures from room to room. He drew a diagram of the floor plan, noting which rooms were the master, the sister's room, and the guest room. He noted that there were two bedrooms on the right and a bathroom on the left, directly across the hall. He lingered in what looked to be Amber's room. Max turned the knob on the desk lamp. In front of him lay open books and study manuals from the police academy. He chuckled. "Following in the family career path, are we?" He took more pictures. He continued on to the next room and peeked around the door. The room was set up as the typical, comfortable looking guest room with a queen-sized bed, dresser, and nightstand. A small desk and wooden chair filled the corner. He continued on. The master bedroom was at the far end on the left with its own bathroom. Max sat at the foot of the bed and bounced a few times as he snickered at her stupid choice of pets. He stared at her birds and had to hold back the temptation to twist their heads off. He didn't want her to know that someone had stopped by.

"So this is where the bitch with the big gun sleeps."

He spat on the bedspread then stood and crossed the

room. He pulled each drawer open until he found her panties and bras. He studied them, ran his fingers across the lace, then sliced several of the panties with his knife. He shoved them back in the drawer and closed it. Max returned to the family room and snapped more pictures of the deck entrance, the front entrance, and every closet. The large eat-in kitchen was directly across from the family room. A door beyond the pantry caught his eye.

Hmmm...what's this?

Max turned the knob and pulled the door toward him. A flight of steps going to the basement lay ahead. He hit the rocker switch on the wall, and the staircase lit up. He followed the steps down while he counted each one then jotted that information on the piece of paper. The basement was unfinished and held plenty of hiding spots. Max snapped a few pictures of dark corners and their locations relative to the staircase, then went back upstairs and turned off the basement light. Off the kitchen were the laundry room, a powder room, and the two-car garage.

Typical floor plan, but good to memorize.

With a final walk-through of each room and a few more pictures, Max wiped the marks from his gloves off the glass sliders, secured the door, and sneaked out the front. He hugged the side of the house until he reached the back then disappeared into the woods.

Chapter 50

Amber and I waited at Concourse D. Dad always flew Delta and probably had a free ticket for this trip. We watched, each with a coffee in hand and a hot one waiting for him.

"Oh my God, Jade, there's Daddy, and he's using a cane."

"That damn knee is a lot worse than he let on. I had no idea it was that bad."

Amber waved from a distance and gave me a concerned look. "He'll be okay after the surgery, won't he?"

"Of course he will, but he's still going to get a good scolding for letting it go this long. It has to hurt like hell for him to suck it up and use a cane."

Amber waved again as he got closer.

He grinned and waved back.

"Finally!" Amber said when he reached us.

I elbowed her, and she gave me a dirty look.

"I didn't mean it that way. I meant he's finally here again." She embraced him in a tight hug. "Hi, Daddy."

"Hi, sweetheart." My dad kissed Amber's cheek, then kissed mine.

"Let me take that bag, Dad. Do you need to sit for a minute? That's an awful long concourse."

"Yeah, good idea."

"Over here, Daddy." Amber led the way to a table, and we sat. I handed him his coffee.

"Thanks, honey. I can't wait to get this knee fixed. It sure is a nuisance right now, especially with this cane."

"We'll have you as good as new in no time, Dad. We're meeting Kate and Jack for brunch at the Washington House. I hope you didn't eat on the plane."

"Only three bags of pretzels. What are there, four mini pretzels in each bag?"

I smirked. "Yeah, if that. How was your flight, other than early and long?"

"It wasn't bad. I think I slept through most of it."

I stood and threw my coffee cup in the garbage can. "Do you have the same suitcase as last time?"

"Uh-huh, the tan one."

"Okay, you guys stay put and enjoy your coffee. I'll go downstairs and get it. Thankfully, the car is parked close by. I'll be back in a flash."

A half hour later, I pulled in line at the airport exit and paid the parking fee. We were on our way to North Bend.

"I'm sure glad winter is over with here. I'd hate to be gimping around on wet, icy sidewalks."

"I've been thinking about moving to San Bernardino, more and more every day, Dad. I could transfer to your sheriff's department."

Dad looked surprised. "Why would you do that, honey?

You just bought a brand-new condo."

"Yeah, Jade, why would you do that? Are you just going to ditch me like yesterday's trash and move to sunny California?"

I chuckled. "I'm thinking out loud, that's all. San Bernardino County is the largest county in southern California. You have more bad guys to get off the streets and a lot more resources. It just sounds like a good fit for me. You both know how much I hate winter too."

Amber huffed. "I'll buy you a heavier coat for Christmas."

I exited the freeway at the North Bend ramp. Downtown was only a few minutes away. I pulled up in front of the Washington House and let Amber and my dad out of the car.

"I'll meet up with you in a second. I see a parking spot across the street."

A minute later, as I walked toward the restaurant, I saw Kate approaching the bench Dad and Amber waited on.

Kate grinned when I caught up with her. "It's pretty cool that it only takes me two minutes to walk here, right?" She stuck out her hand to shake my dad's. "Good to see you again, Mr. Monroe."

"Kate, how have you been? You're looking much happier than the first time I met you."

"I definitely am, and I can thank Jade for that. She's amazing."

Kate squeezed my arm.

"Mr. Monroe, did you know that Amber and I go to the police academy together?"

"I sure did. You girls can tell me all about it over brunch."

I scanned the street and saw Jack pulling his Charger into a parking spot.

"Jack's here. I'll wait for him if you guys want to go ahead and get seated."

I watched my family go inside then took a seat on the bench. I wanted a few minutes alone with Jack.

"Hey, partner, any news?" I asked when he got closer.

Jack sat down. "That tip from the bar last night was a false alarm."

"I figured as much. I doubt if Max is that reckless. Anything else?"

"A few tips came in this morning that may be worth checking out. Somebody in Mequon thinks a new tenant in their building could be Max. Somebody else in Saint Francis called in. They swear they saw him in a Walmart on South 60th Street. I have the store pulling up their surveillance tapes. Saint Francis PD is going to check it out. I think after lunch, I'll head in for a few hours and answer tip line calls."

"Maybe I should too."

Jack cocked his head and frowned at me. "Your dad just got here, Jade. Take a break for the day. We have this covered. Believe me, you'll be busy enough between work and helping out after his surgery. Cut yourself some slack."

I groaned with frustration. "You know, we're so limited with what we can do."

Jack gave me another odd glance. "What does that mean?"

"I mean Max could be right over the county line, but then it isn't our case anymore. He could have left the state, and it's out of our hands. We're stuck within our own boundaries."

"We always have been, Jade. So what's really eating at you?"

I looked out at the downtown area I loved, and had, my entire life. Farmers' markets took place every Saturday between May and October. Settler's Square often held live music performances. I loved my town, and other than the cold winters, something else was gnawing at me—pulling me to do more. I had to catch the bad guys no matter what, but I felt stuck.

"Jade, we were able to help in Green River Falls. That's far from our own county."

I smiled. "You know damn well we weren't welcome there. It's only because we know Judge Gardino and Clark asked us to check on him as a courtesy. No matter what, the outcome was horrific."

"You can't save everyone, partner."

My eyes stung with tears, and I quickly brushed them away. "But I'd like to try."

Jack nudged me and jerked his head toward the door. "Come on. Let's go inside. Your family is waiting for us. We'll talk about this later. Right now, be in the moment. It's all we have. Hell, your old man is here. What could be better than that?"

"I know you're right. I'm just having an early midlife crisis."

Jack laughed and gave me a hug. "You'll feel a lot better once you've guzzled down a couple of those Scottish Ales." He opened the door for me, and I passed through. "For now, I need to reconnect with your pop."

Gabi stood behind the hostess podium and reached for two menus. I could tell she recognized Jack and me.

She smiled and nodded. "Detectives, right this way."

Once we were in the dining room, Amber saw us and lifted her hand to get our attention.

I pointed. "We're with them."

"Wonderful, and it looks like you have the best table in the house. Would you like me to light the fireplace?"

Jack raised his brows. "What do you think?"

"I think my dad would really like that. Sure, Gabi, go ahead."

We each ordered the brunch special, and the waitress went to fill our drink requests. Jack and my dad yucked it up, and Amber and Kate were as thick as thieves. I happily joined in on the conversations—work issues could wait. That afternoon, my friends and family took center stage.

Chapter 51

I pulled into the garage at two thirty. Brunch was fun, but by his tired eyes, I knew my dad was ready to wind down. He had been up since three a.m. California time.

We entered the house, and I rolled the suitcase into the guest room for him.

"Feel free to take a nap if you want to, Dad. Amber and I aren't going anywhere. Knowing her, she's probably already planning the dinner menu."

"You sure you don't mind? A couple of hours would do me good."

"I don't mind one bit. I'll wake you up at four." I closed the door at my back and joined Amber in the kitchen.

"I started the coffee," she said as she pulled out her favorite recipe book.

I grinned as I leaned against the wall, my arms crossed. "What's for dinner?"

"I'm thinking a vegetable, cheese, and bacon quiche. How does that sound?"

"It sounds delicious. I'm going to change into

something relaxing now that Jack has me on house arrest."

Amber's eyes twinkled when she laughed. "He's right, you know."

"Yeah, yeah." I walked down the hallway and stopped just before my door and stared. I'd never left that door open. I wouldn't take a chance of Polly and Porky being in the same room with Spaz. After all, cats eat birds. Luckily, they were fine.

"Amber, come here a sec."

She walked down the hallway toward me. "What's up?"

"Did you have any reason to go in my bedroom before we left to pick up Dad? Was there laundry to put away or something like that?"

"No, why?"

"My bedroom door was standing wide open." I walked in, and Amber followed. "Look at my bedspread, it's all messed up. Spaz had to be in here."

"That's never happened before. Thank God Polly and Porky are okay. Maybe the latch didn't catch when you closed the door."

I eyed the room and door suspiciously. "Yeah, maybe."

After I changed my clothes, I shut the bedroom door tightly and gave it a slight push. The latch held just as it should. I went to the sliding door in the family room and jiggled the handle. The lock was secure.

"Coffee is ready. Want a cup?"

"Huh? Oh, yeah, coffee sounds good." I sat next to Amber at the breakfast bar and scanned the room.

"You're freaking me out. I can tell you're anxious about something. What gives?"

"Nah—I'm fine. I think I'll check into security systems and have something installed."

"You've been saying that since last summer, Jade. Aren't they expensive? I thought your gun was our security system."

"Yeah, I know, but I'm not always home."

"I have a gun too, and this *is* North Bend you're talking about. Last time I checked, this town didn't make the top one hundred on the most dangerous cities list."

"True, but you can never be too careful. Maybe we should go to the range tomorrow evening when I get home from work. That would be fun, wouldn't it? You can show Dad how good of a shot you are."

"Yeah, I'd like that a lot"

That night, sleep eluded me. I couldn't turn off Max Sims. I saw him every time I closed my eyes. We had to catch this crazed killer. He was too dangerous to be out on the streets doing what he loved best—murdering anyone he wanted to. I rolled over and checked the time—11:12. I called Jack.

His voice sounded groggy when he answered, and I immediately regretted making the call.

"Jade, is something wrong?"

"Damn it, I'm sorry, Jack. I wasn't sure if you'd be asleep yet, but by the sound of—"

He interrupted. "It's okay, partner. What's up?"

"Is Clark going to continue running the news segments on Max?"

"Yeah, he said he was. He wants to get as much publicity

as he can on the case. We have to keep Max's face on everyone's mind. We need to see where we are with the identification of the bones too. I guess we're going over that tomorrow. Some families have claimed the remains, yet there are plenty of bones that are still unidentified. We're expecting Dr. White to release all the data tomorrow. After we hear what he has, we might need to think about running more 'ID the Missing' events."

"Okay, that sounds like a good plan. So the few leads we had for Max were duds?"

Jack groaned. "Yeah, none of them have panned out yet. He's either staying under the radar or has left the area. We'll get him, Jade. At some point he's going to slip up, and we'll be waiting with our guns drawn."

"I hope so. Sorry I woke you. I'll see you in the morning. Good night."

"Night, Jade."

I punched my pillow until the indention felt right under my head. With the blankets up to my neck, I tried to turn off the images of Max Sims and think about anything else.

I woke to the happy voices of my dad and Amber. Even though I had a restless night, I was glad to start a new day and get to work. I slipped on my robe and joined my family in the kitchen.

"Morning, guys. Coffee smells good." I opened the cabinet to the left of the stove and pulled out a coffee cup. I filled it three quarters full and topped it off with half-and-half. Amber and my dad sat at the table. His cane was propped against the wall behind him. I pulled out my usual chair and took a seat. I noticed my dad studying my face.

"You don't look very refreshed for just getting up."

"I couldn't get Max Sims out of my head enough to sleep peacefully, Dad. So far, the news bulletins haven't produced any viable results."

"Unfortunately, catching criminals isn't always a slam dunk, honey. Oftentimes, the worst of the worst slip between the cracks, and that's reality. It isn't always an easy pill to swallow."

"I know, but it still weighs on my mind. Anyway, do you want to go to the shooting range tonight?"

"That sounds like fun. Once tomorrow comes, I'll be gimping around on crutches for the next few weeks."

"Who wants French toast?" Amber pushed away from the table and went into the kitchen.

"I think we both do," I said. "I'm going to get showered before breakfast, though." I rose and kissed my dad's cheek. "It's good to have you home, Dad."

"And it's good to be here, honey."

I arrived at work at nine o'clock, later than usual, but I had left a message on Clark's voicemail telling him in advance. I wanted to have a casual, peaceful breakfast as a family. Most mornings, Amber and I crossed paths as we filled our coffee cups and said a quick goodbye as we walked out the door. Tomorrow morning would be hectic with Dad's surgery. We needed that quiet morning together, just the three of us.

Once at work and back in the bull pen, I dug in. I listened to all of the tip line calls that had come in over the weekend and dismissed the ones that had already been checked out.

"What about the sighting at the Milwaukee bus terminal earlier? Did anyone check into that?"

Billings answered the question for everyone. "The downtown precinct said they'd take care of it."

"And?"

"And we haven't heard back from them yet."

"Did anyone check to see if an actual ticket was purchased in his name and where it was going?"

"I called the Greybus terminal myself, Jade. They said no ticket was issued to anyone named Max Sims."

"Maybe he bought it a few days ago to throw us off. He could have used a false name or bought it online. Did anyone check his credit card statement? Weren't you in charge of that, Clayton?"

I saw Chad roll his eyes at everyone, then he chuckled. "Man, she's like a dog with a bone."

I pushed back my chair and stood. "Hey, smart-ass, you weren't there to see the carnage he did. Green River Falls is now one deputy short. Talk smart to that dead man's widow. Or how about the decomposing girl half buried in the ground with her forehead smashed in? What about Theresa Gardino that had a ball gag jammed in her mouth while her dead body was splayed out across the room with blood everywhere, or Deborah French and Amy Patterson? Don't tell me I'm like a dog with a bone! Max Sims needs to go down, and I'll shoot that son of a bitch myself if I get the chance."

The room fell quiet. My hands shook, and everyone stared at me. Clark came out of his office and put his arm around my shoulder. He jerked his chin at Jack. "Get her a glass of water. Jade, come inside and sit down. The rest of you, get busy. Clayton, check out Max Sims's latest credit card purchases."

Jack knocked on the closed office door, and Clark waved him in. He entered and placed the glass of water on the desk, then turned to leave.

"Jack, have a seat," Clark said. "I'm putting you two in charge of Max Sims, nobody else. You don't need to worry about any other task or case—only Max. You'll be in charge of following up with other law enforcement agencies when tips come in. Keep the news stations active on his case. Get flyers out, hold a press conference, and do whatever you need to do. We're going to flush him out of his hole. I don't care where he's hiding. Got it?"

I stared down at my folded hands in my lap. "Got it, sir, but I have to go apologize to Clayton first."

"He's a big boy. No apology necessary. If he can dish it out, he can take it too. Drink your water, regroup, and dig in."

I was ashamed. I'd lost my cool, and to one of my own colleagues, no less. Jack and I exited Clark's office, and everyone looked up. I sat at my desk and began a list of things I needed to do. Clayton rose and walked over. He took a seat in my guest chair.

"Jade?"

"Yeah, Chad?"

"First off, I'm sorry."

I smiled sheepishly. "I am too. My outburst was uncalled for."

"And I was an insensitive jerk."

I chuckled. "Okay, we both were. So what have you got?"

"You were right. Max Sims did use his credit card just yesterday. He purchased a one-way bus ticket under the passenger name Josh Manyard."

"Where was it going?"

"To Denver."

"No kidding? Did you print out the information?"

He handed me the sheet of paper that sat on his lap. "It's right here. The bus left at seven this morning. It doesn't stop until it gets to Burlington, Iowa, at five p.m. The passengers have dinner there, and then another driver takes over until they reach Denver. The bus pulls into the Denver station at four thirty tomorrow morning."

"Okay, thanks, Clayton. I'll take it from here."

I called the Burlington, Iowa, police department and explained everything there was to know about Max Sims, then I faxed them a copy of the sketch Marie had drawn. The police would be waiting at the station for that bus to arrive, and they'd check every passenger that disembarked. I felt a sense of relief for now. I still wanted to see that video footage of Max actually boarding the bus. I called the bus station downtown and asked about their video surveillance. They told me two Milwaukee police officers had picked up the tape an hour earlier. They said they'd have their tech department clean up the grainy image of the passengers the best they could. I called the downtown precinct and asked for the tech department. I explained who I was, wrote down the names of the officers that picked up the tape, and thanked them. I'd go through the proper channels and have the officers get in touch with me. I left my contact information with them. They would either confirm or refute the identity of the individual in question. Once again, my hands were tied. I couldn't pursue Max Sims on my own.

Chapter 52

That should keep North Bend's finest busy for a while.

Max climbed off the bus when it made an unscheduled stop. A pregnant woman on board felt ill and needed to use the ladies' room. The bus pulled into a truck stop to wait, and the driver called out that this would be only a ten-minute stop. The scheduled fuel stop would be in Naperville, Illinois. If anyone needed to disembark, they should do it quickly. Inside the diner and gift shop, passengers quickly used the lavatories and bought snacks before returning to the bus. One seat remained empty when the bus took to the freeway again.

Max stared out the window at the bus until its taillights disappeared. Once he was satisfied it was gone, he approached the counter attendant and asked if any bus lines that went to Milwaukee stopped at their location. She explained that the Kenosha to Milwaukee bus line did, and she would be happy to look up the time for him.

"The next bus going north picks up passengers here at ten o'clock, sir. You have about an hour and a half before it arrives."

Max pulled off the cap and rubbed his bald head with the back of his forearm. "Yeah, that's good. I'll enjoy a leisurely breakfast while I wait. I'll take a ticket for one."

With his grand-slam breakfast and two cups of coffee finished, Max paid his tab and browsed the gift shop. He had twenty minutes to kill before the bus was scheduled to arrive. A book on the shelf caught his eye. The title, *Murderous Intentions*, almost made him laugh, so he bought it. The book would provide an hour of reading entertainment while he rode the bus back to Milwaukee.

Max heard the air brakes engage as the northbound bus slowed to a stop. He looked out the window. Several passengers exited the bus while others waited their turn to climb aboard. Max went outside and stood in line. Once inside and seated, Max watched as the driver closed the door, walked the aisle, and collected the tickets from the new passengers. Max handed his to the man, got comfortable, and opened the book. He'd probably get through ten chapters if he was lucky. He caught himself a few times when his head bobbed and hit his chest. Next thing he knew, he woke to the sound of the brakes hiss as the bus pulled into the Milwaukee station. He rolled his neck and yawned—the book had fallen into his lap. He remembered reading through chapter four. Tonight he'd pick up where he left off.

Max exited the bus and flagged down one of many taxis parked along the curb. He climbed in and, twenty minutes later, was dropped off at the Northside Motel, his most recent residence. He went inside to kill more time.

Chapter 53

My desk phone rang right as Jack and I were walking out. After lunch, we'd planned to meet with a few of the families whose loved ones had been identified. They had to decide what to do with the few bones that remained. The logical suggestion would be cremation and a memorial service.

"Hold up, Jack. I better see who's calling." I walked back to my desk and answered as I grabbed a sheet of paper and a pen.

"Hello, Sergeant Jade Monroe speaking. How can I help you?" I sat in my chair and listened.

An Officer Brad Littner from the downtown Milwaukee precinct was calling. He and Officer Pat Reynolds were the two that had picked up the videotape in question. Comparing it side by side with the image and description of Max Sims led them to believe he was indeed the man that boarded the bus.

"Is it possible for you to email me a video file of that tape so I can see it myself? I know this man personally, and I'd like to be one hundred percent certain it's him."

"Absolutely, Sergeant, I just need the email address you use on your work computer."

I gave it to Officer Littner and thanked him. He told me the file would be coming within minutes.

"Jack, have a seat. I want to see this video before we go anywhere."

"Coffee, then?"

"Sure, thanks."

I tapped my fingers on the desk and waited as I constantly refreshed the screen. The email finally showed up as the most recent one in my in-box.

"Here it is." I sat straight up in my chair and whispered a short prayer. "Please, God, let it be him."

I clicked on the file. Everyone crowded at my back and watched over my shoulder. The technical department at the downtown precinct had done a great job of cleaning up the footage. The man's height compared to the other passengers seemed correct. If this was indeed Max, his size was right. I paused the footage when he looked toward the camera. I slid the zoom bar to the right. I knew the more I zoomed in, the fuzzier the image would become. I only needed a little more clarification. The man wore a baseball cap, making it more difficult to see his face, but I could say with eighty percent certainty he was Max.

"Okay, guys, your opinions? I don't want to go by wishful thinking." I looked at each face that surrounded me.

"You and Jack are the ones that saw Max up close and personal. What's your gut telling you?" Clark asked.

"Jack?"

"I agree. I think it's Max."

"Okay, I'm going to call the Burlington, Iowa, police department again and tell them it's a positive ID. They need to have all hands on deck and be extremely careful when they apprehend him. There are other passengers to consider."

Clark spoke up. "Tell them to wait until he's off the bus and separated from everyone else. Nobody wants this to turn into a hostage situation."

"Roger that, boss." I dialed Burlington, Iowa, again.

After the phone call, Jack and I headed out. We had four families to talk to that afternoon. We stopped at Bub's Bar and Grill for lunch since it was on our way out of town. The hostess seated us, and the waitress brought two glasses of water to our table. Once our order was in and the waitress had left, Jack spoke up.

"Can I be candid with you?"

His question took me by surprise. "Well, sure, I guess. Is this about earlier with Clayton?"

Jack sighed and took in a deep breath. "Jade, don't go off the rails about Max Sims. What makes him so different than the other criminals we've captured?"

"Just that—he *hasn't* been captured, and he's a serious menace to society. I'm not going to rest until he's behind bars. How many people do you think have died at his hands?"

Jack shrugged. "I know, he's super dangerous. Between Max and Darryl, there could be twenty, maybe more."

"That's exactly right. I'm glad Clark handed him to us.

Now, I can focus entirely on Max Sims. With any luck, he'll be apprehended tonight and brought back to Wisconsin to stand trial for multiple murders."

Jack nodded.

I waited to continue until the waitress left. She brought our burgers to the table, refilled our coffees, and then walked away. I leaned forward toward Jack. "I wonder if Darryl intends to make the four o'clock call. Maybe he already knows Max has left the area."

"Even if he does, we won't get the taped audio file from WSPF for days. Do you have any idea how many convicts use those pay phones on a daily basis?"

"All of them?" I asked, half joking.

"Damn near. Red tape slows things down."

We finished lunch and forty-five minutes later, were back in the cruiser and on our way to the first home. We were about to begin the difficult discussions with family members that had waited years for news of their loved ones.

There was nothing we could do about Max Sims until tonight when we got word that he was in custody.

Chapter 54

We ended the conversations with the families at four thirty and headed back to the station. I was excited, yet nervous, to hear the news of how the apprehension went. I didn't want anything to go wrong. The bus was scheduled to arrive at the Burlington station in a half hour.

Jack and I entered the bull pen. He took his seat, and I poured out the stale morning coffee and started a new pot. I did whatever I could to stay busy for the next twenty-five minutes. The light on my desk phone flashed, indicating I had a message. I checked it. A call came in from Amber, wanting to know if I'd be home for dinner and telling me not to forget about our scheduled appointment at the shooting range at seven o'clock.

I made a quick call back to her. "Hey, sis, I should be home by six at the latest."

She sighed into the phone. "Good to hear. I was hoping you wouldn't cancel on Dad and me. I made a tuna casserole for dinner with garlic bread and green beans."

"That sounds delicious. I'll see you in a bit." With my

desk phone's receiver back on the cradle, I checked the time again. Fifteen minutes to go. "This is torture," I said as I rose from my chair and poured coffee for everyone. I looked at my emails, shuffled papers on my desk, inspected my cuticles, and drummed my fingers. A few minutes after five, my desk phone rang. Clark gave me a nod, and I answered, then hit the speakerphone button. "Sergeant Jade Monroe speaking, how can I help you?"

"Sergeant Monroe, this is Captain Frank Black calling from the Burlington, Iowa, police department. We're at the main bus terminal right now. All of my officers were staged at different spots with a clear view of the bus that just came in from Milwaukee. Your suspect never disembarked with the other passengers."

"You can't be serious! Did your officers board the bus and check every seat?"

"We did, ma'am, and he wasn't there. He must have left the bus during one of the fuel stops and never got back on."

I felt like ripping my eyeballs out and my head began to pound. I had to take a few deep gulps of air to calm myself.

"Captain, do you know where the fuel stops are?"

"My officers are talking to the driver right now. We're digging into that information. Would you like a callback when we know more?"

"Absolutely. Please take down my cell phone number too, and thank you, sir." I hung up and buried my face in my hands. "That son of a bitch got away again."

The lieutenant coughed into his hand and cleared his throat. "Jade, you have plans with your pop tonight.

Tomorrow is going to be an early morning because of his surgery. I'd suggest you take the entire day off. You're going to drive yourself crazy with all this pressure. Jack can keep you updated hour by hour if necessary."

I glanced at Jack—he nodded. "It's the right thing to do, Jade. I promise to keep you abreast of the news as it comes in."

Clark jerked his head toward the door. "That's an order, Monroe. Go home and be with your family."

I sucked in more air to clear my head. "Okay, boss, you win. My dad's surgery will take a few hours." I pointed at Jack. "I'm calling you as soon as they wheel him into the operating room."

"You got it, partner. I'll talk to you tomorrow."

I packed up my belongings and dropped my phone into my purse. "See you guys on Wednesday."

I walked out into the fresh evening air and paused. I took in the coolness against my skin—it felt good, and I needed to be revived.

Be in the moment, like Jack said. It's all we have, anyway.

The rest of the night, I put all my energy into my dad and sister. We had a delicious dinner, then went to the shooting range for an hour. I was happy to see how much Dad enjoyed his time with us. Our laughter lit up the shooting lanes as Amber bragged about her skills and Dad fed right into it. He was in his element, and his face radiated with pride to see how his daughters had followed in his footsteps. I had to admit, I was thankful that the lieutenant sent me home. It felt good to get Max out of my head and put all of my focus on my family, at least for the next full day.

That night, before I turned off my bedside lamp, I made a final call to Jack.

"Hey, partner. Sorry, I know I'm a pest."

"Nah—don't worry about it."

I yawned into the phone. "Anything on the fuel stops?"

"I guess the only scheduled fuel stop was in Naperville, Illinois. They were going to pull up the video footage to see if anyone that looked like Max got off the bus and didn't get back on. We're still waiting for confirmation. Get some sleep, Jade. You sound beat."

"Okay, I'll talk to you in the morning."

"Tell your old man I said good luck."

"Will do. Good night." I clicked off and set my phone on the nightstand.

Chapter 55

I woke to my alarm clock buzzing at five forty-five. It was set only as a backup plan since I was certain Amber was dressed and already making breakfast. We were both taking the day off to be at our dad's side.

From my bedroom, I heard Dad and Amber talking in the kitchen. She apologized for cooking in front of him. He said she shouldn't worry about it. Since he had to fast before surgery, Dad was limited to hot tea and nothing else.

With my bathrobe and slippers on, I entered the kitchen and joined them. A cup of coffee sat on the breakfast bar, waiting my arrival. The cream, in a small stoneware pitcher, sat next to it.

"I swear, you should own a bed-and-breakfast, Amber. You're the best hostess ever." I kissed my sister's cheek and walked to the table, where I kissed my dad. "How'd you sleep, Dad?"

"Like a baby."

"Yeah, I never understood that analogy. I thought babies woke up at all hours of the night." I chuckled and sipped my coffee. "I hope you're making something simple, Amber. I'd hate to rub Dad's nose in the fact that we're eating in front of him."

"I'm making oatmeal."

"That'll work."

After eating and showering, we left the house at six forty. St. Joseph's Community Hospital was five miles door to door. After Dad filled out his paperwork, he was ushered into a room where they prepped him for surgery. Amber and I were allowed to wait with him once his IV was hooked up and he was comfortable. Dr. Dumont entered the prep room and shook our hands. He gave me a few minutes of ribbing and told my dad what a horrible patient I was last summer when he had to stitch up my foot after the dog bite. He chuckled, then went into the explanation of Dad's surgery, what it entailed and what to expect afterward. He said he would be in the recovery room when Dad woke up and go over the post-op instructions. He shook our hands once more and left.

"It's time, Mr. Monroe," the nurse said. "I'm going to start the sedative in your IV. You'll get sleepy very quickly. Ladies." She pointed at the exit.

"Okay, bye, Dad. Good luck." I kissed him and waited at the door.

"We'll see you in recovery, Daddy." Amber kissed him too, then we left.

Downstairs in the cafeteria, we bought two coffees and two doughnuts, then sat at a table facing the serenity garden. It was peaceful and calm.

“I hope Daddy won’t be bored at home afterward.”

“The alternative would be worse, Amber. He’d be alone, and he wouldn’t have any help. He’ll be fine. Dad is a tough old codger, and he’ll be as good as new before he leaves to go back to California.”

“Jade, what’s this talk about moving? I don’t want you to leave.” Amber cupped my hand with hers. “I can’t join the FBI until I have a few years of law enforcement under my belt. I was hoping to join the sheriff’s department and work with you and the guys. I know everyone already. It would be awesome to work together.”

I smiled. “You wouldn’t be a detective right away. The reality is, you’d likely have your butt planted in a cruiser all day, pulling over speeders on the freeway.”

“I don’t mind. You have to start somewhere. Kate can join the sheriff’s department too.”

“Sure, she could. You’d both be great deputies. Do you remember the name of the agent Dad talked about in the serial crimes unit?”

“You mean his friend, the supervisory special agent in the FBI?”

“Yeah, that guy.”

“Um…” Amber stared at the ceiling. “Oh yeah, his name is Dave Spencer. I ought to write that down so I don’t forget. Why?”

“Just a thought. Maybe I’ll give him a call.”

“On my behalf?”

“Not exactly. I’ll be back in a sec, hon. I need to get an update from Jack.” I exited through the glass doors and entered the serenity garden. I sat on a bench among flower beds and called Jack.

"Hey, Jade, calling for your update?"

"You know I am. What's the word?"

"Max is in the wind. He didn't show up in the footage at the Naperville fuel stop. Nobody that fits his description exited the bus. The driver didn't make any stops after that until they arrived in Burlington, and you know the rest."

"How is that possible?"

"I don't know. All we can do is push the news channels to keep airing the segment, do a write-up for the paper, and hold a press conference. Let's work on that tomorrow. We'll distribute more flyers too."

"Damn it. It isn't like he's going to walk into a local police station and turn himself in anytime soon. I guess we have to do what we can."

"How's your old man?"

"He's in surgery right now. Dr. Dumont gave me a hard time."

Jack laughed. "And rightfully so. You were a pain in the ass last year when you had your bum foot."

"Whatever. Anyway, I have to get back to Amber and do some sister bonding while I have the time."

"Sounds good, and call me after your dad wakes up."

I clicked off and slid my phone into my back pocket, then went inside where Amber was waiting. She faced the TV that was mounted on the wall in the cafeteria. The channel was turned to the news.

"See anything about Max?" I asked as I took a seat.

"No, this is CNN, not a local station. They've been showing a huge storm that's heading down from Canada. We're supposed to get severe wind and rain throughout the afternoon and evening."

"Seriously? I guess I haven't paid any attention to the forecast. As a matter of fact, other than the broadcasts about Max, I don't think I've watched TV for a few days. The storm sounds bad." I glanced out the window and saw heavy cloud cover moving in from the north.

"That's what they're saying. At least we'll have Daddy home and snuggled in before the rain starts. After we get him home, I'll run out and pick up more food and fill his prescriptions. I'm thinking he'll do best on the recliner, that way he'll be in the middle of everything. If he wants something to eat or drink, he can tell one of us, and he'll have the TV remote next to him too."

"Good idea—that's if the power doesn't go out." I stood and tipped my head. "Come on. Let's head back to the waiting area." I grabbed a stack of gossip magazines as I passed the rack. We still had an hour-and-a-half wait.

Chapter 56

"Daddy, how are you doing?" Amber sat next to our dad as he lay in the reclined recovery chair. Blankets covered him to his chin.

"What?" His heavy eyelids barely opened and then closed again.

I watched him as he gradually woke up. His face was as white as a sheet, and he was still very groggy. Several heated blankets covered his entire body. The nurse came in and switched out the top blanket for a newly warmed one. I checked his monitors. His heart rate and pulse were strong.

"Let's give him a minute, sis. He's still out of it."

We sat for another fifteen minutes. I read the latest gossip about famous celebrities, and Amber scrolled through her cell phone.

"Hey, girls." My dad's voice sounded thick, and he spoke slowly.

"Your surgery is over, Dad. The doctor should be in soon to talk to us. I know you're pretty groggy, but we'll listen to every word he says."

"That's good. Thanks, honey."

"He'll give you a release instruction sheet, anyway, and Amber has volunteered to pick up any meds he might prescribe."

My dad reached out and squeezed Amber's hand.

"You're going to be dancing with me in a week, you know," she teased. "We're going to light up the family room, play some hip-hop, and let it rip."

He coughed when he laughed. "That sounds like a plan, kiddo."

Dr. Dumont entered the recovery room. "Tom, I see you're waking up. How do you feel?"

"Like I've had too many Brandy Old Fashioneds."

Dr. Dumont laughed. "Now I know where Jade gets her personality. Anyway, the surgery went fine—no complications. You'll be on crutches for a few weeks. I know these two are going to be hovering." He raised his right eyebrow at Amber and me. "But you do need to get up and exercise, so ladies, don't hover too much."

I nodded.

"No driving for those two weeks, either. After you see me again, if everything looks good, I'll get you fitted with a knee brace. That will be on for six weeks, but you can go about your business and walk without the crutches. Mind your manners and you'll get a release from me to go back to work at the two-week mark."

"Understood. Thank you, doctor."

Dr. Dumont handed me the post-op instruction sheet. "Make sure he follows this religiously. Here's the prescription for an anti-inflammatory and a mild pain pill. I'll see you in two weeks, Tom." He shook our hands before he walked out. "Make sure to set up your next appointment with my nurse."

The nurse entered the room, took Dad's blood pressure and pulse, and asked him what he'd like to eat and drink. She offered him a choice of cranberry juice, apple juice, or water, and a granola bar or pretzels.

"I think I've had enough pretzels for a while. I'll take the granola bar and apple juice, please."

"You got it, Mr. Monroe." She looked back from the door. "Need another warm blanket?"

"Yeah, that sounds good too."

After dad had spent an hour in recovery, a young man from the orthopedic department came in to measure Dad for crutches.

"Mr. Monroe, I'm going to lower the footrest on the recovery chair for a few minutes. When you're sure you don't feel dizzy, I want you to stand for me."

"Yeah, okay."

Dad pushed back the blankets and sat on the edge of the chair. He nodded, and Amber and I helped him stand. I glanced at his right knee. Thick bandages wrapped multiple times made it as big as a football.

"Okay, sir, I just need to adjust these crutches to your height and position them properly under your arms. Got it. Okay, you can sit back down."

Dad did, and I raised the footrest and covered him back up.

The nurse returned a few minutes later with his release papers and the appointment reminder card.

"I'll get you a wheelchair, Mr. Monroe. You can get dressed and leave as soon as you feel up to it."

Chapter 57

Max sat on the threadbare chair cushion and faced the television. He leaned forward and watched the weather forecast with his head propped between his hands and his elbows on his knees.

Static and pixilation scrambled nearly every channel. Max rose and pulled the wand on the blinds. He peered out at the ominous sky through the smudge covered window. Bending tree branches indicated the wind force had increased at an alarming rate. Max reached for his cup of coffee and turned his focus back to the television screen.

Through the choppy weather report and the TV's abrupt freeze-frame, he got the gist of what to expect from the approaching storm. People were advised to stay indoors, avoid low areas due to flash floods, and watch for downed power lines if they had to venture out. High winds and torrential rain was expected to begin right after sunset.

Humph—sounds like my kind of night. Nobody's focus will be on me since everyone will be glued to their television set and watching the weather channel.

Max thought back to the call he'd received yesterday afternoon. Darryl's hearty laughter echoed through the phone lines when he talked to Max. He used his words cautiously, especially when he explained who his most recent visitor was.

"Lies, lies, lies, that's all they do. I put that bitch right in her place, then she stormed out. She was caught in the act of being a bald-faced liar, and she couldn't handle it. I wish you could have seen her expression—it was priceless." Darryl mentioned again how pleased he was with the outcome of the most recent events, and now, he stressed the urgency for Max to finish task number two.

"I've been thinking about different scenarios that might work out well for this assignment. I aim to please you, Pa."

"You'll please me real good when number eight happens."

Max checked the code on the sheet of paper spread out on his lap. Number eight asked when the second set of instructions would be completed.

Max responded, "Number eight will take place before our next conversation."

"Very good—I'll touch base on Friday."

Back in the moment, Max began scratching out notes. He had a task, a short time to complete it, and now he needed a plan. He lifted the coffee cup to his mouth, took a sip, and then rubbed the tic above his left eye.

Chapter 58

I backed my car into the garage so Dad could get out on the side closest to the door that led into the kitchen.

"Amber, jump out and help Dad with his crutches. I'll come around and open the kitchen door and make sure Spaz is out of the way."

It proved difficult to get Dad up the two concrete steps that went from the garage floor to the kitchen, but with our help, he made it.

"Daddy, do you need to use the bathroom before you get comfortable on the recliner?"

I grinned when I saw my dad's face blush bright red.

He stammered out a thank-you, then hobbled in the direction of the powder room, the closest bathroom to the family room. He closed the door behind him.

I chuckled. "Did you see Dad blush?"

"Yeah, I guess there's a first time for everything. I'll get him some blankets and his bed pillow."

Once Dad was comfortable on the recliner with the remote and a cup of coffee within reach, Amber left to fill his prescriptions and get a few groceries. I took that time to call the lieutenant and check in.

"Hi, boss, what's new?"

"Nothing on this end, Jade. How's your pop?"

"He's relaxing. The surgery went fine, and Amber just stepped out to fill his prescriptions. Any word on Max's whereabouts?"

"The bus driver is being interviewed again. I guess he was a bit dumbfounded last night with all the police presence. He's back in Milwaukee, and several of the guys from the downtown precinct are going over the course of events with him again." Clark sighed. "We aren't giving up, Jade. If we keep the pressure on him, he'll slip up."

"Is Jack putting together anything for the press conference?"

"Hold on."

I heard Clark yell to Jack in the bull pen.

"He wants to talk to you himself. I'll transfer the call. Tell your old man we have to get together over the weekend."

"I will, boss. You're welcome here anytime."

I waited as Clark transferred me over to Jack's desk phone.

"Hey, partner. Is your dad safe and sound at home now?"

"Yeah, we just got in about a half hour ago. How's the press conference speech going?"

"Slowly. I've been pushing the news stations to keep showing Max's face. They're balking a little."

"Why would they do that?" I passed my dad's chair and noticed he had fallen asleep. I turned the TV off and went to talk in my bedroom.

"Because there's a big storm brewing, and they want to focus on that. They said we haven't given them anything new to report on Max now that he's off the grid."

I huffed. "Great. I'll put something together myself. It isn't like I'm going anywhere. Why don't you focus on the news stations and take a bunch of flyers to *City News*? Talk them into inserting them in tomorrow's paper."

"Good idea, Jade. I'll do that right now before the weather turns. So you'll take care of putting the press conference together?"

"Absolutely, and I'll start on it right now while it's quiet in the house."

I hung up and snuggled on the couch with a blanket, a cup of coffee, and my legal pad. I began to write the profile of our most recent serial killer, Max Sims.

After an hour of fervent writing, which included plenty of disturbing adjectives describing Max, I had put together a three-page profile that I planned to present in a press conference tomorrow. I looked forward to it, and I prayed it would give Max plenty of publicity. I sent a quick text off to Jack to alert our local columnists and TV stations that I'd hold the press conference at the sheriff's department tomorrow at two p.m.

A text came in from Amber saying she was almost home. My help with the grocery bags would be greatly appreciated. I got up and crossed the kitchen to the garage door and opened it. I hit the button on the wall and lifted the overhead right as Amber pulled into the driveway. She gave me the thumbs-up as she slid her car in next to mine and parked.

"Great timing, sis. I think the storm is about to start. I heard plenty of rumbling coming from the north, and the sky is really getting black. The lightning just began too."

"Then it's a good night to hunker down and play cards with Dad after dinner. I'm thinking of something decadent for dessert."

She smirked. "Mind reader. I picked up a box of double-fudge brownies with nuts."

After that two-hour nap, Dad looked better, the color came back to his face, and he seemed relatively comfortable. I helped Amber in the kitchen while he tracked the latest news reports on this storm that was intensifying by the minute. Rain pelted the windows, and the glass sliders chattered when a direct wind gust slammed against them. I had the police scanner tuned to the North Bend stations.

"It's getting bad out there, girls. Do you have flashlights and candles in case the power goes out?"

I flipped on the deck lights and peered out at the woods. Thin branches had snapped under the constant wind pressure and hung to the ground. "Sure do, Dad. I'll gather a few things after dinner. Let's get busy, sis. I'd hate for the electricity to go out in the middle of cooking."

"I'm on it," Amber said. "It'll be ready in ten minutes."

I set the table then checked on Dad. "Do you need a pain pill yet? If you do, you should take it with food."

"Yeah, my knee is starting to throb."

"Okay, I'll get it." I placed a glass of water and a Tramadol tablet on the table where my dad would sit, then I helped him off the recliner. "Here are your crutches."

Amber dished up the chicken Alfredo and set a tossed salad on the table. Dinner was delicious, and the brownies were too. Dad listened as Amber explained everything she was learning at the academy. I saw pride spread across his face.

I cleared the table after dinner and set out a deck of cards. Amber placed the flashlight on the breakfast bar—just in case. The lights had already flickered a few times. Lightning cracked so hard it sounded as if it had hit a tree in the woods.

Dad looked toward the sliders. "Geez, it's really getting nasty out there."

Amber squeezed his hand. "Your call, Daddy. What do you want to play?"

He rubbed his hands together briskly in his typical gesture. He had full confidence he would win. "Texas Hold'em, of course."

The scanner crackled and came to life right as we started the game. My ears perked as I listened to the code on the 9-1-1 call. Dispatch alerted deputies to the scene. The caller said a crazed, tall man wielding a knife had just attacked him in his house. He was bleeding badly.

"What the hell!" I jumped from the table and called Jack. "Did you just hear that report? It could be Max."

"I'm already on my way."

"What's the location?"

"Jade."

"Jack, I swear to God—"

"Okay, okay, it's off of Highway 60 going west, 4290 Timberline Road."

I clicked off and grabbed my gun, rain jacket, purse, and phone. I looked at my dad and sister and hated the fact that I was leaving. "Amber, keep your eye on Dad. That pain pill could make him woozy. Are you two going to be okay?"

Dad waved me off with a laugh. "Stop hovering—we'll be fine. Just go, honey, and be careful out in that weather. Make sure you catch that maniac, and do your old man proud."

With a final look back, I ran out, pressed the overhead, and jumped in my car. The rain and wind would slow my drive a bit—the roads were slick, and the visibility was bad.

I prayed out loud as I left the subdivision and headed to the highway. "Please, God, let this be Max, and please don't let the caller die."

Chapter 59

Max retreated deeper into the dense woods and took cover. He could have been seen when she turned on the deck lights. He was lucky—that would have ruined his surprise. Now, as he watched her speed away to that crank call of the nearly fatal knife attack, he had all the time in the world to complete task number two.

He secured the hood of his black rain slicker over the headlamp he wore. Even though he was soaked through and through, having the hood up was still a small improvement. He'd improvise and cut the electricity himself since the storm hadn't cooperated enough to cause a power outage yet. He knew exactly where the electric box was located after that surveillance mission on Sunday.

Max went through the process in his mind again. Jade was gone, and that left the sister and Tom Monroe in the house alone. He remembered going through Amber's room and seeing the police academy manual and textbooks on her desk. He knew the protocol—every student had to have their own handgun. She would need to be disabled first, and quickly. The old man had just had knee surgery, so he was useless—cop or no cop. Max chuckled at the image in his mind. He thought back to that afternoon when he'd watched Jade and Amber from a distance. They wheeled the pathetic Tom Monroe out of the hospital and into Jade's waiting car. The old man wouldn't pose a problem—he'd be lucky if he could even stand on his own.

Max used the trees as cover and stayed in the shadows while he inched closer to the house. The electricity and phone cables were located on the west outer wall of the condo. He'd cut the lines for both to be on the safe side. That would leave only the cell phones—he'd have to move quickly and destroy them.

When he was close enough, he slunk down and ran for the side of the house. His wire cutter and skinning knife filled the large left pocket of the rain slicker, and the ball gag and rope filled the right. A stubby claw hammer with finger grips hung from the loop in his cargo pants. Max lowered the hood on the slicker and illuminated the headlamp while he snipped wires at the electric box. Within seconds the house went black.

He moved quickly and charged up the steps to the deck, then with the force of a two-hundred-seventy-five-pound man and all his might, he kicked the slider. Glass sprayed in every direction, and shards shot throughout the family room.

Amber screamed and ran to the kitchen. Tom yelled out and fell to the floor when he tried to stand under his own weight. The crutches were beyond his reach.

A cell phone sitting on the side table next to the recliner caught Max's eye when his light beam hit it. Tom tried tipping the table toward him, but Max was much quicker. He threw the phone to the floor and stomped it with his heavy boot, then went after Amber.

She stumbled through the blackness and crashed into the closed bedroom door, stunning herself for a second. Max was only steps behind her. She turned the knob and ran into her bedroom then slammed the door at her back, but she was no match against the strength of his enormous body. Max powered through that wooden barrier and shattered the frame, leaving Amber with nothing to use as cover. She frantically felt for something, anything that would protect her against that monster. In less than a second, Max was on her and threw her violently against the wall. She fell quiet.

Tom's yelling was of little help. The torrential rain and wind silenced his cries. Lightning strikes and rolling thunder drowned out his pleas for mercy. Max returned to the family room after finding Amber's cell phone and gun. He jammed the gun into his pants pocket and stomped the phone. His focus returned to Tom Monroe. It was time to complete task number two.

"Get in that chair, old man, and sit your ass down."

"Who are you, and what do you want? I'll give you anything, just leave us alone. Amber, Amber! Can you hear me, honey?"

Max laughed. "The bitch can't hear anything. Now get in that chair like I told you to."

Max watched as Tom limped to the recliner and sat down. "So you have no idea who I am?"

Tom shielded his eyes from the bright headlamp. He couldn't see who was behind the light. "No, I have no idea who you are! What did you do to my daughter?"

"I'm not here to talk about your youngest bitch daughter, Tom. I'm here for you, and only you. You do remember twenty years ago when you testified against Darryl Sims, don't you? You and Judge Gardino sent him to prison for life."

"But that was two decades ago. He deserved to be sent to prison. He murdered his wife and mother-in-law, for crissakes."

"What you didn't know is that he killed plenty more than those two. They were just the last ones." Max cocked his head and smirked at the anxiety written across Tom's face. "Darryl Sims taught me everything I know. He's somebody very close to my heart and the one calling the shots. As a matter of fact, he says hello, and since he can't be here to exact revenge himself, being locked up and all, I'm going to fulfill his long-overdue requests. I'm Max Sims, Tom, Darryl's son, and I'm here to kill you."

Max leaned in and straddled the recliner. He hovered over Tom and pressed him deeper into the chair. With his fist coiled back, Max punched Tom's face hard and fast and knocked him unconscious. He wrapped the rope around Tom several times and knotted it behind the recliner. Max wanted the scene to look perfect when Jade arrived home and found her father. He pulled the ball gag from his pocket and jammed it into Tom's mouth, then secured it behind his head. With a final look of approval and a click of his cell phone camera, he plunged the skinning knife into Tom's gut and ended his life.

In the kitchen, Max yanked out drawers until he found paper and a pen. With the pad of paper on the breakfast bar, he wrote a note to Jade.

Tit for tat—isn't that what they say, Sergeant Monroe? You should have stayed home and protected your family with that big gun of yours. Now that guilt can be your very own prison sentence. It's a real shame, you know—your old man could have been a worthy adversary if it wasn't for that bum knee of his. I wonder who will be next. How about you, Jade? Wanna play?

Max read the note twice and decided it was perfect. He placed it on Tom's bloody chest, walked through the shards of glass, and disappeared into the stormy night.

Chapter 60

The deputies surrounded the two-story residence on Timberline Road and moved in. Lights shined through the lower level windows and indicated that somebody had been there, or still was. One car stood parked in the driveway near the garage. With every side of the house covered, Jack, three deputies, and I approached the front door. I turned the knob—it was locked. With our guns drawn, I nodded and kicked in the door.

A startled man, woman, and two children jumped at the sight of us rushing the family room.

"What the hell is going on?" the man yelled out as he shielded his family.

I pointed at the two adults. "You and you, get on the floor, now. Deputy Knowles, get these kids out of here." I waved off the other deputies. "Search this house top to bottom and have the guys outside search the perimeter." Deputy Knowles took the crying children to another room while I did a quick scan of the immediate area. Nothing seemed amiss.

Jack called the deputies stationed outside. "Make sure everything is clear, including that shed out back." He knelt over the man and woman on the floor. "What's your names, and who called in the knife attack?"

The man looked up at Jack. "Knife attack? What in the world are you talking about? Nobody from this house called in a knife attack. Who in their right mind would be outside on a night like this, anyway?"

"What are your names?"

"Jesse and Lynn Bryant. Our kids are Missy and Braden. What the hell is going on? You scared the shit out of us."

I spoke up. "I'll ask the questions, Mr. Bryant. Do you have a house phone?"

"No—just our cells."

"I need to see them now."

I turned when Deputy Knowles approached me. "Sergeant, the deputies cleared the house and grounds. Everything looks normal."

I nodded. "Both of you, get up. Deputy Knowles, pat them down."

"Is that really necessary?" Lynn asked.

I raised my brow and gave her a longer than necessary scowl. "Yes, it is."

"They're good, Sergeant."

"Okay, where are the cell phones? I need both of them now."

"May I?" Jesse asked as he jerked his chin toward the kitchen.

"Deputy, go with him."

Mr. Bryant and Deputy Knowles rounded the corner and returned a minute later. Jesse had both cell phones in his hand.

"They were on the chargers in case the power went out. We wanted fully charged phones. They've been in the kitchen for over an hour."

I took them and handed one to Jack. "Check the recent outgoing calls."

We both scrolled the call logs. There hadn't been an outgoing call since four o'clock on Jesse's phone and two o'clock on Lynn's.

I sighed with frustration. It wasn't Max after all. It was nothing more than a crank call by some idiot that sent us out on a wild-goose chase on the worst night of the season. We apologized to the Bryant family and left.

As the deputies climbed in their squad cars and drove away, Jack and I stood on the covered porch alone.

"What do you make of that call?" I asked. "Somebody just happened to think it was cool to send half of Washburn County out to a possible murder scene? I swear I'll never understand people."

Jack shook his head. "I hear you, partner." He squeezed my shoulder and tipped his head toward the cars. "Go home and get out of those wet clothes. Enjoy the rest of the night with your family. Tomorrow morning comes early enough, and we'll have a busy day ahead of us. Drive carefully, Jade."

"Yeah, see you bright and early." I ran to my car and climbed in. I'd be back in the thick of that card game in twenty minutes. I was sure my dad was winning.

I called Amber's phone as I drove. It went straight to voicemail.

Well, that's weird.

I called my dad's phone and his did the same, but I left a message, anyway. "Hey, Dad, ask Amber to make a pot of coffee. The call was a false alarm, I'm soaked, and a cup of coffee would taste really good right now. See you in a few minutes."

I tossed my phone on the passenger seat and continued on.

Ten minutes later, I turned into Ashbury Woods, and as I neared my house, I noticed all the lights were off. I looked left and right at the other homes in the cul-de-sac, and they all had electricity.

What the hell is going on? There's no way they went to bed already.

As I pulled into the driveway, I hit the button on the remote to open the overhead. Nothing happened.

Damn batteries.

I pressed the button again. It was as dead as a doornail.

"Oh for Pete's sake." I killed the engine and got out. I clicked the fob to lock my car and ran for the front door. As I fumbled with the house key, I realized the porch light was out too. I turned back and looked at all of the houses on the street one more time—fully lit. "Okay, I'm totally not understanding this." I unlocked the door, turned the knob, and stepped into the foyer. "Amber, what's going on?" I flipped the light switch up and down. The house was pitch black. "Dad? Amber? Where are you guys?"

I remembered Amber had placed the flashlight on the breakfast bar before I left. I felt my way through the dark with my outstretched hands. I bumped into drawers pulled out in the kitchen as I slid my hand along the breakfast bar for the flashlight. I finally felt its shape and wrapped my hand around it, then clicked it on. I turned around and did a quick scan with the light.

"What the hell?"

Every drawer in the kitchen was pulled out. Wind and rain blew through the family room. My gut instantly knotted with fear, and my heart pounded in my chest.

"Amber, Dad, where are you?" I screamed out their names but got no response.

I jammed the flashlight under my arm and pulled out my pistol. As I stepped around the breakfast bar, glass shards crunched under my feet. I flicked the light back and forth, then caught the image of the recliner. A double length of rope wrapped the chair and was tied at the back.

"No, no, no, no. Please, God, no, no, no!"

I ran to the chair and shined the light. The sight in front of me was indescribable. I screamed at the brutality and ached with pain at seeing my dad that way. I spun around and shined the light through the family room. I didn't see Amber anywhere.

"Amber, Amber! Please, God, Amber, where are you?"

I hugged the wall as I slunk down the hallway. The flashlight's beam hit Amber's phone, smashed and lying on the floor in front of her bedroom. Spaz hissed as he scurried past me. A low moan came from Amber's room. I shined the light at the broken door then panned the area. A glimmer of hope caught in my throat when I saw her. Amber lay under the window, wedged between her bed and the desk. She was alive but injured. I had to call for help.

"Amber, honey, don't try to move. I have to get my phone and call 9-1-1."

Tears blurred my vision as I raced back to the kitchen, where I'd dropped my purse. I wiped my eyes so I could see the numbers on my phone.

The operator answered at the police department's emergency number. "9-1-1, what is your emergency?"

I could barely talk, but my police training kicked in. I had to speak clearly so the operator could understand me. "This is Sergeant Jade Monroe with the sheriff's department. I need an ambulance at my house fast. One officer is down, and a civilian is badly injured. Hurry!" I gave them my address and hung up, then called the sheriff's department. I recognized Bob Kennedy's voice when he picked up at the dispatch desk. "Bob, it's Jade. I need everyone at my house immediately. It's an emergency. Get a generator too. There's no electricity here. I have an ambulance dispatched already. Bob, it's bad—really bad. Call Jack, call Clark, call everyone!"

I quickly cleared the house then ran back to Amber. A few minutes later, I heard the faint sound of sirens in the distance.

I comforted Amber through my sobs. "They're coming, honey. Just hang on for me. Dad would want you to fight."

I lay on the floor next to her and cradled her injured

body. I couldn't help my dad—it was too late for him, and my heart broke with agony. I didn't know if I could get through the pain.

The sound got closer, then broke through the roar of the thunder and lightning cracks. I heard the shrill siren outside, then people charged through the door. They were here—they'd save Amber, and I could take another breath.

Jack's voice was the first I recognized. "Jade, Jade, where are you?"

My sobs echoed through the hallway. "Jack, I'm in Amber's bedroom. She needs the EMTs."

I held the flashlight up so he could see us when he entered the room. The EMTs were right behind him.

"Over here, guys." Jack pointed at Amber then cleared a space for them to get through.

"Do you know what her injuries are, ma'am?"

"No, it's too dark, I can barely see anything." I screamed out through my tears. "We need some light in here!"

I heard Clark's voice in the family room as he was directing people in. "Get that generator going so we can see what we have. We need lights up, now!"

The sound of a gas engine started, and a few rooms lit up.

"Ma'am, we need you to step back so we can get her on a gurney."

Amber was moaning, and I was living my worst nightmare.

Clark yelled out orders from somewhere in the house. "Go through this house and make sure it's clear. Somebody get the electric company out here to restore power and call a repair service. I want this patio door sealed up, now!"

Jack helped me up and led me down the hall. I didn't want to see what lay ahead of us.

Clark stood in front of the recliner to block my view. He yelled out to Horbeck, "Get that blanket off the couch and cover Tom up. Holy Mother of God!"

My knees buckled beneath me. Jack helped me to a chair and sat me down. I buried my face in his shoulder and wept.

Chapter 61

Two days had passed since that devastating night. I sat in Amber's hospital room and held her hand while she slept. Our mom sat on a chair to my left. Amber would be okay, thank God. Her shoulder was dislocated, and the doctor wanted to monitor the head injury she'd sustained when she was thrown against the wall. The concussion left her with seven stitches in her hairline, and she was still confused and dizzy, but she was getting better. The doctor said she'd make a full recovery, she just needed time and rest.

My phone buzzed in my pocket. I pulled it out and checked the screen. A text from Jack said he was in the hallway by the nurses' station.

I stood and tiptoed toward the door. "I'll be back in a few minutes, Mom." I pulled the curtain closed behind me.

Jack saw me and headed my way. "Need a coffee?"

"Yeah, thanks."

We took the elevator to the lower level where the cafeteria was located. Jack bought two coffees, and we sat at the table facing the serenity garden. I remembered only a few days ago when Amber and I sat in the same spot while Dad had his surgery.

I broke down and cried. "Jack, what am I supposed to do? We have nothing on Max. There haven't been any sightings, there's no news. He killed my dad and nearly killed Amber, and now he's trying to pull me into his game—he's taunting me. You read that note. He wants me to come after him."

"Jade, let law enforcement do its job. Don't take this on by yourself."

I pounded the table and spilled my coffee. "Law enforcement didn't save Theresa Gardino and the countless others he's killed. Hell, I couldn't even save my own dad from that monster. I let that son of a bitch kill my dad, Jack." I buried my face in my hands. "I can't do what I need to do—I'm stuck within Washburn County boundaries."

Jack reached for my hand and squeezed it. "What does that mean?"

"I mean I'm resigning from the sheriff's department."

"Jade, give it some time. Your pain is so raw. It's too soon to make life-changing decisions, and Amber really needs you now. Judge Gardino just buried Theresa, and we still have to get through your dad's funeral. I'll help you figure out what to do about his home and belongings, but there's no rush. Let's take things one day at a time. I'll always be there for you. Just say the word—I'll help you with anything."

"I appreciate that, Jack, and I'm going to hold you to

that promise, but I've made up my mind. Tomorrow, I'm going to have the toughest conversation I've ever had in my life with Lieutenant Clark."

Chapter 62

We sat in the conference room together, just the lieutenant and me. I wanted to keep our conversation private. I knew everyone would be watching through the wall of glass if we had conducted our meeting in the lieutenant's office.

We took the first half hour discussing necessities. How was Amber? Did I call about getting an alarm system installed? Did I order new glass and wrought-iron patio doors?

We discussed the funeral plans for my dad. The mention of him being dead still made my breath catch in my throat. I could barely talk about it without breaking down or becoming physically ill.

Many of Dad's colleagues from the San Bernardino County Sheriff's Department were flying in for the services. He would have a formal police escort all the way to the cemetery by the North Bend police and sheriff's departments.

"What about your dad's home, Jade?"

"I'll figure it out in time. His mortgage was paid off, so for now I'll hire a service to keep an eye on the place. Boss—"

"I'm not sure I want to hear what you're going to say, Monroe."

I gave him a weak smile. "Jack's already clued you in?"

"Tell me you aren't resigning."

"I can't. I have to do what I have to do. Other than going rogue, which I won't, I need to spread my reach a little farther—like the entire United States."

"So, what are you saying?"

"Originally I thought of going to California, living with my dad, and joining his department or southern California's local branch of the FBI. I know it's something Amber wants to do down the road too."

Clark nodded. "I've heard her mention that."

I wiped my eyes. "I guess there's no need to go to California anymore. Boss, this is something my gut has been telling me to do. I've already spoken with a friend of my dad's from the FBI. Dave Spencer is his name, and he's a supervisory special agent in the serial crimes unit. He's here for Dad's funeral, and we met up last night. He was sure he could pull the right strings to get me located at the Milwaukee field office after my training is complete. Having their resources at my disposal is the only way to put Max Sims away for good. I'll never be able to do my dad justice and honor his legacy unless I catch his killer."

Clark handed me a tissue.

"Please don't make it harder on me, boss, by trying to talk me out of it."

"I understand your reasoning, Jade, but being in the FBI

isn't necessarily going to give you Max Sims on a silver platter."

"I know that, but I will find him, and when I do—"

"Jade, I don't want to hear the rest of that sentence. Your job as a public servant is to uphold the law." Clark got up and closed the door. "You do understand that, don't you? Tell me you aren't going vigilante."

"I won't—I'm just venting, but I do have a request, if you don't mind."

"Go ahead."

"Amber and Kate have both expressed their desire to work under your supervision when they finish the academy."

"Consider it done. They'll make fine deputies. What about Jack? He'll need a new partner."

"I think Horbeck would be a good fit."

Clark rubbed his chin and sighed. "You were a good fit. Jack is going to take this really hard."

"Boss, I'm not leaving North Bend. I'll just buy warmer winter wear."

He chuckled.

"We'll still get together for patio parties in the summer and dinners anytime. You know what a great cook Amber is."

"That is true. What about Amber while you're at Quantico?"

"I'd like her to stay at my mom's house until I get back. I think she'd feel safer, and I don't want her living alone while I'm gone."

"Well, you know she's like a daughter to all of us. We'll keep our eyes on her too."

"And you're like a second dad for us, and the guys are the brothers we've never had. You're my extended family, and always will be."

"All right, there's no need to prolong the agony. Let's go to my office and sign the papers."

Chapter 63

The void in the family room where the recliner had sat sent me into a round of tears every time I walked by. I moved an end table to that spot and added another chair.

Today would be the hardest day of my life. We were burying our dad.

After I dressed in my formal uniform, I helped Amber get ready for the services. The dislocated shoulder made it difficult for her to lift her arm above her head to get dressed. Mom came over to help.

The house was filled with wall-to-wall flower arrangements, cards, and casseroles. Kate took care of phone calls, food, and flowers while Mom and I took care of Amber.

"Jade, it's time to go," Kate said as she peeked around my bedroom door.

I looked at Amber and tucked the strand of misplaced hair behind her ear. She couldn't hide her misery—those swollen red eyes gave her away, and I'd carry that heartache forever.

Mom took both of our hands and led us to the waiting

black cruiser that Billings drove.

The funeral home was standing room only. Amber, Mom, Bruce, and I sat in the front row as a family, and directly behind us sat all of our brothers and sisters in law enforcement. It seemed as if every person my dad had ever known from Wisconsin and California was in attendance. Minister Harland from St. John's Church, the church we grew up in, conducted the service. Mayor Gleason, Lieutenant Clark, and Sheriff Matthew Link, from San Bernardino Sheriff's Department where my dad was the captain, gave the eulogies.

At two o'clock, the funeral home emptied out to the sidewalk and parking lot. The sun peeked out from the clouds and lit the sky with beautiful rays. My dad was smiling down at us—I felt it, and I wanted to linger in that warm glow.

Hundreds of uniformed officers along with people from North Bend lined both sides of the street. My dad grew up with these families and protected them in his twenty-five years of service in North Bend. They were friends, neighbors, colleagues, and people Amber and I went to school with. They waved small American flags as they stood in reverence on the sidewalk.

The street to the cemetery was closed to through traffic. From the funeral home, it was a short five-block walk. Dad's flag-draped casket was placed in the hearse, and then the car slowly pulled out onto the street. Amber, Mom, and Bruce walked behind the vehicle. I followed with my arms locked in solidarity with Lieutenant Clark, Jack, Clayton,

Billings, Horbeck, and Jamison, all in dress uniforms. Officers from North Bend's police and sheriff's departments walked behind us, with hundreds of law enforcement officers from San Bernardino County and many other cities, counties, and states taking up the back of the procession.

St. John's Cemetery was a large, tree-filled place of serenity with beautiful gardens dotting the landscape. The parklike setting gave me a certain sense of comfort—peace in a way. I knew I'd come often and sit with Dad. I always needed his advice, and just because he wasn't here in the flesh anymore wouldn't change that.

We followed the hearse to the Monroe family plot, where a spot had been prepared for Dad. Six pallbearers carried his casket to the site. Sheriff Link placed Dad's service hat and badge on the casket then took a seat. Minister Harland said a few words about his friendship with Dad and led a final prayer, then several close friends shared their own amazing stories of our father. When it was time, the bagpiper played *Amazing Grace,* and the honor guards folded the American flag and handed it to me along with Dad's service hat and badge. I passed them to Amber.

I wondered if Max Sims watched from a distance—if he was out in the crowd somewhere with a smile across his face. He had done his father proud. I squeezed my eyes tight and erased him from my mind. Thoughts of him didn't belong in that place of reverence. He'd get what was due him soon enough.

I stood, along with my brothers and sisters in law

enforcement, and saluted our fallen officer—my dad, the man that taught me everything I knew—while the bugler played *Taps.*

My tears flowed freely as I squeezed Jack's hand and silently vowed to bring Max Sims to justice—even if it meant doing it my own way.

THE END

Thank you for reading *Exposed*, Book 5 and the final book in the Detective Jade Monroe Crime Thriller Series. I hope you enjoyed it!

Keep your eyes open for the new Jade Monroe FBI series coming soon.

Stay abreast of my new releases by signing up for my VIP email list at: http://cmsutter.com/newsletter/

You'll be one of the first to get a glimpse of the cover reveals and release dates, and you'll have a chance at exciting raffles and freebies offered throughout the series.

Posting a review will help other readers find my books. I appreciate every review, whether positive or negative, and if you have a second to spare, a review is truly appreciated.

Again, thank you for reading!

Visit my author website at: http://cmsutter.com/

See all of my available titles at:
http://cmsutter.com/available-books/

Made in the USA
Columbia, SC
22 June 2021